Just Say Yes

Book Two of the Just Say Yes Series

Jen Andrews

Dedication

This book is dedicated to my fellow Indie Authors in our Indies Round Table group and the amazing ladies from The Indie Erogenous Zone. Without your support every single day, my sanity would be further out in La-La-Land than it already is.

This book is also dedicated to Kay Manis and Jessica Guerrero because without all the crazy antics and texts between the three of us, life surely would be boring.

Chapter Thirteen is dedicated to all you ladies who love fast cars and hot men!

Acknowledgements

I have many people to thank now, since the release of my first book, The Reason. I have met so many new people since then, and I cannot thank all of you enough for your support!

My Snowflakes Street Team: Bree, Danielle, Emma, Jessica, Ashley, Sandee, MaryAnn, Alyssa, Shawna, Kendra, Karen, MaRanda, Karrie, Joyce, Andrea, Julie, Sandee, Melissa, Heather, Tiah, Chelle, Stephanie, Sarah, Karen, and Joyce.

My beta readers: Jessica, Kendra, Julie, Kelly, Andrea, MaRanda, Karrie, Bree, Chelle, Emma, Melissa, and Missy.

There are several blogs I need to thank for their support and for allowing me to hijack their pages for takeovers:

Summer's Book Blog, Panty Dropping Book Blog, Livin' Simple Promotions, Beautifully Broken Book Blog, Bibliophile Book Reviews, Amanda's Book Club, This Mommy Loves to Read, Romance Obsessed Book Blog,

Two Ordinary Girls and Their Books, Book Talk with Amanda, Fallen for Books, The Book Enthusiast, Just One More Page, and Sandwich Making Book Bitches.

Phew! I think I got everyone, but if I missed anyone, I am truly sorry! Just know that your support is truly appreciated and I look forward to working with you.

Special thanks to Kay Manis and Lorrie Anson for their last minute reading and suggestions to help make this book what it truly should be.

Sprinkles on Top Studios, you have done another amazing cover for me and I love working with you.

Integrity Formatting, I cannot thank you enough for making the interior of my books as beautiful as the outside,

If I missed anyone at all, I am so sorry. These last four months since the release of The Reason have been pure insanity.

Prologue

I lie in the silent darkness on a bed that is not my own. My body feels heavy, like a lead weight. I am unable to move, but my mind is fully awake. The touch of his soft lips press against mine, the rough texture of his warm hands caress my cool skin. The gentle, soothing whispers of his voice in my ear make me want to fight. He's begging me to come back to him, and I want to.

Please, God, let me come back. He needs me to come back. His need far outweighs my own. He can't lose me. If he does, he will suffer. Oh God, he will suffer the unimaginable. Again.

I can't stand to hear the pain in his voice. I try to move, yet again, but nothing happens. If I wake, I will never tell him no. I will always say yes to him. If I can make it through this, I can make it through anything.

He is my reason for being, my reason for living, my reason for everything.

Chapter One

January 2012

My head throbbed and my body would not cooperate with me when I wanted to move. I could not force my eyes to open, and people spoke quietly around me. *"She should be awake by now...Oh God, please let her wake up..."* Andy's cologne permeated the darkness of my mind. I sensed his presence nearby.

From somewhere to my left, I heard my mom praying in Spanish and I envisioned her clutching the rosary beads she'd had since she was a child. I recognized the voices of my family and friends all around me.

Whatever happened to me, it had to have been bad.

"Andy, you need to go home and get some rest." Justin's voice was sympathetic and concerned when he spoke to Andy.

"I can't leave her, mate. I need to be here for her when she wakes up..."

Why won't she wake up? The question repeated over and over in my head, with a different person's voice asking it each time. Through my closed eyes, I was aware that the room was bright. From the obvious scent of the liquid cleaner used to keep everything sterile, to the steady beeping sound of my own heartbeat coming from a machine near my head, I could tell I was in the hospital. *Why am I here?*

Andy held my hand, rubbing his thumb back and forth across it. His warm lips brushed mine. *"Zoey, please..."* he whispered, pleading for me to do something...anything. *"Please wake up, Beautiful. I need you to come back to me. I can't lose you, too."*

Why couldn't I talk? He needed to know I was okay. *Shit, am I okay?*

It was nearly dark in the room when I finally opened my eyes. My legs tingled and ached like they were asleep. I tried to move them but couldn't. *Oh God, why can't I move my legs? Am I paralyzed?* Fear ripped through me and I forced my head up to glance down at my legs.

The light from the hallway outside the open door illuminated the room just enough that I could barely make out Andy. He was sitting in a chair so close to the side of my bed, his upper body and arms were sprawled across my legs. He was sound asleep, faced toward me, with his cheek on my knee. Relieved that his weight was probably what caused my legs to feel the way they did, I slowly lowered my head back down onto my pillow.

Just in case, I forced myself to make sure my legs worked properly, straining to wiggle my toes. I couldn't see them past Andy, but they moved. I was in so much pain, an involuntary whimper escaped from my mouth. I squeezed my eyes shut, hoping I would pass out again and not feel anything. I'd only closed them for a split second when the weight lifted from my legs and I heard the sweetest sound.

"Zoey, you're awake. Oh, thank God. I'm calling the nurse. Don't move, okay?" Andy jumped from his chair and fumbled around with something next to my bed. He let out a long, trembling sigh then took my hand in his. I couldn't bring myself to close my eyes, so they remained on Andy. A few moments later, a nurse came into the room and flipped on the overhead light.

"Miss James? My name is Maxine. How are you feeling?"

"Not good. Everything hurts. What happened?" I whispered as she checked my pulse. My eyes closed part way as the words left my mouth. My throat was dry and scratchy, and it felt like I was going to cough. I attempted to swallow any saliva I had in my mouth, but it just made it worse. Maxine noticed and filled a cup with water from the small pitcher on my bedside table.

"We'll explain everything in a few minutes, sweetie. I'll go get the doctor so he can get you something for your pain after we get you a sip of water for your throat," she said as she added a bendy straw to the cup and held it to my lips. My eyes closed again as the cool water soothed my dry mouth and throat. *Ahh, heavenly.*

Maxine set the cup on the table and left the room to get the doctor. Gradually, I reopened my eyes to see Andy sitting next to my bed in the chair. He was rubbing his jaw—his eyes were bloodshot and tired. For as handsome as he was, he looked like hell. His face was pale with dark circles under his eyes.

"What happened?" I remembered talking with Jess and Sasha outside of dance class, but nothing else. "Did Rob do something to me?" I asked, scared that maybe he'd hit me with my own fucking car. I didn't know why my first thought was that he'd hurt me, because he wasn't like that. But, with him following me and causing trouble, I just wasn't sure what he was capable of anymore.

Andy stood over me to push my hair gently away from my face. The simple light touch from his fingertips brushing across the side of my head comforted me.

"No, it was a freak accident. All we know is the police were chasing a guy on foot near the dance studio and he came around the corner then ran in to you from behind. He knocked you in between your car and the car in front of yours. You crashed head first in to the bumper of your Audi. When you landed, you ended up smacking your head on the road too."

"That's it? That's what hurt me? A person? How stupid!" *Well, technically it was my Audi and the road, but still.*

Pain spread like wildfire through my body when I made an idiotic attempt to sit up, so I stayed motionless. *Who gets knocked over by a man and ends up in the hospital? Apparently me...*

He inhaled deeply and let it out, along with a little chuckle at what I'd said. Before he spoke again, he breathed a long, sigh of relief. "God, Zoey, when Jess called to tell me what happened, I thought I'd lost you. She was crying so hard she could barely speak. All I knew was you were hurt and lying on the road."

His eyes watered and I didn't want to see him upset like that. I tried to reach out to him, but a flash of pain shot through me, causing me to wince. He cringed but didn't take his eyes off me.

"Please, don't move," he begged.

The doctor arrived at that moment with Maxine hot on his heels carrying an IV bag in her hand.

"Miss James, I'm Dr. Waits. How are you feeling?"

Like shit. "I'm in a lot of pain. Is anything broken?"

Maxine hung the IV bag on the stand then hooked the tube from it to an IV port that was sticking out of my arm. Some type of clear liquid was being pumped into my body through the tube that was already hooked up. I assumed it was the standard IV fluids instead of pain medication since every part of my body hurt like hell.

"You're very lucky, Miss James. You hit your head twice. Your hip, shoulder, and ribs are badly bruised because they took the full force of your weight when you landed on the street. You're going to have some pain and discomfort for the next several days, but nothing was broken. Do you understand what I'm saying?"

Thank God the doctor was using small words because I didn't think I could comprehend anything with my head pounding so badly. I mumbled something that might have sounded like a yes then gave him a curt nod. Not a good idea. It hurt like hell, making me dizzy and sick to my stomach. I winced again, making myself so queasy I wanted to throw up.

"We'll keep you here for a day or two because of the head trauma you suffered then send you home with medication to keep your pain level at a minimum. You will need to take it easy for a week or two, so nothing strenuous. No work, no heavy lifting. Just try to rest and let your body heal."

Maxine finally did something to the tube coming out of the IV bag next to my bed. Within minutes, the throbbing pain slowly started to subside. *That's some good shit in that bag,* I thought and tried to chuckle. Another bad idea. I flinched as pain shot through me again.

"Just press this button when the pain gets too much, it will administer a dose of pain medication for you," he said, handing me a round tube-like thing with a button on the end. "I'll be back to check on you later, Miss James. We'll run more tests in the morning to see how you're healing and we'll go from there." Once I thanked him, he and Maxine left the room, leaving us alone.

"Andy?" I whispered.

"I'm here, love. What do you need?"

"My purse...I need a mirror," I answered, not quite sure if I wanted to see myself. My head hurt like hell, so I could only imagine what I looked like.

"Zoey, you hit the side and back of your head, not your face."

I did? "But I tasted blood."

The pain meds were taking effect, making me a little confused. Andy found my compact in my purse, opened it, and handed it to me. My face was pale with purplish-black, puffy bags under my eyes.

"Holy shit, I look like death."

He frowned and looked away, making me feel terrible for my choice of words. I ran my tongue over the inside of my cheek, finding it lumpy and very sore. Apparently, I bit it at some point, causing it to bleed.

Carefully, I pulled my hair back on the side of my head where it hurt, discovering a large bruise on my scalp. Running my fingers across the back of my head where it bounced off the ground, I found a large, very sore lump.

Andy dropped onto the chair at my bedside then raked his hands up and down his jaw. He did the same uneasy gesture any time we talked about his family. I'd seen it several times and recognized it instantly.

"Hey, don't do that. I'm fine." I reached out for his hand but didn't care how bad it hurt that time. I needed contact with him, to comfort him so he knew I was okay.

"I'm just relieved you're awake. When Jess called, she said you were hurt and unconscious..." He trailed off as a sickened expression washed over his face. He swallowed hard then didn't finish what he was saying.

"How long have I been here?"

"Since Thursday night." Andy's gaze dropped to the floor and he ran his fingers through his hair, making it stand on end, even as short as it was.

"What day is it?" I whispered, completely confused. *How the fuck long have I been here?*

"Saturday." He flipped his wrist to look at his watch. "Two a.m. It's been a little over twenty-four hours."

"I've been out for that long?" I was completely flabbergasted and a sudden surge of adrenaline moved through my body from the shock.

"Yes. Jess said the man who hit you was the size of an NFL linebacker. They said he knocked you several feet before you hit your car."

"Did they catch the guy?"

Andy nodded. "Yes. After he collided with you, he lost his balance then fell down. The police weren't too far behind him, so they were able to tackle him back down to the ground when he tried to get up. He was twice my size so it took five cops to keep him down. They arrested him and hauled him off to jail."

Holy shit, that's a big motherfucker. Andy was six-foot-three and two hundred twenty pounds of sexy, muscled man, so the guy must have been a giant.

Thoughts of my family began running through my head. Oh God, my parents. They were probably freaking out.

"My family..." I trailed off, wondering where they were. "Where are they? Do they know I'm okay?" I didn't want to move and had no idea where my phone was to call them.

"Everyone went home, Beautiful. The hospital wouldn't let them stay past visiting hours because they crowded your entire room. The doctor convinced them you needed to rest so they would go home. Somehow your mum persuaded them to let me stay with you."

"She did?" Tears pricked my eyes because of her thoughtfulness. *Dear God, thank you for giving me such a wonderful mother.* "Can you call her?" He nodded as he stood to pull his phone out of his pocket. "Wait," I said. "How long have you been here?"

"Since Thursday night, I couldn't leave you," he replied, his voice faltered when he spoke. Just looking at him, I could tell he was exhausted. The only sleep he'd probably had was when he was sprawled across my legs.

"Come here," I whispered. Without moving my arm, I patted the bed with my hand. Andy shook his head just slightly to say no, but I could tell how tempted he was to crawl onto the bed with me. All I wanted was for him to lie next to me and get some sleep.

"Zoey, it's not a good idea. I don't want to bump you and hurt you."

He didn't budge. I looked him in the eyes, pleading with him. Fine, let me try his tactics on him for a change.

"Just say yes," I sang quietly with my scratchy voice. When he smiled at me, I swore I heard the little beeping noise on my heart monitor speed up.

"Oh, I see how it is. You're gonna sing Snow Patrol to *me* now, are you?" He reached out and caressed the side of my face, gently pressing his lips to my cheek.

Instead of getting into bed with me, he said, "Let's call your mum and dad. I promised to let them know as soon as you woke up."

He found my parents' phone number and pressed the speaker button. The phone rang only once before my dad answered it. I forced myself to concentrate, so I could stay awake long enough to speak to my parents.

"Dad, I'm awake."

"Baby girl, we were so worried about you. How are you feeling?" He sounded relieved and I heard my mom in the background anxiously telling him to put their phone on speaker so she could talk to me too.

"It feels like I got hit by a bus, but from what I heard, it was only a linebacker," I joked. "I must have missed the memo about the NFL drafting me."

My dad chuckled quietly at my joke.

"Zoey, it's so good to hear your voice," my mom said. "We've been so worried about you." Her voice trembled as she spoke, and when she sniffled, I knew she'd started to cry.

"Please, Mom, I'm fine. Hold the waterworks or you're going to make me cry too."

"Sorry, Mija, I don't want you to be in any more pain than you already are. Andy, honey, are you still there?"

He tilted his cell toward him. "Yes, I'm here."

There was a moment of silence. "How does our girl look?" she asked. "Is she really alright?"

He looked over at me then smiled slightly as he laid his warm hand on mine. "She's beautiful. The doctor gave her pain meds, so she's about to fall asleep, but she's fine."

"Thank you, Andy. For everything," she said, her voice cracking again. "We'll come see you in the morning, Mija. Andy, you go home and get some sleep, okay? You've been at the hospital almost as long as Zoey has."

I couldn't believe he'd been with me the whole time. But, I knew if the tables had been turned and he was the one lying in a hospital bed, I wouldn't have left him either. I loved him far too much to let him wake up alone.

"Sure. I'll try to later," he said, sounding unconvincing to me.

"Goodnight, Mom and Dad." I yawned. *Ow!*

"Goodnight. We're so happy you're awake," my dad added before we ended the call.

"Andy, go home," I pleaded. "You need some sleep, a nice hot shower, and probably some food, too."

When I finally realized he'd been there for so long, I asked where our cat, James, was staying.

"Justin and Will are taking care of him. Your friends have been a big help to me, especially since I didn't know where the hospital was. They drove me here when I got the call from Jess. I honestly don't know what I would have done if they hadn't been home that night."

My eyes grew heavy and I smiled sleepily at my blue-eyed man. "Remind me to cook them dinner when I break out of here."

"I don't think you'll be doing too much for a while," he stated flatly, his expression distressed.

Whatever sort of drug cocktail that was in the IV bag began to flow through my body, and suddenly it felt like I was floating, my body light as air. My vision blurred slightly, almost like I was drunk, but the drugs were making me sleepy, too. I drifted off for a split second, then jerked awake. *Ouch.*

"Go home, okay? I'm going back to sleep for a while." I was losing my fight against consciousness, but needed him to know how much I loved him before I fell back to sleep. "I love you," I slurred.

"And I love you," he replied and kissed me softly again before I drifted away.

When I woke next, the sun was shining brightly through the windows. I was alone in the quiet hospital room; the only sounds came from the IV pump next to the bed. I vaguely remembered the night before and recalled waking up in pain then pushing that magic button a few times.

I remembered Andy being there; calling my mom and dad, but that was about it. Hopefully, he'd gone home to get some rest, shower, and eat something.

My purse was on the rolling table next to my bedside within reach of my good arm. I dug through it, found my birth control pills, and popped the ones I'd missed from being in the hospital. Crap, there went my plans for Andy and me before I left for vacation.

The whole right side of my body ached, but nowhere nearly as bad as it had when I woke up the first time. I was feeling better, so I stretched out the neck of my hospital gown and looked down the front to see why I hurt so much.

Ugh. No wonder everything hurt. I was one solid bruise from the top of my ribs to just below my hip. The side of my freaking boob was even bruised! I'd been in the same position in my bed so long my back was starting to ache. Unable to change position on my own because I couldn't put weight on my injured shoulder, I pushed the nurse's call button just as the doctor walked in.

"Miss James, you're awake," he voiced.

"Please, call me Zoey." I hated it when people called me 'Miss'. I was just plain Zoey.

"Of course," he said politely. "I am going to send you up to radiology for a follow-up CT scan of your head right now and if all is still well, you can go home later this evening."

Oh, thank God.

"How are you feeling this morning?" he asked as he thoroughly examined my visible injuries.

"I'm better," I replied. "My back was starting to hurt, so I was calling the nurse to see if she could come help me roll over. How sad is that?"

He chuckled and flipped through my chart, added notes, then glanced back up to speak to me. "Considering what you've been through, it's not sad at all. You've experienced quite the ordeal."

"Can you tell me again what happened, doctor? The details are still a little foggy." For some reason I dreamt about football all night and it made no sense why, especially since I hated football.

"Well, Zoey," he said, as if he had a memory of something amusing. "When you get run over by a man the size of 'The Fridge,' chances are, you're going to get hurt."

Who the fuck is 'The Fridge?' "Sorry, Doc, I don't get it," I smiled in utter confusion. "Who is *'The Fridge?'*"

Dr. Waits quickly flipped my chart open, scanned over it and looked back up at me. "Ah, you're too young to know who he is. He played NFL football for the Chicago Bears and the Philadelphia Eagles. He was only six foot two, or so, but weighed over three hundred pounds."

Holy shit, Andy was right. "Awesome. Please tell me I am the only person in history to have been hit by a running appliance." I made myself laugh at my own stupid joke and Dr. Waits even laughed with me.

"You are definitely my first, Zoey," he chuckled again. It didn't seem like being hit by a *person* would cause so much pain, but after he described how I slammed headfirst against the front of my car before landing and hitting the back of my head on the street, it made more sense.

The doctor and I spoke for a few minutes before a giant, male nurse pushed a wheelchair through the doorway of my room. "Are you ready for some tests so we can get you out of here?"

"Let's get this over with," I laughed. *This is gonna hurt.* The nurse introduced himself as Allen as he helped me from the bed to the wheelchair. Allen wheeled me to the elevator, then up to the radiology department where they performed another CT scan, just to make sure nothing changed from the one they did when I was admitted.

As Allen wheeled me back to my room after I was done, I noticed Andy waiting for me just inside the door. His short hair wasn't sticking up from running his fingers through it like it had been the night before. He'd changed into clean clothes, looking as gorgeous as ever. The smell of his body soap and cologne infiltrated my senses the closer I came to him. However, I wasn't confident he'd slept any. His blue eyes were tired and he still looked drained.

"Hey, you," I said to him as Allen pushed me to the side of the bed.

"Good morning, Beautiful." He smiled widely, obviously happy to see me out of bed.

"Are you ready to stand, Miss James?" Allen asked. I nodded in response and that time it didn't hurt nearly as bad as before.

Allen locked the wheelchair in place and helped me to my feet, steadying me as I turned to sit on the bed. A draft of air grazed my bare skin, as my gown became untied and fluttered open.

Andy took in a sharp breath and looked away as Allen re-tied my gown, helped me onto the bed, arranging the blankets for me. After he left, I eased to the side of the bed as far as possible, then patted the empty space next to me.

"Come up here with me, please," I pleaded, tapping the bed. Andy pushed the button to recline the bed a little so I would be comfortable.

Andy slipped off his shoes and slowly eased himself up next to me, carefully wrapping his arm around my shoulders. I nestled into him, losing myself in the constant warmth of his body, knowing that next to Andy was the only place I wanted to be.

"Did you get some sleep?" I asked.

He chuckled quietly while he very carefully tried not to move. "I'm the one that's supposed to be worried if *you* slept, not the other way around. This is one of the reasons I love you so much. You're lying here in the hospital with a head injury, and worried about me instead of yourself. You are incredibly selfless."

He kissed the top of my head and I burrowed into his side a little more until I felt a twinge of pain. I pushed the magic medicine button so the pain didn't worsen then laid my arm across Andy's stomach.

We rested together for quite some time and it felt nice to be in his arms. He was warm and smelled wonderful from his shower. "You smell good," I whispered groggily. I felt him lay his head back against the bed then we both drifted off to sleep.

Chapter Two

My parents woke us later when they came to visit. Andy slowly started to get up from the bed, but my dad spoke first. "You look comfortable. Stay where you are, son. Sorry we woke you, but we're glad to see you get a little rest too, Andy."

My dad turned to me. "As for you young lady, I'm so thankful you're going to be okay." His eyes were teary when he bent over and gently kissed me on the forehead.

He stepped back to give my mom her turn to see me. She squeezed my hand lightly. "Mija, we were so scared for you."

I smiled up at my mom and dad. "I'm fine, I promise. I'll be sore for a while, but they're only bruises. Nothing's broken at least."

We talked for a while longer and I let them know about the tests they ran that morning. Andy was still on my hospital bed with me and I expected to feel uncomfortable with my parents there, but I wasn't. As they were getting ready to leave, the doctor came in with my test results.

"Good news, Zoey. It looks like you'll get to go home later today. Your CT scan has been reviewed and everything appears to be normal," he said. "We'll get someone up here to get you checked out soon and I'll send you home with some pain medication to take if you need them."

What a relief it was to be going home. I needed a nice hot bath and something decent to eat. I was ready to go to my quiet apartment to spend some quality time with my man.

My parents kissed me goodbye and Andy spent the day in my hospital bed with me watching TV. We were still waiting for the discharge papers when my dinner was delivered. One glance at what was on the tray and I wanted to gag. They had brought the same thing to me for lunch earlier that day. Broth, a hard bread roll, and Jell-O. *Gross.*

"Just eat it," Andy said softly when he saw the look of disgust on my face. "You haven't had much since Thursday, so you need to eat it. I'll fix you something better when we get home."

"Okay, bossy. I'll eat it." Luckily, the hospital released me shortly after dinner.

Andy brought a pair of sweatpants and my favorite hoody for me to wear home. I smiled at the fond memories of him pulling that hoody over my head the last time I wore it. He helped me change out of my hospital gown and I didn't miss the pale, sickened look on his face while he helped me get dressed. The bruises really bothered him.

He gathered all of my belongings, packed them in my bag for me then left to pull my car around to the hospital entrance. I waited patiently on the bed for my wheelchair ride out of the hospital when a nurse whom I'd never seen before entered. After a quick introduction, she wheeled me out the door to my waiting car.

"So, did my hard head leave a nice dent on my Audi?" I asked Andy as I painfully stretched forward to see if I could find any damage.

"No," he answered gruffly, obviously not wanting to talk about it. He opened the car door and helped me in. When I tried to buckle my seatbelt on my own and couldn't, he leaned over and did it for me.

The ride home from the hospital was miserable, but I was ready to be home in my apartment. No matter how small each bump in the road was, I felt it. Andy parked as close to the lobby doors as possible and then helped me into the building. My bruised hip and leg made climbing the flight of stairs tortuous. I could barely put any weight on it, so Andy carefully picked me up and carried me. I rested my cheek on his shoulder, breathing him in all the way up the stairs.

He situated me on the couch then turned on my iPod before making me a sandwich. I was famished and the broth and Jell-O at the hospital only made it worse. I pretty much devoured the sandwich and guzzled a glass of water in a matter of minutes. After I finished, Andy brought me the package of Oreos I kept in the back of a cupboard for PMS emergencies. He didn't know that's what they were for, but I demolished an entire row of those too.

Andy kept himself busy tidying up my already clean apartment while I sat alone in the living room eating my dessert. He was being helpful and taking care of me, but he seemed a bit distant. There was definitely something going on in that head of his. Once I was finished with my cookies, he was right back at my side to see what I needed next.

It was nice to be home, but I felt gross from not showering in three days and desperately needed a nice hot bath and a toothbrush to clean my teeth.

"Can you help me with a bath, please?"

"Of course I will," he replied, his voice strained. "Stay here and I'll go start it for you."

Since the bathroom in my bedroom only had a shower, he went into the guest bathroom and started the water in the large, garden tub. I watched as Andy went back and forth across the hallway, each time taking an armload of products and towels to the guest bathroom. When I heard the water shut off, he came out to collect me.

"Ugh, I feel like an invalid," I groaned as he helped me stand from the couch and walk down the hallway. While I held on to the bathroom counter for support, he stripped my clothes off me, dropping them in to a pile on the floor.

"Get in with me?" I invited. He said nothing and shed his clothes. "I really need to brush my teeth first."

On the bathroom counter, my toothbrush and toothpaste were laid out for me. Tasting blood again as I brushed, my eyes wandered over my injured body in the mirror and I noticed where the bruises were darker over each rib. Andy and Sasha were right. I needed to gain some weight. It was creepy to see the outline of every rib because of the bruising on my skin.

I felt Andy's gaze on me. He was sitting on the edge of the bathtub watching me intently, his eyes roaming over my bruised body. He glanced up and I met his gaze in the mirror. It was almost like he was the one in pain instead of me. He swallowed hard then averted his eyes away from me as he ran his hands up his face and through his hair.

I quickly finished brushing and spit the bloody toothpaste from my mouth into the sink, rinsing with a mouthful of water before making my way over to the tub. It upset me to look at Andy because he was still wearing a distressed look on his face. He very gently took my hands and pulled me between his thighs, placing kisses on my bruised ribs.

"Are you in pain? I can get you a pill if you want one."

I shook my head slowly. "All I need is you and a bath. I'll be as good as new in no time."

He stepped into the tub first to help me over the side. Andy sat down on the edge and helped me down to a sitting position then eased in behind me. The hot, vanilla-lavender scented water swirled around us. *Ahh, heaven.* A hot bath with a gorgeous man, what more did a girl need?

Somewhere he'd found a large plastic cup and filled it several times, pouring the hot water over my hair to wet it. Once it was drenched, he leaned forward and kissed my bruised shoulder. I reclined back onto his chest, relaxing against him.

After soaking a while, he stirred and took in a deep breath before he spoke. "Let's get your hair washed."

Once he helped me sit up straight, he wet my hair again then lathered it up with shampoo. He took great care when he washed the sore areas of my head. Once he rinsed and conditioned my hair, he squeezed body soap into his hand, gently massaging it onto my back and shoulders.

He eased me back on his chest then squeezed more soap on his hands to wash the rest of my body. I raised my uninjured arm up, wound it around the back of his neck, and ran my fingertips through his short hair. After he'd finished bathing me, he skimmed his wet, soapy hands back up over my breasts—my nipples hardened even more from his touch.

No matter how much I hurt, my body still craved him and the way he made me feel. "Please," I whispered. "I need you."

He lightly teased my breasts, gently working my nipples with his strong, masculine fingers. It felt wonderful. I let out a quiet moan as I closed my eyes and let my upright knees fall open to rest on the insides of his legs. Andy took the hint, letting his hand slide from my chest, down my stomach and under the water to caress and stroke me. His fingers began moving in a slow, agonizing, circular motion.

"Are you sure this is okay? I don't want to hurt you."

"Mmm, feels so good," I whispered breathlessly. "Please, don't stop." His fingers were driving me mad and it felt like he hadn't touched me in weeks. Finally, I couldn't take it anymore. I needed to be with him right then, so I pulled myself upright, not caring how bad it hurt.

"What are you doing?" he asked, startled, when I started to get up.

"I want to be with you, right now. I can't stand it anymore," I whispered, hearing the desperation in my own voice.

His eyebrows rose in surprise when he realized what I wanted, then they furrowed with worry. "No, you're too bruised. I don't want to hurt you. Come on. Lean back and I'll finish what I was doing."

Damn noble man.

"Can you forget about being such a good guy for five minutes? I promise it won't take any longer than that," I laughed. Suddenly, I was glad he said no. I'd forgotten about missing my birth control when I was in the hospital.

"Sit," he commanded in a very sexy tone as he indicated for me to take a seat between his legs.

When his eyebrow rose, I rolled my eyes at him, but did as he instructed. "Who's bossy now?" I grumbled and moved back to my previous position against his chest. His hand dipped back under the water and like the good guy he was, he did as promised and brought me to orgasm within minutes.

Afterward, we relaxed, soaking in the tepid water. "Let's finish our bath and get you back into bed," he said.

Bed was the last place I wanted to be. It felt like I'd been in bed for a week straight. He rinsed the conditioner out of my hair before he rose to sit on the edge of the tub, leaving his feet in the water. Quickly, I washed my face with fresh water from the tap. Andy handed me a towel to dry off when I was finished.

Andy looked incredibly delicious sitting there with his golden, tattooed skin and long lean muscles on full display. While he scrubbed my legs and feet, he was growing hard as he touched me but was trying to hide it. He shifted his legs several times in an attempt to block my view, before he finally just grabbed a towel and draped it over his lap. When he was done, he gently set my foot back down in the water to rinse off the soap. As he did, the towel covering his lap fell into the tub leaving him completely exposed to me.

Since he'd taken such good care of me, I wanted to take care of him, too. I folded my legs to the side, and using my hands I slid across the slick bottom of the bathtub, until I came to rest between his knees. He had a knowing expression on his face when I looked up at him.

"Zoey, I know what you're doing. I don't want to hurt—"

I snaked my hand up out of the water and took hold of him. "Shh. I don't want to hear another word out of you," I said, staring up at him deviously. He raised his hands in surrender.

He was slick from our bath, so I caressed him slowly, my hand sliding easily over his smooth hardness. I moved closer, taking him into my mouth. I teased the head of his cock with my tongue and drew him in the way he liked it, stroking him and lightly squeezing his balls with my other hand. Andy's breath quickened as he watched me while I pleasured him. I found it erotic. I liked to watch him as he watched me.

The man just brought something out in me I'd never felt before. I wanted to do everything with him and experience things I'd only read or heard my friends talk about. Sure, I'd been with a few people before him, but none of them did to me what this man did. Every inch of his body was something that I wanted to explore—to find out what he liked and what he didn't—to make sure he was always satisfied, and never longed for anyone's touch but mine.

One thing was for sure, Andy liked to run his fingers through my hair while I gave him blowjobs. I tasted his saltiness on my tongue so he was getting close. I pulled back and teased the head of his cock with my tongue and lips as I pumped him at the same time with my hand. He came with a deep, throaty groan moments later then slid back down in the tub with me as I swallowed.

"You're in so much trouble now," he said as I washed him off under the water.

"Fine with me," I smiled. "It was well worth it."

He helped me out of the tub and dried me off.

"I could get used to this, you know?"

"The next time you want me to bathe you, don't put yourself in the hospital. Just ask me, okay?" he muttered as he toweled himself off.

Holy crap, was he mad at me? Did I imagine it or was I just tired and in need of a pain pill?

"Fine," I said as I attempted to lift my bruised leg to pull on my pajama pants. A sharp stab of pain shot through my hip, causing me to grimace. I gripped the edge of the countertop and dropped my foot back to the floor before I lost my balance.

"Jesus Christ, Zoey!" Andy growled as he lunged toward me to catch me if I fell. "Would you let me help you instead of trying to do everything on your own?"

He is mad at me!

"Why are you mad at me?" I asked defensively.

Andy helped me get dressed. "I'm not mad at you. I wasn't prepared to see the bruises all over you. I'm sorry if you think that. I want you to take it easy and let me take care of you. I don't know what I would do without you. You're all I have and I can't lose you too."

He rubbed his hands up and down his jaw in frustration. *So that's what this is about.* I wrapped my arms around his waist.

"I'm not going anywhere. I promise you I'm okay." I embraced him tighter. It hurt, but I didn't care. He didn't hug me back. "Why won't you hug me back?"

He sighed. "Because, I don't want to hurt you. You're covered in bruises, remember?"

How could I forget?

"I'm taking a pain pill then going to bed." I turned and left him standing naked in the middle of my bathroom. My brain was getting foggy from the pain and I wanted to forget about what had just happened.

In the kitchen, I refilled my water glass then swallowed one of the pills the doctor gave me. After I took the pain pill, I decided to get James since he would let me cuddle him without being scared of hurting me. I hobbled next door and knocked on Will and Justin's door

Will answered a minute later. "Zoey, oh my God, you're home. Justin, she's home!" he called toward their kitchen. "Come in! Come in!"

The boys each held an arm and helped me sit on the couch between them. We chatted a bit about what happened the night of the accident.

"I also want to thank you guys for helping Andy get to the hospital and for taking care of James for us. As soon as I'm back to normal, I'll cook you two anything you want, I promise."

They both smiled graciously, but I could tell they were keeping something from me. "We needed to get him to the hospital A-SAP so he didn't have a stroke. I've never seen a man so distraught in my life. I wasn't about to let him drive," Justin admitted.

Seriously? That made me feel guilty for being irritated with him earlier.

Will stood and went to get James for me. "We're glad you're home, Z. We were so worried about you," Justin said as Will came back into the room, holding my tiny, orange fluff ball kitty.

"There he is. I've missed him." I stupidly raised my arms to take him from Will and pain traveled from my shoulder all the way down my arm. "Ow."

Justin's eyebrows rose with concern. "You alright?"

I nodded. "Yeah, I'm good. Still waiting for the pain pill to kick in."

Andy came barreling through their open door with a very pissed off expression on his face. "There you are, Zoey. You could've told me you were coming over here."

"Sorry, I came to say hi and pick up James," I said, full of remorse for worrying him. I turned back to Will and Justin. "I'd better get back home, guys. Looks like I've been busted for sneaking out."

Andy turned and walked to the door to wait for me. *Not so patiently, I might add.* He was not happy with me.

Justin stepped forward to help me stand. "Z, give the poor guy a break. He loves you. You didn't see him the other night after Jess called him. I thought he was going to break down our door from beating on it so hard. He didn't know where the hospital was and all he wanted was to get to you."

Knowing what Andy's reaction was to my accident made me feel incredibly guilty for the way I acted toward him. I nodded at Justin, understanding. "Goodnight. Thanks for taking care of my two favorite guys for me while I was away."

Once we were back in my apartment, Andy locked up and we headed to the bedroom in silence. I crawled into bed, set James on top of the covers, and watched as he playfully chased my hand. Andy sat next to us, brooding.

"Will you please talk to me, Sexy?" I used my nickname for him to try to get him to relax. He rubbed his hands down his jaw again. "Andy, stop doing that, please. I'll be healed up in no time."

"I can't help it," he admitted. "I swear to you, when Jess called me and she said you were hurt...that you weren't waking up...I thought you were *dead*. You don't know what that felt like for me."

It made my heart ache to know that was how he felt, even for just a second. I wanted to move over and wrap my arms around him, but my pill hadn't taken effect and it wasn't possible to move without him noticing I was hurting. I needed to convince him I was okay.

"I'm sorry you had to go through that, but it's not like I asked to be tackled and put in the hospital. Besides, I was given a clean bill of health, remember? You were there." James became bored with me, hopped onto Andy's lap, and fell asleep. *Lucky little shit.* I wanted to crawl up on his lap and fall asleep in his arms.

"I'm sorry, too," he said as he looked at me with shame in his eyes. "You're right. I'm being a selfish prick. I don't know what I'd do if I lost you. You're all I have."

Screw the pain, I thought as I scooted over to him and wrapped my arm around him. At least he was sitting on my left side, so the dull throbbing wasn't as bad. "I swear you'll never lose me," I whispered to him.

"I'll be right back." He waited for me to let go of him, then stood up and took James to his bed in the laundry room.

While he was gone, I maneuvered around until I was comfortable. It looked like I would be sleeping on my left side until my body was healed. Andy came back in and stripped down to his boxers. He started to get in bed when I stopped him.

"Hey, you practically live here, you know? You can sleep in whatever you want, even if it's nothing. In fact, I'd prefer it," I said with a smile. "I want you to be as comfortable here as you are at your place."

Andy stuck his thumbs under his waistband, made a show of bending completely over at the waist, and pushed his boxers to his feet. Standing back up, he dangled them from his index finger, twirling them a few times before dropping them to the floor with a smirk.

"Whatever makes you feel better, Zoey." He turned off his lamp and slipped under the covers. He faced me, but didn't touch me.

"I'm not going to break. You can touch me."

He leaned over and caressed my cheek with his thumb. "Someday I'll comprehend that," he whispered morosely before he kissed me goodnight, moving back to his position across the bed.

Chapter Three

The next several days raced by much too fast. It was Friday and in two more days, Jess, Sasha, and I would be on our way to Cabo. My bruises were a lovely shade of greenish-yellow, with some purple mixed in on the worst of them.

Thankfully, I didn't need the pain pills as much as before. They worked well, but they made me feel groggy and I found myself not remembering things that happened, or things I said. Andy was a big help during the week, but he was increasingly broodier the closer it came to Sunday, the day I was leaving for Cabo.

Because we'd both been so out of sorts, I'd made the decision that I needed to try to put us back in sync with each other before I left. The only way I thought we could do that was to be together intimately. Originally, I wanted it to be without the use of condoms, like we'd talked about at Christmas when we first got together. But, the accident screwed up my original plan because I'd missed a few days of my birth control pills. There was no way I was risking a pregnancy just to be with him, bare and uninhibited.

We needed our connection back before we were driven so far apart we couldn't be repaired. I couldn't lose him.

I had an appointment with my therapist, Dr. Jensen first thing that morning. Not being allowed to work, I was bored to death, so I went shopping afterward. The store at the top of my priority list was Victoria's Secret, where I purchased an off-white, sheer, baby doll nightie with matching thong panties I knew would drive Andy wild. On the way home, I made another stop at the store and bought several candles of all shapes and sizes to set a romantic mood for us.

And even though I hated the thought of using them, I bought a box of condoms.

When I arrived at home, I quickly hand washed my new nightie and panties, then hung them up to dry near the heater vent in the spare bedroom. I arranged the candles on every level surface of my bedroom and changed the sheets on my bed. Once that was finished, I took a nice, long shower to ready myself for what I hoped would be an unforgettable night.

Andy would be off work soon so I texted him and asked him to go home to shower before coming to my place. I mentioned to him that I wanted to go out for dinner since I'd been cooped up in my apartment all week. As soon as I heard Andy's key in the lock, I rushed to the bedroom as quickly as my still-sore hip allowed, sat back on my heels on the center of the bed, and waited for him to find me.

"Zoey?" he called out.

"Back here," I responded as I arranged my tiny nightie over the large bruise on my hip. My hair fell in loose waves all around my shoulders and I'd put on a bit of makeup to enhance my eyes and lips. The box of condoms was tucked into the drawer of my nightstand next to my bed so I didn't have to see the damn things. They were the only thing that would put a damper on the evening and I couldn't even stand to look at them.

I'd lit every single candle I bought, letting them cast a romantic glow around my large bedroom. I closed all the curtains on the enormous windows for added privacy because I didn't want Andy to see into my bedroom when he came over from his apartment. I'd never offered myself to a man before the way that I was giving myself to Andy. I didn't know how he was going to take in the situation, especially as strained as our relationship had become.

His footsteps echoed down the hallway and he stopped dead in his tracks when he entered the bedroom. He glanced around, taking everything in before turning to face me. "What's this all about, Zoey?" he asked coyly as he stepped over to the foot of the bed. He stared at me intently and let his eyes travel over my body, then back up to my eyes.

"You're breathtaking," he said in a low voice, but didn't come any closer.

"So are you," I replied anxiously. I couldn't tell which way the situation was going to go, so I made the first move. I rose up on my knees and carefully made my way the few feet to the end of the bed. My hip was still very sore, but I wasn't going to let it hinder my plans.

In typical Andy fashion, he was wearing a button up shirt, so I began undoing it from top to bottom. With each button I let loose, his breath quickened and he shifted in place. When the shirt was completely unfastened, I pushed it off his shoulders, letting it fall to the floor.

"Please, come to bed," I whispered. "I want you to make love to me tonight."

His eyes flickered with pure lust as he reached out and took hold of the silky fabric of my lingerie, running it between his thumb and forefinger. Andy wanted tonight to happen as much as I did. I fisted my hands into the T-shirt he was wearing under his button up and pulled him closer. In an instant, our mouths were devouring each other. My tongue dipped inside his mouth, seeking his, which he willingly gave me.

"Come to bed," I whispered again. Slowly, I backed away from him, still holding his T-shirt. He had no choice but to follow me onto the bed. So there we were, on our knees in the middle of the bed, kissing like two people who had been starved of affection for years. His hands roamed around my body and he gave my bare ass a nice, gentle squeeze as he groaned against my lips. My heart swelled in my chest because we were finally taking our relationship to the next level.

He chuckled when I moved to his side and gave him a little shove so he'd lie down. When I shifted, my hip strained, causing me to grimace. Andy didn't notice since he was in the process of lying down. I scooted off the bed, took the box of condoms out of the drawer, and set them on top of the nightstand. Andy gave me a confused look when he realized what the box contained so I explained why we needed them.

"I missed taking some of my birth control pills because of the accident." He gave me a curt nod of understanding when I eased myself back onto the bed. When I did, another twinge of pain shot through my hip. That time Andy saw me wince, but didn't say anything. I lay on my side facing him and gently pulled his face to mine. The steady thump of my heart sped up when he finally touched me.

Within seconds, I had him on his back, pushing his T-shirt up his torso. He lifted himself so we could get his shirt off. I took my time kissing and licking every inch of his gorgeous, upper body, restoring to memory what I'd lost in the days since we'd last touched. His hands tangled in my hair as he kissed me with so much hunger, my body throbbed and hummed with anticipation.

With a groan, I sat up quickly, and worked the rest of his clothes off. He pulled me back on top of him and slipped his hand down the front of my panties as he kissed me. Andy massaged my clit then slid his fingers in and out of me as he whispered, "I love you so fucking much, Zoey. I don't know what I'd do without you."

His words dulled the ache in my heart from the tension that had grown between us since my release from the hospital. I rocked my hips forward against his hand. The movement forced me into the throes of orgasm and I gently bit his neck as it subsided.

"I've missed your touch so much," I breathed into the side of his neck as I reached down, taking his dick in my hand. He was hard and ready to go, so I grabbed a condom, ripped it open, and rolled it down the length of him.

"Zoey, are you sure it's okay? I can tell you're still in pain," he said as I fumbled, trying to get my panties off without straining my hip. I decided to leave my baby doll nightie on to hide the bruising so he couldn't see them and put a stop to my plans.

He was right. My hip was hurting because I'd been on my feet all day, but I didn't care. I wanted to be with him. I eased down next to him, urging him to take the lead.

Our hands roamed over one another's bodies while we kissed and loved each other, making up for lost time. As soon as Andy lifted his body over me, positioning himself between my legs, my hip gave out and pain shot from my pelvis all the way to my knee. I tried to hold in the whimper the pain caused, but it was too late.

Andy scrambled off the bed, facing away from me. His shoulders slumped, then I heard the snap of the condom being pulled hastily from his body. He took in a sharp breath because it had to have hurt him. Shock and confusion filled my mind when he bent over, picked all his clothes up off the floor, and redressed himself.

"I'm sorry, but we're not doing this until you're fully healed. You're covered in fucking bruises and I can't touch you without hurting you. This never should've happened," he muttered as he raked his hands through his hair. Not looking at me once, he stalked into the bathroom, shutting the door behind him.

Hot tears of rejection spilled down my cheeks as I went to my dresser, took out my pajamas, and pulled them on. After tossing my new lingerie set into the empty trashcan next to my small desk, I limped around the room blowing out all the candles I'd lit earlier. The room filled with smoke before I realized it would set off the alarm, so I opened all of my windows in an attempt to air it out. I flipped on a single lamp, sat on the edge of my bed, and waited for Andy to come out of the bathroom.

When he finally did, he looked more pissed than upset. I didn't know if he was upset at me or at himself, but I couldn't take it anymore. The emotional distance between us was too much for me to bear and I just wanted to be alone. I glanced up at the man I loved more than anything and said something I never thought I'd say to him.

"Please leave."

"Zoey, I'm sorry, but I can't—"

Tired of hearing those words from him, I put my hand over my mouth as a sob escaped it. "Andy, please go. I need to be alone right now. I...I need some time to think about things."

"Think about what?" he asked quietly. He stood in the center of my bedroom, still as a statue while he waited for my answer.

"Us."

"What do you mean by 'us', Zoey?" he asked and came to kneel in front of me. The alarm in his eyes revealed to me that he was clueless about what my words meant.

My hurt turned into anger at that point because he just didn't get it. We were falling apart. How could he be so blind?

"Just fucking leave," I cried. I couldn't even look at him.

Andy stood and walked away, but stopped at the doorway. "I love you," he said, just before turning on his heels, leaving me alone in my apartment.

An hour later, I was still perched at the edge of my bed, so very confused about my life with Andy. What had gone so horribly wrong? My mind was overwhelmed from the way the night turned out. All I wanted to do was sleep, so I went to the kitchen and took a pain pill for my throbbing hip.

The smoke was cleared from my bedroom, so I closed the windows. As I did, I noticed Andy sitting on the top step in front of his apartment. I stood at my window and watched him as he sat and watched me. Were we over?

Was there still hope for us? More than anything, I wanted there to be. I closed all but one set of curtains, lit a single candle in a small holder, placing it on the wide, brick windowsill as a peace offering. I crawled into bed, shut off the lamp, and fell into a restless sleep.

The next morning when I woke up, I found my gorgeous man, fully clothed and lying behind me, his body molded to mine. He had come back while I was asleep.

"I'm going to miss you so much," he whispered.

"I'm going to miss you, too. What are you going to do while I'm gone?" I asked, trying to give myself some time to wake up and figure out where we stood after what happened the night before.

"Worry," he replied dryly. I rolled over and moved in close to him.

"*Please*, don't," I begged as I rested my forehead against his and closed my eyes. "This is too intense. Last night was horrible."

Andy took in a deep breath and let it out. "I'm sorry, Zoey. I'm still freaked out after the accident, and now you're leaving for a month. I'm afraid something is going to happen to you and I can't touch you without hurting you—"

"Then let me touch you," I whispered with the unwavering need to prove to him that I was okay and nothing would happen to me.

After last night, I knew he wouldn't have sex with me, so I held his face in my hands and kissed him hard. He parted his lips, deepening our kiss, letting our love for each other take over. I slowly slipped my tongue inside his mouth to meet his, thankful when Andy *finally* wrapped his arms around me. He had barely touched me all week aside from helping me bathe. His refusal to make love to me the previous night hurt worse than the injuries. He hadn't harmed me on purpose, but the rejection still stung.

No matter how badly I still wanted to be with him, he would refuse. However, I was still more than willing to give him what he needed. I ended our heated kiss, unbuttoned his jeans, and slid the zipper down, knowing he wouldn't turn down what I wanted to do to him.

I tugged his pants and boxers down as he lifted his hips, freeing his erection. Wasting no time, I took him in my mouth. He groaned as I sucked, drawing him further inside. I wanted to do this to him every day. I loved the way he tasted and the way he watched me. I stroked him while I ran my tongue and lips over the head of his cock then took him deep inside my mouth.

When the tip of him hit the back of my throat, I swallowed. He took in a sharp breath, closing his eyes while he knotted his fingers in my hair. He must have liked that. *A lot.* I continued sucking him and pumping him with my hand, increasing speed and pressure until he was close to coming, then I'd back off for a bit. I wanted to prolong his experience since it was probably the last time I'd touch him until I returned from Cabo.

Looking up at him, I found he was watching me again, his eyes glazed over with lust. I ran my hand up his warm chest, and on the way back down to his muscular abs, I teased his nipple with my fingertips. He moaned quietly at my touch, so I did it again.

His breath came in rasps the closer he came to his release. His body jerked slightly and he mumbled my name as he came. I swallowed and released him, crawling back up to lie beside him. He wrapped his arm around me and we drifted off to sleep.

It was late Saturday and almost time for our dinner and karaoke night with all my friends. Andy was going to be there too so we could spend as much time together as possible. He hadn't left my side since he'd come back in the early morning hours after our horrendous fight, and I was pretty sure he had no plans to until I was on the plane.

My hip felt better after a day of rest so I was well enough to cook dinner. Will and Justin were bringing a salad, I was making lasagna, and Jess and Sasha were bringing garlic bread and dessert. I felt a little wimpy for needing Andy to lift the pots and pans full of food for me because they were too heavy to lift with a sore shoulder.

His mood was still not right and it was obvious he was worried about me leaving because he kept asking me if I was sure that I was okay. I did everything in my power to try to get through to him so he knew I was, but it didn't seem to help.

When my friends arrived, the six of us enjoyed dinner gathered around my dining room table. Andy finally loosened up after a few beers. I pulled out a half bottle of Johnnie Walker and the guys proceeded to knock back the rest of it. I wasn't drinking because I didn't know if I'd need a pain pill that night. Not to mention the fact I needed to wake up early to get to the airport.

Later on, we set up the karaoke machine. We always played a game where we took all the names of the songs, printed them out, and put them in a hat. Each person drew out a strip of paper and no matter what was on it, you had to sing it.

Andy was being shy and a bit quiet. I wasn't too sure if he was ready to join our game or not. I'd heard him sing several times when he didn't know I was listening. He had a great voice and I begged him on many occasions to sing me something, but he never did.

I had yet to hear him play his guitar either, for that matter.

After everyone except Andy sang a song, my turn came up again. Jess pulled out a slip of paper, handing it to me. I opened it and read the song title.

"Oh, hell no. You assholes do this to me every time. I swear I'm going to delete that song from the list."

They started clapping and cheering for me, obviously wanting to see me make an ass out of myself. I put my hands over my face to hide my shame as I laughed hysterically. I couldn't help it. It *was* funny.

I looked over at Andy who was waiting for someone to tell him what was going on. He was nearly drunk and seemed to be having a good time. Not wanting to ruin his night, I decided to suck it up and do the song my so-called best friends gave me.

"Let's get on with it, bitches," I teased. *Dear God, how am I going to get through this sober?*

Jess found the song on the karaoke machine then pressed play. The music started, along with the cheers and applause. Once Andy realized what it was, he joined in with the rest of my friends. I knew the song by heart, every single word of it. Much to everyone's amusement, I actually did a good job rapping to "Ice Ice Baby" by Vanilla Ice.

While I was singing, Will and Justin thought it would be funny to hop up and do the dance routine Vanilla Ice actually did in the music video. It was hilarious to watch them and I had a hard time finishing the song without laughing.

When my torture was finally over, I was so mortified I collapsed on the couch next to Andy, burying my face in his chest. He put his arm over my shoulder, patting me lightly on the back.

"It's over, Beautiful. Can you do it again?"

"Very funny. You get up and do it now," I joked.

Still laughing, he picked up his glass of Johnnie Walker from the table. "I'd need about ten more of these before you could get me to even attempt *any* song."

He finished his drink and set the empty glass back on the table, then reached over and hoisted me onto his lap, wrapping his arms tightly around me. I was surprised at his actions to say the least.

"I love you so much, Zoey." He sighed, then buried his face in my hair. His warm breath tickled my neck, and the sadness in his voice broke my heart.

I was so relieved that he'd finally chosen to touch me I couldn't let the moment pass by. I wrapped my arms around his neck, rested my cheek on his head, and sat there, unmoving. I didn't know what else to do. He wanted to hold me and I was damn sure going to let him because I needed it as much as he did.

Justin cleared his throat. "Hey, party people, we better get home and let these two lovers be alone."

Andy and I sat there while everyone packed up to leave. I didn't get up from his lap and neither of us broke our hold on each other.

"Don't forget, our flight leaves at twelve-thirty, Z," Sasha called over her shoulder.

"I'll see you girls tomorrow at ten then," I answered quietly as everyone made their way out my door.

Once everyone left, I decided to give Andy the gift I'd bought him. While I was away, I didn't want him to forget about everything we'd begun to build together.

"Andy, I have something for you. Wait here. I'll go get it."

Chapter Four

Since I was going to be away on Valentine's Day, I bought an iPod for him as a gift. Of course, the stores started selling Valentine's cards before Christmas, so I picked one up after an appointment with Dr. Jensen.

I gave him a kiss on the lips, went into my closet, and pulled the little black gift bag out from behind a stack of shoeboxes.

During the week while he was at work, I worked on getting his new iPod set up. The doctor said no work for me so I would heal faster for my trip, which left me to find things to do around my apartment.

Fuck, I even went over to the shop and sat in the lounge to read the new magazines that came in the mail because I was so bored. That was after I attempted to play a few songs on my guitar, but couldn't get it situated on my lap comfortably enough to play it without some body part hurting. The entire week had been pure hell.

I added music to the iPod I bought him on the day we went shopping for his laptop so we could Skype while I was on vacation. I made him several playlists of songs that were special to me, and songs that reminded me of him.

Back in the living room, I resumed my favorite spot on his lap.

"I know it's not Valentine's Day yet, but since I won't be here...I bought this for you." I handed him the card first. It was one of the mushy cards and it actually made me tear up when I picked it out.

He opened the card and read it as a genuine smile spread over his entire face. "Thank you. I love it," he whispered, wrapping his muscular arms around me.

"I have a present for you too," I said, handing him the tiny bag.

"Zoey, I didn't get you anything."

"You don't need to get me anything. Open it." I was anxious to see if he liked it.

He pulled the tissue paper out of the bag and took out the box containing the iPod. I'd wrapped it in black paper and tied it with a silver bow. He pulled off the ribbon, then the paper.

"You bought me an iPod?" he asked, as he looked it over. "No, you bought me the most *expensive* iPod. You shouldn't have spent so much money on me."

I looked him in the eyes. "Don't worry about my money, okay? I did it because I love you and wanted to get you something nice, but that's not the best part." I took the box from him, opened it, and pulled out the black iPod. I chose the black one for him because it reminded me of the black paint on his Camaro.

After I powered it on, I scrolled to the song menu. "Look, I preloaded it with music for you." I moved on to the playlists I'd made for him. "All the songs on this list remind me of you. They're special to me and I want you to listen to them while I'm away. I made this one with some of your favorites too."

He sat in silence for a minute after I handed the iPod to him. "It's perfect, Zoey. Thank you."

"Turn it over," I said.

Earlier in the week, I'd taken the iPod to a local store that engraved items. I wanted him to remember the night of my birthday when we danced in my apartment. The night the walls I'd built around me briefly crumbled. The night I realized I loved him. He turned it over and read the back, a look of confusion washing over his face. "It's a lyric from the song that was playing when I realized I was falling in love with you," I admitted.

It was also the very same song he unknowingly quoted the line: *Just let me love you.* He put the iPod aside and we sat and held each other for what seemed like hours. Unfortunately, it was getting late and I needed to be up early in the morning for our flight.

"Let's go to bed before you pass out on the couch. I can't carry you," I teased, because his eyes were as sleepy as mine were.

"Very funny," he replied dryly. I was still sitting on his lap, but in one quick movement, he was standing upright with me still in his arms. He walked down the hall to my bedroom and laid me down on the bed. "I'll be back after I lock up."

By the time I was ready for bed, Andy was back, wearing only boxer briefs. I was going to miss seeing him in those every night. Well, I would mostly miss seeing him *out* of them. Lying on his back with his fingers entwined together behind his head, he stared at the ceiling. I hated that he was still being so distant and quiet.

I rolled over to him, laid my head on his chest, and began tracing his tattoos with my fingertip. "Please don't be mad at me. If I'd known I was going to meet you, I would have never planned this trip. You know that, right?"

"I know, and I'm not mad at you. It's going to be a long month. That's all."

Tell me about it. "For you *and* me," I sighed.

He stirred and I raised my head so he could roll to his side and face me. "I'm sorry. I'm not trying to make you feel bad for leaving. I feel like an asshole about last night. I want you to have a good time and take all the time you need. Remember, you were going on this vacation for a reason."

"Yes, I remember." *How can I forget?* I was stressed out and the accident had made my life extremely unbalanced again. It seemed like for every good thing that happened, something bad followed.

My mind drifted back to the memory of being dressed up in pretty lingerie for my special night with Andy. Because of my injuries, he'd flipped out and I threw him out of my apartment. I shook my head to get the memory of the devastating night out of my thoughts because it still hurt to think about his rejection of me.

Once again, I was overwhelmed. Andy knew it, and I knew it. I needed a break from my life. I didn't want to leave him because it felt like our relationship was hanging by a thread about to snap, but I knew if I didn't take some time to de-stress, I would be no good to either of us. It would take a while to deal with all the crap that I allowed to build up for months, not to mention all the new issues between Andy and me.

Things were better since Andy came in to my life. I was seeing Dr. Jensen again, but I still needed some time away, especially after the accident. Plus, I didn't want to become codependent on Andy. It was crucial for me to take care of myself for once.

I realized that I didn't even know who I was. Right then, I decided the sole purpose of my trip to Cabo was to find out. *Have I ever known who I truly am?*

"You know I love you, right?" I asked him, to break the silence. He nodded. "Try to think of this time apart as a way to get to know each other even better. We can talk all the time on the phone and you can use your new laptop so we can see each other on Skype. Just don't go finding someone else, okay?" I teased.

"Zoey, don't say things like that," he said, obviously irritated, but I knew he immediately regretted his words. "I'm sorry. I'm really tired. Can we just go to sleep, please?"

"Good night, then. I love you." I kissed him softly on the lips then watched as he rolled away from me to go to sleep. I didn't want to leave on a bad note, so I let it go.

The next morning, my alarm went off at eight, but most of the night I had stayed awake. Andy hadn't slept much either. He tossed and turned as much as I did. When I rolled over to get up, he was gone. My heart sank, but I didn't have time to worry about what he was doing or why he wasn't there. I took a shower and dressed in some comfy traveling clothes.

After I was ready to go, I found him sitting at the dining room table, staring down at a cup of coffee. He was wearing only a pair of faded jeans, all his golden, muscled, tattooed skin on display...it was going to be a long month.

He looked up at me when I walked in. "Hey," he said quietly as he ran his hands up and down his jaw line. I sat next to him at the table and he slid his coffee cup in front of me. I took a long swallow of it then set it back in front of him.

"Are you okay?"

"I have a headache," he said with an unsteady voice.

I went to the kitchen and returned with a couple of Ibuprofen. I offered the pills to him and watched as he popped them in his mouth without even looking to see what I gave him.

"Thanks. Can I at least drive you to the airport?" he asked warily.

"Andy..." I trailed off. My brother Noah was driving us to the airport so he could see his fiancée, Jess, off.

"How about you pick me up at the airport when I come home? We already planned everything out and I don't want to change anything at the last minute. Do you want to ride with us to the airport?" I asked, feeling bad that he was disappointed.

"Yes," he replied without hesitation.

"I need to eat something before I go. Are you hungry?"

He nodded then propped his elbows on the table and rubbed his temples to try to relieve his headache. I dropped two sliced bagels into the toaster and fixed a cup of coffee for myself while I waited. When they were ready, I spread cream cheese on them then put them on plates.

When I turned around to take them to the dining room, Andy was leaning against the countertop with his hands shoved down in his front pockets. He was barefoot so I hadn't heard him when he came in.

"Sorry for being a dick," he said. "I'm going to miss you. A month is a long time."

I set down the plates and went to him, wrapping my arms around his waist. I laid my cheek on his bare, tattooed chest and breathed him in one last time. His skin was cool on my warm face and he smelled like heaven.

"You're forgiven," I replied as I planted a kiss on his chest.

We broke our embrace and sat down to eat our bagels. "So...what are you going to do on your trip, Zoey?" he asked.

Okay, he's trying. I thought about it before responding. "We planned on doing all the touristy things while the three of us are in Cabo for the week. Depending on the weather, we might go snorkeling one day. Definitely horseback riding, shopping, and lounging around on the beach," I laughed. "You know, girl stuff—"

He pushed his chair away from the table as he popped the last of his bagel in his mouth then went into the kitchen to wash his plate. A few minutes later, he came back in with James. He sat down, putting James on his lap, scratching down his back and behind his ears.

Although I was surprised by what he had just done by getting up and leaving the room when I was mid-sentence, I chose to ignore it. I was leaving as soon as my ride arrived so I didn't want to start a discussion about his abnormal behavior at that point.

"What are you going to do while I'm gone?"

This time, he gave a different answer than the last time I'd asked.

"I have a few changes I want to make on my car before I start racing this year. I thought about going back to Sonoma for a weekend to visit my aunt and uncle."

"That's a great idea. You haven't seen them since you moved and I'm sure they'd love to see you." I wanted him to keep busy so he wouldn't be so moody while I was gone. We talked a while longer about the changes he wanted to make to his car.

The buzzer rang on the intercom while we were talking. *Shit, it's time to leave.* I hopped up and pushed the intercom button. "I'll be right down," I called. "Get dressed. You're coming with me to the airport, remember?"

Andy took James to the laundry room and came back to the living room fully dressed. Since the accident, he'd practically moved in with me, so I had given him his own drawers and space in my closet.

Andy met me at the door. "Zoey," he started, looking down at me with his somber blue eyes. "Have a great vacation. I'll miss you, but we'll talk every day. Call me *anytime*. I don't care what time it is, even if it's the middle of the night and you can't sleep or don't feel well, *call*."

I nodded and wrapped my arms around him as my lips found his. We kissed until the buzzer rang again.

"Freaking persistent-ass people," I muttered. I hugged him again and laid my head on his chest for another moment.

Why did this feel like we were saying goodbye, as in, we weren't going to see each other again? The mood was intense and I didn't like it one bit. He picked up my suitcase for me while I grabbed my purse and laptop bag. Slowly, we made our way down the stairs to meet Jess, Sasha, and Noah, to drive to the airport.

Andy and Noah couldn't go with us once we checked in, so we were forced to say our farewells shortly after we arrived.

I hugged my brother while Andy said bye to Jess and Sasha. I heard him say, "Take care of my girl for me. Make sure she eats, takes her pills, and rests, please."

They agreed then sandwiched him in a bear hug that had them all laughing. He returned their embrace, hoisting them both up. They were so short, their feet dangled in midair as he held them tightly.

Noah and Jess said their goodbyes while Andy and I said ours. I made it brief because I felt like if I didn't, I was going to change my mind about going. We'd said everything we needed to say to each other over the last two days we spent together, so I hoped it would be enough.

He held my face in his hands and gave me one last kiss. "Remember, Zoey, call me anytime. Have fun and be safe. I love you."

I nodded. "I love you. You can call me anytime, too."

As we walked toward security, Andy and Noah stood watching us until we couldn't see them anymore.

Our trip would be my first time away from Andy and it would be Jess's first trip away from Noah. Their goodbye was much easier on them. They were going to be married in June and spending the rest of their lives together. They didn't have all the distance between them that Andy and I had.

Sasha was the first to break the silence while we stood in the security line. I was glad she spoke up because I was getting more anxious the closer we came to our departure terminal. Darkness clouded my mind because my leaving was going to affect my relationship with Andy. It felt like a 'make it or break it' situation.

"You lucky bitches. I need to find myself a man like the two of you have," Sasha grumbled. Her comment instantly brought back the memory of my friend Ben asking for her number.

"Sash, did you get a call from Ben?" I asked, remembering I gave him her phone number during one of our rehearsals for the anniversary party back in December. *Shit. I cannot believe I forgot about giving him Sasha's number.*

"Ben?" she asked, confused.

"Yeah, Ben Ellis. He asked me for your number a while back. Did he not call you?"

She sighed and seemed a little upset. "No, he did not."

I felt bad because I brought it up and now she knew he was going to call her but didn't. I pulled out my cell and shot him a text asking why he never called her. We made it through airport security and went to find a seat at our terminal. We sat for a while talking about what we wanted to do while we were in Cabo.

My phone pinged with a text from Ben. He apologized for not calling Sasha. He let me know the band became busy, but he was going to call her right then to see if she wanted to go out to dinner with him. I sent him a text back telling him she was with me and on her way to Cabo for a week.

Sasha's cell rang as soon as I hit send. She almost hit the ignore button when she didn't recognize the phone number calling her.

"Answer it. It's Ben," I ordered her, with a sneaky grin.

She curled her fingers into a fist and gave me a teasing look, as if she wanted to punch me. I shrugged my shoulders and smiled at her. Secretly, I knew she was thrilled I'd given him her number. She finally answered her phone and pretended she didn't know he was calling. Apparently wanting some privacy, Sasha stood up and walked to the windows to watch the planes take off.

Since we made it through security quickly, we had thirty more minutes to wait for our plane. Jess was engrossed in a book she'd been reading for a few days and Sasha was still on the phone with Ben. I took out my iPod and started the new Snow Patrol album I'd bought prior to our trip. I reached inside my purse and picked out a new book to read.

We were going to be on a plane for five hours, with a quick stop in Phoenix where we had to change planes. I quickly immersed myself in my book and before I knew it, Jess was standing in front of me mouthing something. I yanked out my earbuds so I could hear her.

"They just called our flight, Z. Let's go! Let's go!" she squealed.

Why did I have such an achy, empty feeling in my gut? Even though things were strained, Andy was the best thing to happen in my life, aside from my adoption, and I left him.

"Quit thinking about him. You need to do this for yourself," Jess said as she grabbed my hand and yanked me out of my chair. "Shit. Sorry, Z, I forgot about your bruises. Did I hurt you?"

I laughed so hard I had to hold on to my stomach to stop it from hurting.

"What?"

"First off, you said the word *shit*, and secondly, I was tossed ten feet by a man everyone is describing as the size of an NFL linebacker and I survived. I am pretty sure I can take being manhandled by someone as tiny and puny as you."

Jess put her hand over her heart, her mouth dropping open like she was offended. "Why, you giant, Amazon wench!" she yelled, looking up at me. "How dare you?"

Jess was petite. I don't think she even weighed a hundred pounds soaking wet and was over six inches shorter than I was.

Jess, Sasha, and I were quite the trio. Me being tall, blonde, and slim, Jess was petite with dark mocha skin and black curly hair. Jess was cute, bubbly, and never had a bad word to say about anyone. She never cussed and was the sweetest person I'd ever known.

Then there was Sasha. Sasha had been gothic for as long as I'd known her and wore dark clothes and makeup. Her stick straight hair was styled with perfect bangs that just reached her eyebrows. It was never the same color. Currently, it was black with purple streaks. I wasn't sure I even knew what her natural color was. She was absolutely gorgeous, with her pale blue eyes and dark hair combination. In fact, she reminded me exactly of the character Kenzi from my favorite Syfy show, *Lost Girl*. They had the same look, attitude, and style.

"Hey, Morticia!" I hollered at Sasha, who was still on the phone with Ben. "Plane's leaving without you." Jess and I gathered our purses and moved toward the line.

When she finished her call, Sasha joined us. "Morticia? Zoey, really? That was so high school," she laughed.

It was our turn to board the plane and we slowly made our way down the aisle. Why did it always seem like people went in slow motion once they made it through the door of the plane? We found our numbered row and stowed our purses under the seats in front of us. We chatted excitedly about our trip until the plane was ready to take off.

As the plane slowly taxied toward the runway, I sent Andy a quick text.

> We're getting ready to take off. I'll try to call you tonight when we land. Love you.

I was about to shut my phone off when he messaged me back.

> Miss you already. I love you.

I wanted to have a great vacation, but I felt bad for leaving. We just started our relationship and I felt like I was leaving him at a bad time. We should be working on fixing what had gone wrong, but I was on a plane leaving the country instead.

The pilot's voice came over the speaker, telling everyone to power off all devices. I shut off my phone, threw it in my purse, and found my book. The three of us talked while the plane took off, but once we were in the air we made ourselves comfortable for our flight.

The pilot gave us the all clear to turn any devices back on so I pulled out my phone and powered it up, along with my iPod. I needed to keep my mind occupied, so I put in my earbuds and opened my book to the last page I'd read.

Luckily, my book was good and kept me engrossed all the way to Phoenix where we had to change planes. Unfortunately, we were forced to run to catch our connecting flight to Cabo. By the time we made it to our next terminal, I thought my hip was going to give out on me. As soon as we were in the air, the flight attendants offered us drinks so I asked for water and popped a pain pill.

Chapter Five

We landed at Los Cabos airport around six that evening where my aunt and uncle were supposed to pick us up. "Zoey!" a voice called to me while we waited for our luggage. I turned around and spotted my aunt Maria and my uncle Victor in the crowd. I went over to them and embraced them both.

"It's been too long. I've missed you guys," I cried. It had been a few years since I'd last seen them. I'd never been to their house before in Cabo and they hadn't been to Sacramento since my grandmother died.

Jess and Sasha wheeled our luggage over to where we stood and I introduced everyone. As Uncle Victor loaded our belongings in the back of their van, Aunt Maria said she planned a huge dinner for us that night.

We got on the road to their house. I turned on my phone and sent Andy a text.

> *Hi, Sexy. We're here. On our way to the house now. I'll call you later. They have a big dinner planned so it might be a while.*

I waited for a few minutes to see if he would text me back, but he didn't.

The five of us talked on the way to the house about the things we wanted to do while we were in Cabo. Because we were vacationing in February, my aunt suggested we add whale watching to our excursions. It sounded amazing to me, and it would be calm and relaxing.

Relaxation was exactly what I needed.

It was a busy time of year in Cabo, so we would have plenty to do and new friends to meet. We would definitely have an exciting time if we went out on the town, which we planned to do the Friday before Jess and Sasha left.

We arrived at the house and wheeled our luggage up the sidewalk toward the entrance. It was a traditional cream-colored Spanish style house with a reddish tile roof, located out in the country. There were several lush plants and cacti landscaping the front yard and tiled porch area. The inside of the house was large, but it had a warm, cozy feel to it, filled with bright colors that reminded me of my parents' house.

We rounded the corner near the kitchen and I smelled the mouthwatering food my aunt started preparing before they came to pick us up. "Aunt Maria, dinner smells delicious."

"I made molé for you, Zoey. Your mom mentioned it was one of your favorites."

Oh, yum.

"What's molé?" Sasha asked, looking very confused and a little grossed out.

I laughed as I tried to explain it. "Well...the molé sauce has several different ingredients in it, including plantains and chocolate. It sounds like an odd combo, but it is the best thing you will ever eat. It's filled with chicken and you wrap it up in a tortilla to eat. Trust me. You will love it. And my aunt makes the best rice you've ever tasted. We're in good hands, I promise."

After the girls and I unpacked and settled in, we all sat down to dinner. "Zoey, your mom said you were in an accident a couple of weeks ago. What happened?" my uncle asked.

I explained what happened and my aunt Maria, being the wonderful, concerned woman she was, forced me to stand up and show her my remaining bruises.

"Oh, Mija," she cried, with a pained expression on her face. "You could've been killed from hitting your head like that. Are you sure you're okay?"

"Tia, I'm fine. I have a hard head. I'm not even taking pain pills anymore for it, just when I need them for my hip." I jokingly knocked on my head. "See, hard as a rock."

Thankfully, she smiled and changed the subject to a much better topic. "Your mom also says you have a new boyfriend. Is that true?"

Dang, was my mom the town gossip or what? I laughed at the thought. "Yes, I do. His name is Andy. He's originally from New Zealand."

She seemed pleased. "Good for you. You deserve to be happy."

After dinner, we helped clean up then my uncle made margaritas for everyone. We sat around the fire pit on the back patio talking in to the night. We were drinking and having a good time when I realized I forgot to call Andy. I excused myself and went to my bedroom to find my phone. *Shit, it's after midnight.* Should I call?

Well, he did say to call anytime and I *did* tell him I would call him later. My finger hovered over the button on my phone for several seconds before I finally pressed it. He answered on the third ring. His voice was low and groggy so I knew he'd been asleep.

"Hey, I'm sorry I woke you up," I said quietly.

"I said to call anytime and I meant it. How are you doing?"

"Good," I stated. "The flight was decent. We ate dinner soon after we arrived. Now we're having some margaritas."

"Sounds like your vacation is off to a good start then," he said in his deep, sleepy voice.

I heard James meow in the background. "Are you and James at my place or yours?"

"Mine. I moved him over here while you're gone."

"Probably a good idea. Hey, I'll let you go, since you have to work tomorrow and I woke you up. I wanted to say goodnight and tell you how much I love you."

I heard him moving around, probably trying to get comfortable. "Okay, send me some pictures tomorrow when you're out so I know you're enjoying yourself. Goodnight, love."

Well, he sounded better than before, half-asleep, but better. We ended the call and I rejoined everyone on the patio. I still couldn't help feeling like I drove an invisible wedge between us.

It all started after the accident. I was getting better, but he wasn't. He was distant, broody, and just not himself. I would deal with it another day, when he had more time to get used to the fact that I would be gone for a while. Hell, I needed time to adjust to it too.

The next day we drove in to Cabo and made reservations for all the excursions we wanted to go on while the girls were there. We booked trips for whale watching, horseback riding, snorkeling, and decided to take a tequila boat tour too.

With no set plans for the day, we wandered around town and did some shopping. I picked up souvenirs for Jake and Alex, and Sasha chose Señor Frog's for lunch. We asked a woman at the next table over to snap a few photos of us on our cell phones. I added a *"Wish you were here!"* message to a picture and sent it to Andy.

He didn't respond, so I assumed he was probably just busy at the shop. We finished lunch and did some more shopping, then headed down to the beach to hang out for a while.

The weather was warm and sunny, much nicer than the cold weather we left in Northern California. The ocean was an amazing shade of turquoise, the sky crisp blue, and clear. *What a beautiful day. Wow, when was the last time I thought something like that?*

We lounged at the beach for a while and decided to pack up to head home. Wearing a bikini, I was getting a bit self-conscious of the people staring at my bruise-riddled body. We had just climbed inside the car my aunt let us borrow while we were there, when my cell rang with Andy's ringtone, "Sex on Fire."

Jess and Sasha looked at me with amused expressions on their faces. "It's Andy," I said laughing.

"Yeah, that ringtone is fitting," Sasha said. "Nice choice."

I laughed as I answered the call. "Hello?"

Silence.

"Hello?" I said again.

Silence.

I listened closely and heard the unmistakable sounds of the shop in the background. I said "hello" a few more times, but he still didn't say anything.

When I realized what happened, I chuckled and ended the call. "I think he just butt-dialed me."

At least he finally called me back. *Yeah, that's not funny, Zoey.*

Throughout the day, I sent him a few more pictures, but never heard from him. I still hadn't by the time we arrived home later in the evening. It irritated me, so I typed out a text to him.

> Hope you're enjoying the pics. Let me know when you've had enough. Thanks for the butt-dial. I guess at least you called me.

My feelings were hurt and with how he'd been acting before I left, on top of the one night that went so very wrong, I hit send before I changed my mind.

He called me right back that time, but I let it go to voicemail. Let him see how it felt to be ignored by the person you loved the most. I turned the ringer off and set my phone on the dresser, then went out to eat dinner with my friends and family.

During our meal, I began thinking back to how he'd been acting since my accident. He would go from loving one minute, to distant, and then push me away. It was almost as if he didn't want to be around me at times, but then there were instances where he was being sweet, holding my hand, and being affectionate. I dwelled on the night I'd tried to make things right between us and I ended up kicking him out of my apartment instead.

Later that night, I'd let myself get so depressed I didn't feel like hanging out anymore, so I decided to go to my room. I found my iPod and was in a shitty mood, feeling the need to listen to something brutal. I scrolled through my music, stopping on the metal band, Lamb of God.

They were a bit too brutal, so I quickly changed my mind. I continued scrolling until I found another one of my favorite metal bands, Opeth. Aside from his screams and growling sounds, the singer had an amazing voice. I popped in my earbuds and lounged on my bed, not bothering to check my phone for messages.

I fell asleep and woke up a couple hours later, when the girls staggered in to go to bed. I put my iPod away and took my phone with me to the bathroom for privacy. Andy had sent me a few texts and left a voicemail. I decided to read the texts first.

Call me please!

Sorry...

I love you.

I listened to the voicemail last.

"Zoey, it's me. Sorry about the accidental call. We've been busy today, a typical Monday. Looks like you're having a great time. I guess I'll talk to you later."

I called him back and he answered right away. "Hi," I said quietly, a sick feeling in the pit of my stomach.

"Are you alright?"

I was on the verge of tears. "No, not really. I'm not sure what's going on here, but I'm very overwhelmed right now. I don't know what I did for you to start acting so distant and push me away. One minute you're acting normal and the next minute you're not. I can't keep up with it."

He sighed. "What are you saying, Zoey?"

I didn't know what I was saying. I was so confused.

"Look, I have all these crazy thoughts going through my head right now. I don't know what to do or say because I don't know how you're going to take it. I just know I don't like the way things are going."

Within an instant, I felt horrible for saying it because it would hurt him and that was the last thing I wanted to do. We sat in silence, neither of us knowing what to say. I hated to consider it, but maybe we needed to take a break so we could figure out what to do about our relationship when I came home. The thought of it not only made me sick to my stomach, it made my heart ache.

What other option did I have though? We were both going to be miserable with all the tension between us and with me not even being in the same country as him right then...I didn't see any other choice.

"Andy?"

"Yeah?"

Fuck, this sucks... "I think maybe we should take a break while I'm here. Things have been edgy between us since my accident and I truly don't know what else to do."

He let out a long sigh. "It's not what I want, Zoey, but if it's what you want, then there's nothing for me to say. I guess this is goodbye," he said.

Seriously? He wasn't even going to fight it. He was just fucking giving up.

He didn't even give me a chance to say anything before he ended the call.

Shit. What have I done?

A couple of mornings later, Jess, Sasha, and I hopped on a charter boat with several other tourists then sailed out to sea in search of whales. It was another gorgeous day, but inside my mind, a storm was brewing. I was trying to hold it together in front of my friends and family because I didn't want them to know something was wrong. Inside, I was miserable.

My entire body ached from the tension and anxiety I carried within me. I couldn't think straight and I felt like jumping into the ocean and sinking to the bottom to collect my heart and my guts too, for that matter. I'd honestly never felt so low in my life. I hurt so bad I could hardly breathe.

It felt worse than when I left after my birthday. I knew it was because we were in a relationship and not 'just friends.' Well...we *were* in a relationship, but not anymore.

The three of us gathered near the back of the boat, watching for signs of whales breaking the surface of the water. Jess and Sasha were busy taking pictures and talking to other tourists. All I kept thinking about was Andy. I don't know what the hell happened that night. I didn't want to break up with him, yet I had.

My anxiety was overwhelming me and I felt like I was going to be sick. I desperately wanted to call Dr. Jensen, but there was no cell service when I checked my phone.

We were too far from land. I stood and walked to an empty section of the boat's guardrail, wanting to get some fresh air to see if it helped.

I took in several deep breaths, closed my eyes, and tried to enjoy the day. Besides Andy, the only thing that kept coming to my mind was the song "Run" by Snow Patrol. Just the thought of never seeing Andy and his beautiful blue eyes again made me want to cry. The lyrics were perfect for the way I felt at that moment. *God, this is not helping.*

Over the loudspeaker, I heard the captain of the boat say something, but I didn't open my eyes. People suddenly started crowding around me, talking loudly.

"Look, there it is!" I heard a woman say excitedly.

When I opened my eyes, directly in front of me in the water was a large Blue Whale spraying water out of its blowhole. It was beautiful and surreal to see something so large, wild, and graceful only thirty feet away. I was in complete awe.

The crowd around me started pushing and shoving, trying to get close to the railing to see the whale. I found myself trapped between them and the railing and I started to panic. The anxiety of my deteriorating relationship with Andy, the fact that I was so far from home, and the overpowering sensations I'd had since the accident, brought me full circle to how I felt when I was adopted. I was sad, angry, hurt, emotional, and completely overwhelmed with my life.

A rather large person wearing a Hawaiian shirt and a fanny pack leaned against me, pinning me against the railing in their attempt to see over the top of me. Because I was standing with my arms resting on top of the railing, my bruised ribs pressed directly against it. The pain was excruciating.

I needed to get the fuck out of there, fast. Someone was stepping on my bare toes and another person kept elbowing me in the ribs. Apparently, my ribs were still very tender, because it hurt like a motherfucker.

Come on people. I am not invisible.

My heart thundered inside my chest from the buildup of everything that I'd been thinking about and the sudden swarm of people around me. My lungs tightened and I became lightheaded from being unable to breathe. *Oh, not a panic attack, please.* I started pushing back against the crowd, trying to get away from them. Nearing the edge of the group, I tripped over a backpack someone had dropped in their rush to see the whale.

A second later, I found myself sprawled out on the hard, wooden deck of the boat. I picked myself up as quickly as possible, afraid of being trampled. My palms and bare knees stung from my not-so-graceful landing. I made it to the other side of the boat, sat on a bench, and buried my face in my hands, sobbing uncontrollably.

"Zoey, what happened?" Sasha asked, running over to me. "Are you okay?"

Unable to speak or catch my breath, I was officially hyperventilating. Having been there, done that, I leaned over and put my head between my knees.

Someone, please tell me why I was such a freak of nature. Why did I have to be this way?

Sasha sat next to me and rubbed her hand in a calming circle on my back. "Z, please try to calm down, honey. You're scaring me," she said. I heard Jess ask what was going on, but my head was still between my knees.

"She's bleeding, Jess. Get someone, please." Sasha continued to console me. A few minutes later, one of the boat's medics came over with a first aid kit and cleaned up my scrapes for me.

After I was finally calmed down, Jess brought me a bottle of ice-cold water.

"Z, what happened?" she asked.

Here goes nothing...

Chapter Six

"I broke up with Andy the other night," I blurted out and immediately started sobbing again. Jess walked away, pulling her cell phone out of her purse.

"He's been so distant and moody since that stupid guy hit me and put me in the hospital. I've tried talking to him, but he won't *talk* to me. All he does is say he can't lose me then acts the way he does when we talk about what happened to his family. I've tried to convince him that I'm okay, but it doesn't help. I don't know what to do."

Sasha put her hand up to stop me from rambling. "Z, what do you mean about his family? What happened?"

I didn't want to tell them Andy's business, but I needed to talk to someone. It was killing me to keep it all bottled up. Jess came back and I explained what happened to Andy, his sister, and parents. I explained everything to them about the accident, the move to Sonoma, the ex-wife. *Everything*.

"Zoey, please don't take this the wrong way, because you know I love you," Jess said. "But think about it from his point of view. His *entire* family was taken from him in a split second. He goes to work one day, a newly married, happy man, after that he comes home to divorce papers lying on the table. No warning, no nothing."

Jess sat down on the bench next to me and continued talking. "Then he meets you, falls head over heels in love with you and you end up in the hospital. *You were just standing on the sidewalk, Z.*" Jess stopped talking then picked the conversation back up after a moment. "I feel terrible because I told him you wouldn't wake up after you were hurt. I shouldn't have said that, but I didn't know about his family. Oh Zoey, he asked me if you were *dead.*"

She sighed heavily, a pained expression on her face and tears in her eyes. "Shit!" She stood up and walked off again.

My brain went into overload as I absorbed everything she said. It began to sink in and make sense. I thought back to some of the things he'd said and done when I tried to get him to talk to me.

He kept running his hands over his jaw the way he did anytime we talked about his family, or the accident that killed them.

Did he think about what happened to me in the same way he thought of the accident that claimed his parents and sister? Fuck, why didn't I see it clearly before?

That was it...he thought of me as his family. *Because I am...and he is mine.*

God, I'm such an idiot.

His family was killed in a huge, tragic accident and all I was doing was standing on the sidewalk, talking to my friends. *I was just standing there minding my own business.* If things had gone a different way, my life could have ended. I could've been thrown further out into the street, been hit by a moving car, and killed. I'm sure to him, the possibilities of what *could* have happened to me were endless.

"Z, what are you going to do?" Sasha asked.

Another tear rolled down my cheek, dropping onto the wooden deck at my feet. "I don't know, Sash. I feel so stupid."

Jess came back over, her cell up to her ear and she was talking to someone. Apparently, we were close enough to land to receive cell service again, so I made a mental note to call Dr. Jensen.

"Here she is," she said into the phone before handing it off to me.

"Who is it?"

"Z, just say hello."

The corners of her mouth turned up in a tiny smile when I put her phone up to my ear and said hello as she'd instructed me to.

"Zoey, are you alright?" asked the deep, accented voice I loved so much.

"No," I admitted honestly. I sighed with relief at the sound of his voice. Tears stung my eyes again and trickled down my cheeks. I didn't know what to say to him, so the words "I fell" spilled from my lips.

Jesus, Zoey, is that all you've got? Tell the man you love him and made a big fucking mistake.

The silence on the line worried me. "How are you?" I asked him, to end the dreadful quiet.

"Not good," he answered softly. "Are you hurt?"

Just my heart. "It's only a few scrapes. A crowd swarmed around me and I had a panic attack. Everyone wanted to see the whale so they started pushing and shoving to get to the railing. I got slammed in the ribs and couldn't breathe," I rambled, because I didn't know what else to say.

"I miss you," he said finally, interrupting me.

My chest ached because I missed him too. All I wanted to do was go home, but knew that if I did, we would be right back where we were when I left...drifting further away from each other.

"I've thought a lot about our talk the other night and I think you're right. We should take some time apart," Andy said, his voice dejected.

No! A jolt of emotional anguish shot through my entire body.

"I'm sorry if I pushed you too hard, Zoey. I didn't mean to. I just fell so fast for you. I haven't met anyone like you, ever. When you were hurt, I admit it scared me. I didn't want to be a dick, but for some reason, it happened. I pushed you away because I thought I would lose you anyway, and now, I guess I have."

Tears flowed down my cheeks while I listened to him *finally* talking to me. "You haven't lost me," I whispered.

"Haven't I? You broke up with me."

My heart sank at his words. I wiped off my face with a tissue that Jess handed me. Neither of my friends left my side. They were there to support me.

"Andy, *I love you.* I wanted some time to think. That's all. You were distant and pushing me away. You wouldn't talk to me...I didn't know what to do. I guess I panicked and chose to run. I made a huge mistake and I'm sorry. I did exactly what I was afraid I'd do from the very beginning." I finally took in a deep, calming breath then exhaled.

"So what do we do now?"

I thought about it for all of two seconds. "I want to be with you, but I am on this vacation to deal with my personal issues, and you have some too. I need you to work on them before I come home. Are you okay with that?"

"I'll do whatever I need to make this work. We can take all the time we need to figure out how to do this the right way. You're all I have and I can't lose you over this. We have something really special here. We can't just throw it away."

He was right. Besides my adoptive family, he was the best thing in my life.

Both of us had issues, but now that he was finally willing to talk about it, there was no doubt we would get it right. Andy needed to try separating what happened to me from what happened to his family, and I needed to deal with all the months of crap I'd let build up before I met him.

We had to survive the month apart and each deal with our personal issues individually. Then when I went home, we would get on with our lives together.

Our boat was docking and the passengers started swarming at the exit to get off the boat first. I wasn't going *anywhere* near that scene. Let them get off the boat first. I'd gladly wait.

"We're going to do this, right?" I asked. "Be together, but take time to fix us? We need to go back to one day at a time. No rush. No stress. But we need to talk to each other, Andy. We can't push each other away again and you need to talk to me about what's going on in that head of yours too."

"Yes, Zoey, I'll do what I need to. I give you my word."

All the passengers were almost off the boat, so we needed to get moving.

"Me too. We're getting ready to get off the boat," I said. "I need to go for now, but I'll call you tonight after dinner, if it's alright with you. We can Skype. How does that sound?"

There was an unmistakable smile in his voice when he replied. "Sounds perfect. I can't wait to see you."

I felt my heart slowly start to beat again. "I love you, Andrew James Tate. Please never forget that. I will see you later. Give James a kiss on the head for me, will you?"

He chuckled and it was the sweetest sound I'd heard all day. "I will *not* kiss James for you. I think he needs another bath. But I *will* see you later. I love you."

We ended the call and I handed Jess's phone back to her. Then I jumped up and hugged her. "Thank you. You just saved my life."

I knew it seemed unhealthy that both of us had issues to work on to be in a relationship, but the issues were not *between* us. They were incidents from the past preventing us from moving forward. I loved him and I was willing to do what I needed to do. *I have to get myself straightened out.*

The rest of the day, I had a great time because the weight of everything had been lifted from my shoulders.

The girls and I did more shopping and decided to go for drinks at the Cabo Wabo Cantina.

I felt much better about where Andy and I stood. I didn't know what Jess said to him when she called him, but it helped. I was excited to see him later tonight, but didn't even care that it was going to be over a computer screen. I could see his beautiful face while we talked and I wouldn't need to guess what he was feeling, like I did over the phone.

"Earth to Zoey. Zoooey," Jess whined. "Snap out of it."

I blinked a few times, bringing myself back to the present. On the bar in front of me sat two shots of tequila that were not there before. "Sorry, I'm good. Just got lost in thought for a sec."

My best friends laughed as the bartender set their tequila shots down in front of them. "So we noticed. Bottoms up, bitches," Sasha quipped. We each downed our shots then squeezed limes between our teeth to ease the burn of the tequila. *Yum, I needed that.*

We were hungry, so we decided to order an appetizer off the menu. No one could decide on just one appetizer, they all sounded so delicious, so we ordered several.

As we ate, my mind kept trailing back to Andy and everything that happened over the last few days. I wanted him to understand the way I was feeling earlier on the boat. It was our 'thing' to send each other songs to listen to ever since my birthday so I sent him a text.

> Listen to "Run" by S.P. when you get a chance. Can't wait to see you later.

We finished our lunch and hit the pavement again to shop. I bought a cute pair of sandals and a dress to wear when we went out to the club on Friday night.

Later on in the day, my phone pinged with a text from Andy.

> I'm off work now, listening to the song. I want you to listen to "I Miss You" by Incubus. James says hi. Gonna hit the shower in a few minutes. Can't wait to see you later, too, Beautiful.

I smiled and couldn't stop myself from imagining him naked, glistening with droplets of water, soap cascading over his tattoos down his gorgeous body. I quickly fired off another text to him.

> Thanks. Now I'm going to have to live with that visual the rest of the day.

We were on our way home when my cell pinged with another text from Andy.

It was a picture. *Holy fucking shit.*

He was naked in the shower, holding his cell high up over his head from an angle. He was looking into the camera, smiling that devious, smoldering grin of his. *Fuck me.*

The photo was so small all I could see was down the arm holding the camera, his back, and a tiny bit of the slight roundness of his sexy, muscular ass.

"Holy shit, he's trying to kill me," I muttered, feeling heat creep up my neck and into my cheeks.

Sasha snatched the phone from my hand and looked at the picture. "You are one lucky bitch, Zoey Lynn James. Does the man even have any tan lines?" She tilted the phone sideways to get a better look then passed the phone to Jess, who blushed when she saw the picture.

Nope, there was not one tan line anywhere on his perfect body. He was naturally golden and gorgeous. Sasha was right. I was one lucky bitch. I wrestled my phone back from Sasha, who had a death grip on it, ogling Andy again. Not that I blamed her of course, he was magnificent naked. I responded to his text.

The girls think you're hot, TTYL.

We made it home and relaxed on the patio with my aunt and uncle, who were home from work for the day. I called my mom to let her know how the trip was going so far.

"Is our Andy okay, Zoey?" my mom asked as we chatted about work.

"I think so. Why?"

She took a breath before responding. "Mija, he's been a little out of it at work. Today, after he took a break, he came back and was back to normal. I was worried about him."

Ah, he'd talked to me on his morning break then went back to work. I wasn't happy he was 'out of it' at work though. That is too dangerous in a place like the shop, when you have cars weighing several thousand pounds over your head on car lifts, and handling high-powered tools.

Not good. I would need to talk to him about it, not because I was worried about the shop's liability if something happened, but because I loved him and didn't want him distracted at work by us. That, along with the previous issues with Rob, was one of the original reasons I didn't want to date him in the first place.

That night, the girls helped me cook dinner for my aunt and uncle then clean up the kitchen afterward.

Unable to wait any longer to see Andy, I went to my bedroom and fired up my laptop. I logged on to my Skype account and contacted him. It took a couple minutes for him to login, but when I saw his blue eyes on the screen, my own blue eyes welled with tears.

"Hi," I said. I was so happy to see him. He was sitting on his couch, his laptop on the coffee table in front of him. He was shirtless. *Thank you, God.*

"Hey, love. How are you?"

"Better than I was this morning. You?"

He smiled, his blue eyes sparkling. "I couldn't be better, now that I've seen your beautiful face." Andy looked at me curiously. "Why are your eyes watery?"

I blinked a couple times so the tears wouldn't spill over. "I'm just happy to see you. I truly thought we were over after the other night."

"Zoey, I just want to say again that I'm so sorry for being a dick." His indigo eyes burned into mine with such intensity, I knew he really was sorry. "I didn't sleep at all the night after I hung up on you...which by the way, I am sorry for that too. It was an immature, shitty thing to do. I'm glad Jess called me this morning from the boat. Remind me to thank her later."

I put my hand up so I could say something. "The picture you sent me today was probably thanks enough for her," I laughed.

He looked embarrassed. "Yes, I was going to ask you about that. How did they see it?"

"Sasha's pretty quick and snatched it right out of my hand. I'll need to be more careful the next time you sext me. If there *is* a next time, that is." I let out a breath of relief when he laughed and told me he'd sext me anytime I needed to see his gorgeous body.

By the time we finished laughing, it was time for us to get serious and talk. "Did you listen to the song?" I asked, referring to the text I sent him earlier.

He nodded. "Yes, I did. I understand why you needed me to listen to it. Do you know how happy I am right now to be talking to you?"

His question made me smile. "Hopefully as happy as I am. I'm sorry about everything, Andy. I was stupid."

He shook his head in disagreement. "No, you tried to talk to me and I shut you out. I guess it took actually losing you to put things into perspective. After your accident, I was so scared I would lose you, that I did. I was being stupid, not you."

I listened to him as he talked, refusing to take my eyes off him. I noticed the neck and headstock of his guitar poking out from behind the couch. He must have been playing it then set it on the stand when I called him.

"Have you been playing your guitar?" I asked when he finished talking.

He glanced over his shoulder at his guitar and turned back to me with a happy grin on his face. "Yeah, I was messing around on it, trying to remember the songs I've learned. It's been a while since it's even been out of the case."

"I'm happy you're playing again. Maybe you'll play something for me when I come home?"

He smiled. "Maybe I will." He looked so handsome sitting on the couch, shirtless. I smiled at the thought of tracing over his tattoos with my fingertips.

"Will you finally take me to get a tattoo when I come home, please?"

"Of course," he replied. "Are you getting the snowflakes you said you wanted a while back?"

"Yeah, I think so."

He chuckled. "You better do more than *think,* Zoey. It's going to be on your body for the rest of your life, you know? I still can't believe you want snowflakes because you love Snow Patrol that much. Maybe I'll get another one too."

Yes, please. I laughed. "God, you make it sound like I'm going to get the words 'Snow Patrol' tattooed across my ass, Andy. I just want a pretty swirl of snowflakes, that's all. Nothing major like what you have all over your body."

"You love my tats and you know it," he smirked, causing me to stick my tongue out at him playfully.

We talked for a while longer about our relationship and us. It felt like it did before the accident.

"I wish you were here," I said suddenly. "I think you'd like it here. It's sunny and warm." I sat up a little higher in my seat then moved the screen of my laptop back a bit so the webcam was not cutting off the top of my head.

"Is your hand hurt, Zoey?"

"My hand?"

"You have scrapes on your hand. Is it from when you fell this morning?"

Shit. "Yeah, they're fine though. One of the girls from the boat crew cleaned my hands and knees up." I held my hand back up so he could see it better. He seemed fine with my answer.

"I'm glad you weren't hurt worse. What happened, anyway? Jess called to apologize for what she said to me the night of the accident and to tell me something happened on the boat. Were you crying because of me?" He scooted closer to his webcam, not waiting for an answer. "Zoey, I'm so sorry I was such an asshole to you."

"Stop, please. It's over. We're good now." He nodded and I explained everything that happened on the boat that morning.

"So you tripped over a bag on the deck?" he asked after I finished providing him with the details about my literal boat 'trip'.

"Yep, that's all it was. I was trying to get out of the group of people and my foot hung up on the strap of it. It's no big deal. I am a klutz." I searched his eyes, trying to read him, to see what he was thinking. "You look tired. Are you alright?"

He nodded. "Yeah, I am now. I didn't sleep well last night."

His comment about him not sleeping well reminded me of my earlier conversation with my mom.

"Andy, you need to be careful at work, please. No working when shit like this happens. My mom said you weren't yourself the last couple of days. I don't want you getting hurt at work if you're distracted because of me, okay?"

There was no point in trying to deny the fact we were well past the point of no return. We decided weeks ago that we would try a relationship, even though he worked at my dad's shop.

"Of course, I promise. But, I also don't plan on fighting with you ever again, so we shouldn't have any problems," he laughed.

"Sounds good," I said. "No fighting ever again. I can agree to that."

It was getting late and he had to work the next day. "I should let you get some sleep since you have to work tomorrow. It's good to see you. I've missed you."

He smiled. "I love you, Zoey. I'll talk to you tomorrow."

I didn't want to close my laptop. I wanted just to stare at him, but no sane person would do that. Deciding I wanted to be sane, I finally said my goodbyes to him.

"Sleep well, Sexy. I love you." After our chat ended, I went to find my friends and family.

Chapter Seven

All was right in my world again and for the next couple of days, the three of us lived it up in Cabo. We went on all the excursions we had booked. The horseback tour on the beach was definitely my favorite. The guide gave me the most beautiful gray and white horse to ride. I'd never been on a horse before and instantly fell in love with riding.

We rode down the beach with the sun high in the sky and puffy white clouds off in the distance. The day was absolutely breathtaking. I walked my horse over to Jess and asked her to take a picture of me with my cell so I could send one to Andy and my family back home. Leaving my cell with Jess, I turned my horse around, walking him down to the ocean.

He acted as if he liked the water, so I continued down the beach. His feet seemed to dance in the surf. I laughed and smiled the whole time, finding that I was so at peace in my own little world that I didn't notice Jess had been taking pictures and video of me with my cell.

I could definitely do this every day, I thought. At the end of our ride, we took the horses back to the barn where I convinced the owner of the stable to let me help brush them down. Her name was Josie, and she was a wonderful person who took great care of her horses.

"Josie, what's his name?" I asked, referring to the horse I had ridden and was currently brushing.

"Smoke," she answered with a smile, pushing her bangs away from her sweaty forehead. Her dark eyes sparkled with admiration as she twisted her long, black hair into a bun at the nape of her neck.

"He's amazing. I love the way he sounds when he breathes and the noises he makes. Is that weird?" I laughed when I realized I might sound like a crazy person.

She stopped what she was doing, turning to me with a knowing expression on her face. "Not at all, Zoey. It makes perfect sense to me. I've never found more peace and serenity in my life than when I'm around horses. It's why I do what I do."

As strange as it was, I knew exactly what she meant. "How did you become interested in horses?" I asked.

"I grew up in one of the orphanages in Mexico, then one day, out of the blue, they bussed a small group of kids to a horse ranch to teach us to ride and take care of the horses as part of our therapy." Josie paused, taking in a deep breath before she continued. "I fell in love with horses and when I was old enough, found a job at the ranch taking care of them. Through the years, I worked my way up and became one of the therapists at the ranch, working one on one with the kids and the horses. I retired from the ranch two years ago then spent most of my life savings on the stables."

I swallowed hard, thinking of what she must have gone through but I didn't want to be nosey. From what I'd learned over the years, I was well aware that the orphanages in foreign countries were much worse than they were in the US.

"I'm so sorry, Josie," I said quietly, feeling guilty for bringing up bad memories for her. "I know how hard it must have been for you, not having any family." I thought about how Andy had lost his family and how I was taken away from my mother at age eight.

She studied me curiously for several long seconds then asked me a question I didn't expect.

"Zoey, you seem to personally understand everything I've told you. Do you have experience with orphans?"

"I was one," I admitted plainly without thinking about it first. "How did you know?"

"We orphans have an unknown connection to each other, honey. Whether we want to or not, we're bound together by the lives we had, lost, and started again." Josie studied my face thoughtfully and took in a deep breath before she asked, "Why are you here, Zoey?"

Good question. *Why am I here?* I explained to Josie about my time in foster care, adoption at age fourteen, the opening of my store and marriage to Rob. After that, I couldn't keep myself from rambling on about my problems.

"I see," Josie said when I'd finished speaking. "What is it you'd like to accomplish while you're here?"

"Honestly, my original intention was to come here to take a break from my life. Everything was going well after my divorce, but then something happened and I let my life slip away from me. I fell into a depression for several months, pushing everyone away from me so I didn't hurt them. I started therapy again, but recently I've been having brief episodes of anxiety," I admitted.

Josie nodded her head as her sympathetic eyes met mine. "And what is your intention now?"

"Most importantly, I need to find out who I am. I have an amazing family now, great friends and a new boyfriend who has had a rough life himself. There are things in our lives standing in the way of our happiness...stuff we've both agreed to try to fix while I'm here. I was in an accident recently, which is the reason why my boyfriend, Andy, and I have issues to work out."

I took some time to explain Andy's past, my accident, and how he'd become distant because of it.

"Zoey, I'm pleased to see that you're both aware of how your life and the troubles you've had recently are affecting you and your new relationship. Your boyfriend must be quite the man to realize his own past issues need to be dealt with for you both to move forward," she said. "Do you want to tell me what happened to cause your depression? I'm a good listener."

The way Josie smiled at me eased the tension that started building when we began our discussion. She was easy to talk to so I told her about Rob suing my dad and me, then about him being vindictive, taking my prized possession Chevelle as his settlement payment.

Josie nodded her head in understanding. "That must have been very stressful for you and I can see why you decided to take a vacation. How long are you here for?"

"This is my first week. I'm staying here for a month with my family at their place." I glanced up at the clock on the barn wall, not realizing how late it was. The girls were probably wondering where I'd been since I left them at the corral when our ride was over.

"Wonderful. Will you please come back to visit Smoke and me? You can come every day if you'd like. I would love to talk with you more about your life."

I agreed to come back after Jess and Sasha went back to Sacramento. My aunt and uncle would be working, I had no plans of any kind so the stables felt like the place I needed to be. I left Josie with the horses and went back to the beach to find my friends sprawled out on the sand waiting for me.

"Z, did you have a good day?" Jess asked when she handed my cell phone back to me.

"Yes, it was the most amazing day. Josie invited me to come back here to visit next week."

I wanted to send Andy one of the pictures Jess snapped of me, so I sat on the sand and scrolled through the photos. And scrolled, and scrolled, and scrolled some more. Jess took over thirty pictures of me riding Smoke.

My friends sat on either side of me, watching as I tried to decide what photo to send him.

"That one. Send him *that* one," Sasha stated without hesitation.

I came to a photo of Smoke as he pranced around in the waves, his entire body was in full motion, his mane and tail whipped in the wind. I finally looked at myself in the photo, knowing exactly why they wanted me to send that particular picture to Andy.

They were right. It was the one he would love the most. It was the one I loved the most. In the picture, my face was lit up and I looked content with an enormous smile on my face. My eyes were closed, my head tilted upward toward the sky. The only things in the photo besides Smoke and me were the blue sky, surf, and sand. It was a beautiful picture, so I sent it to Andy and my parents.

"You should take a look at the videos next," Jess suggested.

I watched the videos then started crying. Seeing myself so completely free and truly at peace, shocked me to my core. "Oh my God, why am I so emotional?" I laughed, wiping away my tears as my two friends sandwiched me in a hug. On a whim, I sent one of the videos to Andy too.

We shook the sand off our towels, packed our books, sunscreen, and everything else we'd brought into our beach bags then drove home. By the time we arrived, it was dinnertime and we were all starving.

Thank God my uncle had taken the day off to drive us around after the boat tour yesterday because now we had all the ingredients to make fried chicken, mac and cheese, and fresh green beans. I'd also picked up several large jalapeños, so while the chicken was frying, I halved and seeded them, then stuffed each one with cream cheese. Placing a large shrimp on top of each jalapeño, I arranged them on the special rack my aunt used when she grilled them. Carrying it out to the patio, I placed it on the barbecue pit before calling Andy.

"Hey, Beautiful," he said into the phone when he answered.

Today, I *felt* beautiful. "Hey, how are you?"

"Perfect. Zoey, the picture you sent was...I don't even know how to describe it. You look so happy. Tell me about your day." I could hear the smile in his voice.

I told him about the horses, Josie, and about how I felt simply being around them. It was calming and peaceful.

"It sounds like you've found something that might help you while you're away, then. I've heard about the horse therapies before. There is a similar place near where we lived in Auckland. Sometimes they would ride by us while we were on the beach."

It felt nice talking to him with no pressure or tension. It was perfect.

"What are your plans for tomorrow night?" he asked.

"We're going back to the Cabo Wabo Cantina to go dancing," I replied. "What are you doing tomorrow night?"

"I'm going to play pool and have a couple beers with Noah. I think Jeremy might meet us at the bar too, but he wasn't sure yet."

I was glad he was hanging out with my brothers and they'd become friends.

Sasha chose that moment to yell through the open patio door, "Z, your scrimps are ready! Get off the phone with your fine man and get your skinny ass out here to take care of this shit before it burns!"

Andy cracked up laughing because he could clearly hear my loud-mouthed friend through the phone. "Is she really saying 'scrimps' instead of shrimp?"

"Yep, she saw it in a movie years ago and has called them scrimps ever since," I admitted, thinking back to watching the movie and her spitting out soda when she heard the word. *Freaking Sasha, gotta love that crazy wench.*

"Okay then, go take care of your *scrimps* before they get ruined, Beautiful. Will you call me tomorrow?" I didn't want to get off the phone, but I had stuff to do and I am sure he did too.

"Of course I will. I love you, Sexy."

"I love you, too. Have another good day tomorrow, Zoey."

My friends, family, and I sat on the patio devouring our appetizers and drinking margaritas. Dinner was close to being ready, so I tossed the green beans into the steamer. As we waited for them to cook, I sat next to my aunt and scrolled through my phone, showing her all the memories we'd captured during our horseback ride.

"Those are great pictures. See how peaceful you look?"

"Thank you, Tia." I smiled as I told her all about Josie and Smoke.

Before we sat down for dinner, Sasha pulled me aside. "I thought your aunt's name was Maria. You keep calling her Tia. You're confusing the fuck out of me. I don't know what to call her now."

Holding back a laugh, I explained to Sasha that 'tia' was the Spanish word for 'aunt'. We sat down for dinner a while later, enjoying our meal and talking about the day's events. Later that evening I crawled into bed happy, sleeping through the night for the first time since being in Cabo.

The next day we went snorkeling. I hated it. Well, I only hated one part. The tour guides threw broken up tortillas in the water to lure in the fish, which caused them to swarm around us. It freaked me out because they looked like piranha and I was definitely not in to swarms of *any* kind.

The last straw was when one of them slammed itself against my facemask. Yep, that was enough for me. After swimming away from the 'piranha', I joined a few other people who found some less threatening fish to look at.

Jess and Sasha had one more day before they returned to Sacramento, so our final activity was going out for one last night of partying. We dressed up, me in my new dress and sandals I bought when we went shopping. Sasha wore a black, mini skirt with a matching corset top and red hooker heels, while Jess dressed in a slightly conservative, but short floral dress and gladiator sandals they'd bought the day before. We snapped a couple of pictures for the memories and headed out the door.

Since it was their last night in Cabo, I was the designated driver for the evening. We arrived at the club and were halfway across the parking lot when my cell phone rang with Andy's signature ringtone.

"Hang on a sec, girls. Let me get this really quick." I wasn't sure why he was calling me back so late, since I talked to him earlier. He was supposed to be out with my brother.

I tapped the screen and said, "Hello."

Silence.

"Andy? Hello?"

Silence.

"What's up, Z?" Jess asked.

"I think he butt-dialed me again."

As I pulled the phone away from my ear to hang it up, I heard a woman moan, *"Andy."* What the fuck? I pressed the phone closer to my ear and plugged my other ear with my finger to block the noise coming out of the club. Seeing the horrified expression on my face, Jess and Sasha stepped closer, questioning looks on their faces.

I put the phone on speaker and they heard the same thing I did when the woman moaned again. Their eyes grew as large as mine had. Someone was definitely getting lucky and it was definitely Andy's phone. I was immediately upset in addition to being angry. Was this really happening? He wouldn't. Not after everything...

We continued to listen. The next thing we heard was a man's voice moan, *"Oh, Nicole."*

The voices were muffled, but I refused to listen anymore because it was making me sick. Was he really screwing Nicole, one of Jeremy's old fuck buddies? I thought back to how interested she was in him at Will and Justin's New Year's Eve party, and then when she blatantly propositioned him when he went to the bar with Jeremy a different night. I started to end the call but Jess stopped me with a suspicious expression on her face.

"Hang on a second, Z," she whispered as she whipped out her cell and punched a few buttons.

"Hey, baby, it's me," she said into her phone.

Jess had called Noah. She knew he was supposed to be with Andy at the bar playing pool. "Where's Andy at right now?" she asked my brother.

Jess looked over at me with a relieved expression on her face. "Z, he's standing five feet away from Noah playing pool. It's not him on the phone."

Thank God. She let Noah know what we were listening to on Andy's phone, then handed me her phone.

"Here's Andy," she said.

"Hello," I said into Jess's phone.

"What's going on, Zoey?" Andy asked.

"Where's your phone?"

"It's sitting on the table next to my beer." There was a moment of silence on his end of the line. "No, it *was* sitting on the table. It's not there now."

"Well someone has your phone and called me from it. Whoever it is sounds like they're having a good time with Nicole."

"Fuck," he growled. "Stay on the line. I'm going to find it." He was irate when he let my brothers know what was going on and they went to find his missing phone.

Sasha was holding my cell, which was still on speaker; the two people on the other end were still going at it from the noises they were making.

"I'll call you right back. I think we found it," Andy muttered and ended the call before I could say anything. I handed Jess her phone as we continued to listen in on mine.

The next thing we heard over my phone was a lot of commotion, a woman scream, and more moaning. Except that time, the moaning didn't sound like the *good* kind.

"Zoey, are you still there?" It was Andy, on his phone. Sasha handed my cell back to me and I took it off speaker.

"Yes, I'm here. What happened?"

He was fuming. "It looks like Nicole snatched my phone off the table when she came over to see Jeremy. It was her and Rob in the bathroom, trying to play a little prank on you."

That fucking piece of shit and skank-whore. God, I hated them for what they just did.

"What did you do when you found them?" I asked, silently hoping Rob was lying on the floor bleeding. I would pay Nicole back on my own the next time I saw her.

"The little fucker took a swing at me so I might have punched him...a few times."

Nice. "Is he bleeding?" I prayed he was.

"Maybe a little," he said, chuckling. "Can I just say how good it felt to finally punch him after all this time?"

"Yes, you can, and I hope you got one good punch in there for me," I joked.

"They were all for you, Zoey. Every one of them," he stated matter-of-factly.

Deciding we would talk the next day, Andy went back to playing pool with my brothers and I went dancing with my friends. Andy had done nothing wrong. Rob got what he deserved and Nicole would pay as soon as I saw her nasty face again. I wasn't going to let what happened ruin my last night with my best friends.

Chapter Eight

The morning of Valentine's Day, I woke up missing Andy. Well, I woke up every day missing him, but that day it was worse. I had never celebrated Valentine's Day and it didn't look like it was going to happen this year either.

Jess and Sasha left the weekend before, so it was only me with my aunt and uncle at the house. They worked during the day, so I went to the stables daily to visit with Josie and help where I could. I woke up early, but was feeling rather lazy, so I decided to lounge around in bed to read after my aunt and uncle left for work. It was still before eight, so I called Andy first.

He answered after the second ring. "Happy Valentine's Day," he said, excitedly.

I grinned because he remembered.

"Happy Valentine's Day to you, too. Do you have a hot date tonight to celebrate?"

He exhaled. "Actually, I was going to talk to you about that." *Huh?* "I wanted to go on a date with my beautiful girl, but she's out of the country right now. I was hoping she would have a Skype date with me tonight around seven. Do you think she would do that for me?"

"Of course. She would love nothing more."

We set up our date for that night at seven.

He cleared his throat. "I just realized we've made it halfway through the month. What day do you fly back? I'll need that information since I'll be picking you up at the airport."

I knew down to the exact second I was flying back to him and I couldn't wait to see his gorgeous face in person. "My flight gets back to Sacramento at three on the twenty-sixth. I am so ready to see you."

"I'm ready to see you too, Zoey. Send me your flight information next time you think about it. I'd better get ready for work now. I'll see you tonight at seven for our date. I love you."

"I love you, too." I ended our call, very excited for our date night.

I had less than fifty pages left of my book, and decided to stay home to finish it. With it being Valentine's, the stables probably wouldn't be too busy and I would go visit with Josie later in the day.

After finishing my book, I was hungry for breakfast so I went to the kitchen, cooked bacon, pancakes, eggs, and added a bowl of fruit for something sweet to eat.

I devoured every single bite of it.

Working with horses every day was a lot of manual labor, but I loved it. I dressed in old jeans and a T-shirt then pulled my hair back in a ponytail. After I brushed my teeth, I packed a beach bag with my bikini, towel, sunscreen, a new book, and left for the stables. If it turned out to be a slow day, I would head to the beach, start my book, and relax.

The stables were in full chaos when I arrived. One of the guides called in sick, so Josie was desperate for my help and I was happy to give it. I hadn't thought of giving her my cell number until then, so before I left for the day, I would make sure she had it in case she needed help again before I went home to Cali.

Not only was working at the stables a physical job, it was a dirty job as well. By the time my day was over, I smelled like horses, sweat, and dirt. My body was worn out from the work, but I drove home as fast as possible and hopped in the shower.

Even though I was starving, I wasn't going to have time to make dinner before my date with Andy. I dressed quickly and tried to blow dry my hair, but my stomach was growling so loud, I thought I'd better get food instead. I twisted my long, blonde hair back in a messy bun and jogged to the kitchen where my aunt and uncle were finishing their dinner.

"Zoey, I made you a plate while you were in the shower. It's in the microwave," my aunt said as I was rummaging through the fridge, trying to find something premade.

"Tia, you are a saint," I panted, out of breath from rushing around. "I have a Skype date with my man in two minutes," I announced, looking at the clock on the microwave as I pulled out my plate.

I didn't even heat my dinner up. I would eat it cold. I had somewhere important to be. Laughing and shaking her head, my aunt handed me a fork and napkin as I jogged past her to my bedroom to power up my laptop.

Of course, it decided to take forever to boot up. It never failed that when I was in a hurry it decided to take its sweet time.

"Don't make me upgrade you, you worthless piece of..." The laptop blinked to life at just that moment. *Shit.* I was already late. I logged in, but I'd already missed his call.

I immediately called him back. A minute later, his face popped up on the screen and my heart thudded in my chest at the sight of him.

"Sorry I'm late. This has been a crazy day."

"It's fine, Zoey. I knew you would never stand me up."

"I just stepped out of the shower. Do you mind if I eat while we talk?"

He chuckled. "Of course not. This is a date, remember? You're supposed to eat on dates."

I was wound up from rushing around, so I took a deep breath and when I did, I smelled flowers. I looked around my room only to find the most exquisite bouquet of flowers I'd ever seen on my dresser.

"Did you send me flowers?" I asked as I hopped off the bed for a closer look at them.

The card read:

> *Happy Valentine's Day, Zoey. I love you and hope you enjoy your pressies.*

"I did. Do you like them? Sorry you can't plant them, but I didn't think they'd let you take a live plant home on the plane."

"They're perfect. Thank you. I love them...and you," I replied happily.

"Eat your dinner, please. I'll entertain you while you eat."

Entertain?

I grinned deviously. "Are you gonna strip for me or something?" *Yes please.* He returned my devious look with one of his own. In the next second, he stripped his T-shirt off and tossed it behind the couch onto the floor.

"Mmm, thank you, Sexy," I teased as I wiggled my eyebrows at him.

"Better?" he asked.

"Uh huh. Definitely." He was wearing a chain around his neck with something dangling at the end.

"What is that around your neck? I haven't seen it before."

He looked down, grasped the end of it in his fingertips, and held it up to show me.

"These are my mum and dad's wedding bands. I found them in an old box I hadn't unpacked since we moved from New Zealand."

He didn't seem upset about them. It didn't even seem to faze him when I asked what they were. He must have been dealing with what he wanted to while I was gone. If I had asked last month, he would've gone quiet and rubbed his hands down his jaw. Not today, though. It made me happy for him.

"Do you know how beautiful you are wearing that chain with all those tattoos?"

He chuckled. "You know men aren't supposed to be beautiful. They're supposed to be handsome and masculine."

"Let's not forget sexy, too," I added. "You are all of that and more. When you add it up, it equals beautiful. Sorry, I can't help it. You're just too..."

He put his hand up to stop me from going any further. "Zoey, I get it. I'm too sexy, remember?" He laughed at his own cheese ball joke.

"Actually, you're "Sex on Fire" now. I changed your ringtone ages ago to something a bit more fitting."

He arched his brows. "I guess I'd better check the song out later. Speaking of songs, I want you to sit there and *eat*. I have another pressie for you. Sit tight for a sec."

He moved his laptop back further, then stood and reached over the back of the couch to pick up his guitar from the stand. I was blessed with a nice shot of his gorgeous ass, and stared at it the entire time it was on the screen. As he sat back down, I quickly wiped the smile from my face so he wouldn't notice.

"I've been learning new songs while you've been gone," he said as he sat back down and situated his guitar on his thigh.

Since he'd moved his laptop away, I had full view of his half-naked body from his knees up. He was wearing my favorite jeans, and he was *beautiful*. I don't care what he said.

"Please don't laugh if I suck at singing this, 'cause I'm really nervous."

He's going to sing? I thought he was only going to play the guitar for me.

"I'd never laugh at you. You'll be perfect."

He shook his head and grinned at me. "Beautiful. Perfect. Zoey, you're gonna give me a big ego if you keep it up," he laughed.

We sat in silence while he fine-tuned his guitar. I definitely wanted to remember this day, so I reached down and hit the record button so I could make a video of him to watch again later.

Andy rubbed his forehead nervously with the back of his hand. "Okay, here goes. I'm sure you've heard this song before. It's called "Fade Away."

He took a deep, anxious breath and began strumming his guitar. I didn't immediately recognize the song until he started singing.

His performance absolutely blew me away. The man could *sing*. It was a perfect song too. His voice sounded very much like the man who actually sang the song, deep and sexy.

As he sat on his couch playing and singing, my eyes pooled with tears. I longed to be sitting on the couch next to him while he serenaded me. Listening closely to the lyrics it was clear to me why he picked that song to sing.

The song was amazing when the band Seether performed it, but with him sitting there with only his guitar, and me watching, I had never felt so special and loved in my life.

He finished the song and looked at me apprehensively to see whether I approved or not. By that time, all the tears that welled up in my eyes were running down my face and onto the dinner plate I'd abandoned on my lap.

There were no words. He was amazing.

"What's wrong? Was it so *bad* it made you cry?" he joked. He knew I liked it.

"Ha ha, very funny. Please tell me you have more songs to do."

He smiled. "Just one more, but I need to switch guitars. Give me another minute. Eat!" he demanded with a grin, pointing at my plate.

This time when he stood up, he left my view completely so all I could see was the empty couch.

I heard him in the background rustling around, when James hopped up on the couch in front of the webcam. "James," I called, trying to get his attention. "Hey, James, what are you doing?"

Yes, I was talking to my cat as if he was a person. He heard me and walked to the edge of the couch, trying to decide if he should jump to the table to get closer to the laptop. He was teetering on the edge, still trying to decide, when Andy walked behind the couch with his amp and guitar.

"James, *no*," he stated firmly.

"Hey, be nice to my baby, you big meanie." James became sidetracked by something and jumped to the floor. Yep, our kitty had a short attention span.

Andy chuckled in the background. I still couldn't see him on the screen. "He jumped on the kitchen table last night from one of the chairs and knocked over my cup of ice water," he laughed. "The cup was aimed at me and it spilled all over my lap. It was a bit, um—"

I could not control my response. "I bet it was cold and you had to take your pants off, huh?"

He sat down on the couch, smirking. "I'm not taking my pants off for this song, Zoey."

Damn. "That's too bad. I was kind of looking forward to seeing you without your pants," I joked.

He shook his head as he settled his electric guitar on his thigh then leaned forward to look directly into the webcam. "Zoey, when you get back here, neither one of us will be wearing *anything* or leave your bed for at least two days. I'm tired of taking cold showers while you've been away."

"Sounds good to me," I said because the anticipation was already killing me. "We need to stop talking about this or I'm gonna take matters in to my own hands."

I laughed and wiggled my eyebrows so he *knew* what I meant. At that point, I was not opposed to taking care of my own needs since he was in California and I was in Cabo.

Andy's eyes shot up to mine and he raised a brow, shocked at what I'd said. God, I loved it when he did that. "Did you really just say that to me, Zoey? Oh fuck, the visual from that alone is going to keep me busy later tonight."

My jaw dropped and I giggled, realizing we'd just dirty talked each other over Skype. Andy stuck his guitar pick between his teeth, reached behind the guitar on his lap, and I could only assume he adjusted himself in his pants. When I laughed at the grimace on his face, he playfully glared at me.

"You ready for our song?" he asked after he took the guitar pick from between his front teeth.

Our song? I nodded and hit the record button again.

As soon as he started playing his guitar, my heart started thumping faster in my chest.

He learned to play and sing "An Olive Grove Facing the Sea." Holy hell. I was not expecting it at all. It was wonderful watching him play his guitar because he was so good at it. His long fingers moved smoothly and precisely over the neck and strings.

Vocally, he was flawless. He even hit the higher notes perfectly. It made my heart swell hearing him sing the lyrics aloud after our birthday dance. I would definitely try to get him to sing with me one day.

He finished the song and set his guitar aside. "Well? Did I suck at that one?" he asked.

"Um, no. I don't want you to get a big ego or anything, but...you were perfect. You can sing for me any day, Andy."

"You know I'd do anything for you, right?"

I nodded. "Of course, and I would for you." I missed him so much it hurt. I really wanted to touch him. A long sigh escaped from deep within my lungs. "I wish you were here, even if it was for just a day. We could lounge on the beach in the sun."

His eyes lit up and he smiled. "It would be nice, wouldn't it? It's cold, especially without you here. James isn't much help. I swear he hogs the bed more than you do."

Even if it was at my expense, I loved how he knew to rein me back in when I started to get a little sad.

I am no bed hog.

"Maybe I'll take you home to New Zealand someday," he added.

"Sounds amazing, Andy. Count me in. I'll start saving some money when I get back."

He shook his head. "No, you won't. I said I'd *take* you to En Zed, which means I pay for everything."

I smiled and shook my head. I was definitely going to start saving up for our trip.

Realizing my full dinner plate was still sitting on my lap, I picked it up and set it aside. I hadn't touched a bite of it. I wasn't even hungry anymore.

"Zoey, please go eat your dinner. I'll talk to you tomorrow."

"Alright, bossy. Thank you for the flowers and the songs. I love you."

"Love you too, Beautiful. Happy Valentine's Day."

After we disconnected our chat, I sent him a text.

"New York," by S.P.

It was a song from the newest album, and of course had the perfect lyrics.

The song made me think about what each of us went through before we found each other, the hurt we both experienced and saying we loved each other before we really knew each other, but meaning every word.

It made me miss him, the scent of his cologne and the feel of his skin on mine.

I seriously considered packing my bag that night to catch the next flight home.

For the next several days, I kept myself very busy. I was enjoying myself at the stables working with Josie, but I was ready to go home. I missed Andy, my family, and my friends.

Andy had been mysteriously missing-in-action each day until later in the evening. When I asked him what was keeping him so busy, he always answered "work." I let it go because I was *not* going to be one of those girls who demanded to know where their boyfriends were every second of the day. He did have a life besides me.

When I did speak to him, he was very attentive and loving, but something was up. I also knew he would tell me what was going on when the time was right for him.

We were taking it day-by-day, right? I still had feelings to work through before I went home. I was almost ready, but just needed a few more days.

While I was helping Josie with the horses, she was helping me to get myself back together. I didn't realize she was doing it because she was very good at what she did. She knew it, of course, but she didn't push me. She must have been *really* good at her job as a therapist at the horse ranch. We talked constantly when we were together and I told her about things I never talked to anyone about, not even Dr. Jensen.

The Thursday morning before I was to fly home, Josie invited me out on a ride with her. It would be just the two of us going on one last trip. During our talks, I'd asked her only once to tell me about how she became an orphan. Her response was that she would tell me before I left and *only* after she was certain I'd figured out who I was, since it was my goal. We made a deal that if I didn't figure out who I was by the time I left, she was going to make me go snorkeling with her for one last visit with the 'piranha.'

There was no way in hell I was going to go snorkeling again, so I worked my ass off to figure my shit out.

Finally, after many conversations with Josie, I knew who I was. I was Zoey Lynn James. Daughter of Doug and Luisa James, sister to Jason, Noah, Jeremy, and Adam James. Girlfriend to Andy Tate, the best friend of Jess, Sasha, Will, and Justin. I was not a victim of my birth mom, my sperm donor father, or a victim of Rob. I was my own person, who had my own mind and ideas, and would not think of myself as anyone less than that.

When I arrived at the stables early Thursday morning, Josie had Smoke and her horse, Magnum, tied to the fence for our ride. Noticing they weren't saddled up yet, I went to the barn to see if Josie needed help bringing the saddles out. As I walked through the door, Josie was coming out with a backpack already on her back.

"Ready to go?" she asked.

"Don't we need saddles?"

Josie shook her head. "No. Where we're going we won't need them," she said with a mischievous smile. She called over her shoulder to one of the stable hands, "Carlos, can you give Zoey a boost, por favor?"

"Sí, señora," Carlos said with a grin, as he glanced up at Josie. There was something in his eyes that told me he was quite fond of Josie, and not in a friend-like manner. It was much more than that. It appeared that Carlos had a bit of a crush.

With a smile, I untied Smoke, and stepped beside him to wait for Carlos. In the next moment, a strong hand wrapped around my calf, my feet were off the ground, and I was swinging a leg over Smoke's back. I'd always ridden him using a saddle so I was a little freaked out about falling off.

"Gracias, Carlos," I said with a wink as I waited for Josie to tell me what to do next.

"Just keep your body centered and you'll do just fine," Josie reassured me. In one swift movement, she grabbed a thick chunk of Magnum's mane and gracefully swung herself up onto his bare back. She took the reins in her hand, turned her horse toward the beach and I followed them.

We rode along the sand in silence away from the stables and from the beachgoers. "You wanted to know my story, Zoey, and you've worked so hard for yourself, I'm ready to tell you."

For some reason I was very nervous to hear Josie's story. I knew it was bad, so much worse than anything I could have ever imagined. But, if she wanted to tell me, I would let her. She'd listened to me for the last three weeks. I owed her as much.

"Do you know what coyotes and drug mules are?" Josie asked.

Oh, God. "Yes, I do. My mom is from Santiago, Mexico, and I've heard horror stories." Suddenly, I didn't want her to share her story because I didn't want her to relive it. "Josie, you don't have to tell me."

"It's okay, amiga, I've made peace with it," she said, then started her story. "When I was nine, my parents tried to get my family across the border into Arizona from Mexico. They wanted a better life for us so they found a man...a 'coyote.' They paid him their life savings to take my older sister, them, and me across the border illegally. The coyote loaded my family, plus more than thirty others into a small trailer then drove us out into the desert toward Arizona. In the middle of the night, the driver stopped to let us all out of the trailer. We thought we'd made it to the border, but we were wrong. We were met by men with guns. All the young women, including myself, were separated from our parents and the men from the trailer. We watched as the others from the trailer were lined up next to a shallow ditch then shot to death. Including my parents."

Tears fell from my eyes as I listened to Josie speak, but she continued as if she'd told her account of that night a thousand times.

"The men shoved us into the trailer and took us back in to Mexico where they said if we didn't become 'drug mules' and carry drugs to the US for them, they would either kill us or turn us in to whores for the men in their cartel. Since I was so young, my sister tried convincing the cartel to let me go, but they refused. One night while I was sleeping, my sister woke me and we ran away. She had someone on the inside that she trusted, and they took me to a safe orphanage and left. I never saw my sister again."

"Oh, Josie, I'm so sorry," I cried. She was only a year older than I was when Child Protective Services took me from my mother.

"Gracias, Zoey. This is no time for crying though," she said, seemingly unaffected by the story she'd just told me. "Let's go have some fun and enjoy the rest of our morning."

Getting over my initial shock of what Josie had been through, we had a great morning together. She'd packed us a picnic to eat on the beach. After lunch, we rode the horses into a small lagoon where they swam around with us on their backs. It was exhilarating, freeing, and the best part of my vacation.

When we arrived back at the stables, I invited Josie over for dinner. She accepted, and that night, we shared a wonderful meal together with my family, talking late in to the evening before Josie made her departure.

"Zoey, take the rest of your time here and relax. I cannot thank you enough for all the help you've given me at the stables. If you ever decide to move here, you've got a job."

We laughed, but I knew she meant what she said. "I'll see you tomorrow. I need one more day then I'll be out of your hair, I promise." I hugged her tightly. "Thank you, Josie. You've helped me find myself...I will never forget you."

Friday morning, I woke up feeling like a new person. There was still an ache in my gut, but deep down it was because I missed home. I began the tedious task of packing my clothes into my suitcase and wished I'd brought two so I had more room to pack all the souvenirs I bought.

After breakfast, I left for the stables to go on one last ride. Josie didn't have a full schedule so she'd left Smoke behind for me.

Not bothering to saddle him up since I was comfortable with him, I slipped his bridle on and led him down to the beach. I kicked off my sandals, grabbed the reins along with a handful of Smoke's mane, and swung my leg over his back. Once I was steadied, I turned him toward the beach. I let him prance around in the waves like he had the first day I rode him.

It was so liberating I couldn't help but grin and soon found myself singing quietly. Good thing nobody else was on that stretch of the beach because they would've probably thought I was a lunatic.

I wasn't. I was truly happy...a new and improved Zoey.

After riding a while I hopped down into the surf to cool off, then walked Smoke slowly back to the stables. I took my time and brushed him, feeding him the sugar cubes I'd brought for a treat.

Giving Smoke one last pet and scratch behind his ears, I went to say bye to Josie and all my new friends at the stables. I made my way back to my aunt and uncle's, and when I arrived, I found the house empty. I strolled into the kitchen and found a note on the countertop.

Zoey,

Something came up with Tio's work, and we had to go out to one of his job sites. We won't be home until Sunday.

Sorry about dinner.

See you then

Love Tia

Chapter Nine

Since I was home alone for the rest of the weekend, I heated up leftovers for dinner then tried to call Andy, but the call went to voicemail. He was probably working late again. I decided to take a nice long, hot bath. Filling the tub and adding scented bath oil, I submerged in the water up to my chin.

After a while of luxurious soaking, washing, and conditioning my hair, I took my sponge and scrubbed my skin until it felt clean and smooth. My fingertips were getting wrinkly, so I stepped out of the tub and wrapped a large towel around myself. As I did, Andy's ringtone blasted from my cell phone in my bedroom. I scrambled out of the bathroom to my dresser to answer it.

"Hi, Zoey, how are you?" Andy asked.

I fastened the towel around me tighter. "I'd be much better if it was Sunday and I was seeing you in person."

He laughed. "Believe me, I know how you feel. Did you get the package I sent?"

Thinking back, I hadn't seen anything out of the ordinary when I came home from the stables, but then again, I wasn't expecting anything, so I wasn't looking.

"No, I didn't see anything sitting around inside the house anywhere," I said sadly. I loved it when he surprised me with little gifts or notes. He'd sent me something every week since I'd been gone. I loved him for it because he was thinking about me as much as I was thinking about him.

"Maybe it was dropped off outside the front door," he suggested. "I checked the shipment tracking online and it should be there. Can you go check? It's not something that should be left outside."

I was still wearing a towel. "Yes, of course. Let me change though. I can't go outside like this."

"Like what?" he asked, his voice perking up. "What exactly are you wearing, Beautiful?"

"Well, if you must know, you caught me stepping out of the bathtub, so I am wearing a towel." I hoped he was getting a nice visual, like the one I got a few weeks back from him.

He chuckled, his voice low and gravelly. "Don't they live outside of town? Nobody can see anything. Please go check outside. Besides, I'd like to see you in your towel in a few minutes. We can Skype."

"I'll strip for you if you strip for me," I offered with a laugh as I made my way to the front door.

"That is most definitely a deal I can agree to," Andy said with a hint of amusement in his voice.

When I made it to the door, I swung it open wide, and had a sudden flash of déjà vu from the first time I met him. He was standing in the doorway at his apartment, and I remembered that he was the most beautiful man I had ever seen.

Except this time, it was different. I wasn't in his apartment. I was in Cabo and he wasn't holding a moving box in his hands. He was holding a carry-on suitcase and his cell phone up to his ear.

"Hey," he said as he hung up his phone.

I was in complete and utter disbelief.

He was here.

In Cabo.

Three feet away from me.

In the flesh, and *still* the most beautiful man I'd ever seen.

Simultaneously, I hung up my phone, tossed it on the table next to the door, and launched myself across the threshold into his arms. I squeezed him as if my life depended on it.

"Oh my God, I can't believe you're here! What are you doing here?" I squealed with excitement as I backed up and grabbed my slipping towel before it came all the way off.

"I heard you needed a ride home from the airport, so here I am, at your service," he joked and pulled me back to him.

Yes, here he was, arms wrapped around me, smelling so delicious, all tattooed and incredibly hot. "I need a ride, now. Come here," I said breathlessly, as I slid my fingers inside the waistband of his pants and pulled him closer to me.

I missed the feel of his stubble on my face and his lips on mine, his skin on mine. I unwrapped myself from him and dragged him inside the house, slamming the door. With my fingers still inside the waistband of his pants, I pulled him down the hallway to my bedroom.

"Drop your suitcase," I ordered. "And those pants too, for that matter."

Andy grinned, dropped his suitcase, and pulled me to him. I slipped my hands under his shirt, running them over his hard abs and chest. He wasn't dropping his pants, so I loosened the button and zipper on them myself. I hooked my finger in the top of my towel, letting it drop to the floor at my feet.

Finally, he was getting the not-so-subtle hints I was throwing at him. His arms went around me and he pulled me into a kiss that ignited my entire body on fire. How did I go almost an entire month without touching this man? We devoured each other with our mouths, tongues warm and wet, exploring.

His hands slid down my back, then further down to grip my bare ass as he slowly pulled my hips forward to crush me against his erection. My hands made their way back up his shirt and slipped it off over his head. He needed to be naked as quickly as possible. I was done waiting.

"You will never know how much I've missed these," I said as I began to kiss and trace my tongue over the tattoos across his chest. He was still wearing the chain with his parents' wedding rings. I licked over to his nipple and teased it to harden before sucking it into my mouth.

He drew in a harsh breath. "I love it when you do that," he murmured hoarsely. I trailed my tongue over to his other nipple and flicked it, then nipped it lightly with my teeth, causing him to groan.

Andy had other body parts I wanted to flick with my tongue so I dropped to my knees. It had been way too long. I pulled off his shoes and socks, his hands automatically entwining his fingers through my hair. Yep, he was ready for it too.

I ran my hands up his thighs, then slowly over his erection to his waistband. Without hesitation, I tugged his pants and boxers down, freeing him. As I worked them down his legs with one hand, the other hand guided his cock into my mouth.

I sucked on him, hard; he was delectable after not tasting him in so long. I looked up at his face as he watched me. His gorgeous blue eyes were already glazed over with lust, which instigated a moan from me. I took him further inside my mouth, then pulled back to tease the head of his cock with my lips and tongue.

His hips jerked slightly and he let out a long breath. "Fuck, Zoey. Stop. Come up here," he mumbled.

Stop? Why? I continued what I was doing, but looked up at him, questioning him with my eyes.

"Stand up," he insisted, putting his hands out to help me up.

"What's wrong?" I asked breathlessly as I stood.

"Nothing is wrong. I'm not going to muck this up like I did last time, that's all."

Instantly, I knew he was referring to the awful night we had before I left. It had been a month and I'd let it go, but apparently he hadn't. "I want to make it up to you if you'll let me." I nodded because if he felt he needed to atone for it, I would let him.

He sat on my bed and pulled me to stand facing him. His eyes roamed my body then back up to meet my eyes.

"You're so beautiful," he whispered. "I can't believe you're finally standing here in front of me."

His hands on my hips, he trailed kisses from my belly to my breasts. He followed my previous lead and sucked each hardened nipple into his mouth, teasing them mercilessly with his lips and tongue.

My arms wrapped around his shoulders, where I gently grazed his back and neck with my fingertips. One hand still on my hip, he slid his other hand between my legs to massage my clit. I was aching and so hot for him I nearly had an orgasm the second he touched me. I let my head fall slowly forward, pressing my forehead to his. I breathed in the scent of his shampoo and tangled my fingers in his short hair.

"Please, I need you now," I whispered against his lips. He pushed himself further back onto the bed, lifting me to straddle his lap. My knees sat on either side of his hips, and my breasts pressed against his muscular chest.

He positioned me over the head of his long, thick cock and I slowly eased down onto him. I hadn't been with anyone since Rob, or anyone as large, so my body slowly stretched to accommodate his size. I lowered myself a few inches then raised back up enough to where he almost slipped out.

"Zoey, *please*...it's been too long," he groaned as he grasped my hips and guided me back down, then up again.

Andy slowly eased himself further inside me each time. It was pure ecstasy. He stopped pulling me down, but my body craved for him to fill me. I lowered myself until I couldn't take anymore of him. I rocked my hips forward, sliding up and down, taking more of him inside me each time.

He liked it so much he gripped my hips hard, urging me to do it repeatedly. "Fuck, that feels so good," he growled.

We found our desperate rhythm and began kissing again, his hands gripping my hips. As I raised and lowered myself on him, using my arms around his neck and shoulders for balance, my nipples grazed his hard, muscular chest, causing the most glorious vibrations to trail between them to where our bodies joined.

He slipped a hand between us and found me with his fingertips. He began to stroke me lightly. I yearned for more, so I moved faster. Each time I lowered myself, his fingers bumped my clit harder, sending the most erotic sensations through me. He began breathing faster and buried his face in the crook of my neck.

"Mmm, Zoey," he moaned in between his quick breaths. The sounds coming from him and the sensation of his moan rumbling in his chest against mine sent me over the edge.

I gasped and rolled my head back, my body burning and clenching around him as my orgasm reached its peak. He flicked his tongue over my hardened nipple and then sucked it delicately. *Oh my God.* He wrapped his arms around me, holding me close, slightly rotating his hips until my orgasm subsided.

My legs were tired from the sudden exertion, and I could barely move. As he slowly slid himself out of me, I nearly had another orgasm from the leftover sensations still pulsing deep inside me.

"Lie back for me, Beautiful," he said calmly. His voice was sweet and soothing.

"My legs are shaking so bad, I can't get up just yet," I giggled.

"It's alright. I've got you."

He lifted me slightly and guided himself back inside me. My arms still around his neck, he stood up, holding my legs around his hips, then laid me gently on the bed. He eased me onto my back, never moving his lips from mine.

Everything seemed to be moving in slow motion.

The weight of him on me felt like heaven. His elbows propped him up just enough, so it wasn't too much. I adored the fact that I could watch his beautiful face while he made love to me.

"I love you, Zoey," he said as he started slowly thrusting his hips.

My legs were still shaking when I pulled his face down to kiss him. "I love you, too," I whispered as our bodies moved together in a slow, easy pace.

His eyes went from a bright blue to a faded blue, dripping with lust. The song "Fallen Empires" crossed my mind as I watched his face. He rose back up on his elbows just enough and started thrusting his hips harder and slightly faster. All the while, his eyes burned in to mine. I could not look away and neither could he. Forgetting about my shaking legs, I ground my heels down on the bed, thrusting my hips up to meet his.

Balancing on his elbow and forearm, he reached down with his other hand to grasp me behind the knee. He pulled my leg up to wrap it around the back of his thigh so he could deepen his thrusts. His lips found mine then traveled south to torture my breasts.

"Andy, that feels so good. Don't stop," I gasped. He continued driving into me and slowly started rotating his hips, so he was grinding against me. He would do it every few times he would thrust.

His breath came in quick, short huffs and I knew he was close. I was close to coming again from watching him. Wondering what he would do, I ran my nails lightly down his back, careful not to scratch him too hard.

"Fuck, do it again, Zoey," he gasped and thrust harder.

I did it again. "*Harder...*" he groaned.

So I did as he asked, much harder that time. It turned him on, so it turned me on.

He rotated his hips again, and another orgasm began to pulsate inside me. He gave one final thrust as my body tightened hard around him, then collapsed on top of me, his own orgasm taking over.

"*Ahhh fuck, Zoey...*" His cock throbbed as he came. His hips continued to rotate until my orgasm faded and every last drop of him was inside me.

Andy groaned against me, his breath cooling my sweat-slicked neck...was I dreaming? I was in the freaking bathtub thirty minutes ago, and now I lay shaking, completely spent, with a gorgeous, sweaty man on top of me. I couldn't have been happier.

We laid there catching our breath, with his head next to mine on the pillow as he playfully nibbled on my neck and the ticklish area just behind my ear. He gave me one last kiss on the cheek before he finally rose up on his elbows.

"Hi, Beautiful," he said, alternating kisses between my lips and cheeks as I squirmed beneath him. "I feel like I'm crushing you." He rolled off me and pulled me on top of him, where I rested my cheek on his tattooed chest.

"I don't know what brought you down here, but I'm glad it did."

He lazily stroked my back with his fingertips as his heart rapidly beat against my cheek. "Zoey, *you* brought me here. Our conversation a while back, when you told me you would love to relax with me on the beach, even if it was for only one day...it sounded amazing. Then you sent me the text with the 'New York' song. I talked to your dad the next day to see if he would give me today off. I busted my ass since then at work to get all my jobs done so I could fly out this afternoon. Now here we are."

I rested my hand under my chin across his chest to look him in the eyes. "Thank you. I'm happy you're here. We have the whole house to ourselves until Sunday."

He turned his wrist to look at his watch. "Actually, we need to get out of here. We have reservations."

I eyed him inquiringly. "What do you mean *reservations*?"

He reached up, pulled the chain off over his head, and unclasped it, sliding his parents' wedding rings off.

"What are you doing?" I asked. He pulled my left hand out from under my chin and slipped the smaller of the two rings onto my ring finger.

"Andy?"

He grinned. "Don't freak out, but I made reservations at one of the resorts here for tonight and tomorrow night. It's all inclusive, private beaches, and I booked the honeymoon suite. We don't have to leave the resort at all if we don't want to."

I was speechless. I sat up, wrapping the bed sheet around myself.

"So, for the rest of the weekend, we'll be Mr. and Mrs. Andrew J. Tate," he said.

"Andy, this belonged to your mom. I don't want to lose it." I tried to pull the ring off, but he took my hand in his to stop me.

"No, please don't take it off, Zoey. It's only for the weekend, I promise. It'll look funny if we're not wearing rings while checking in to the honeymoon suite. That's all."

He handed me his dad's ring and held his left hand out for me to put it onto his finger. Silently, I slid it on him then brushed my lips over the ring. "I love you."

Andy sat up then patted his lap, so I moved over to sit on him. I wrapped the bed sheet around us and he held me tightly as he combed his fingers through my still damp hair. "Please don't take this the wrong way, but how can you afford to do all of this? It was last minute travel, so I know it wasn't cheap." Suddenly, I felt horrible for asking. "Sorry that sounded bad, didn't it?"

He laughed. "No, it's fine. Let's just say, I've been thinking about some things in my life while you've been gone. For one, I opened the box from New Zealand and found the rings, and I know if you thought about it for a second, you'd realize where the money came from for the trip."

The money from the life insurance. Andy previously mentioned he hadn't touched a penny of it since he received it ten years ago.

"Good for you," I said. "I'm glad you're doing something you wanted to do with the money. I know you would rather have your family, but it's there if you need it for anything. I'm happy for you."

The conversation was getting a little heavy, but we were both fine with it. He had changed in the last month, right along with me.

"Zoey, I can't think of anything I'd rather spend all of my money on than you and me. Now let's get to the resort so we can get back in bed."

With a chuckle and a smack to my ass, he practically shoved me off the bed to take a quick shower together. He made sure we only washed ourselves instead of each other, because we both knew where it would lead. Not that either of us would've minded, but apparently we had somewhere to be.

I packed a few different outfits into Andy's half-empty carry-on suitcase and we headed to the resort in his rental car. Sitting in the passenger seat of a brand new Camaro, with my hands folded on my lap, my fingers spun the wedding band around my finger.

"It feels weird having a wedding ring on again," I admitted. "I mean, I know it's not for real, but..."

"Yeah, it does feel strange, doesn't it?" he replied, glancing at his left hand.

All I could do was smile. I was thrilled he was there with me in Cabo for the next two days. Andy surprising me, just having very intense, almost desperate sex, was a huge step in our relationship, and I was so very ready for it.

Chapter Ten

Andy pulled his rental car into the parking area of the resort, we went in to the reservation desk, checked in, and found our room. "I need food, Zoey. Do you want something from room service?" he asked as he sat down on the edge of the bed after we checked out all the amenities of the honeymoon suite.

I shook my head. "I ate before you came to the house. What do you want to eat? I can order for you."

I scanned over the desserts before handing him the room service menu, then straddled him on the edge of the bed. "Maybe I'll just eat *you* for dessert, Mr. Tate," I whispered.

"I think I'll let you, Mrs. Tate."

He tossed the menu onto the bed and pulled me into a deep, passionate kiss, letting his hands leisurely roam my body.

And then his stomach let out a loud growl, interrupting us. I ordered him a steak dinner and a piece of chocolate cake for each of us. There was a bottle of champagne chilling in the room when we arrived, so we popped the cork on it and waited for his food. I considered changing into my pajamas, but I knew I wouldn't be wearing them for long.

He had given me fair warning neither one of us would be wearing *anything* for at least two days when I came home.

When the food arrived, he dug in ravenously.

"When was the last time you ate?" I joked before I took a bite of my cake.

"This morning before I went to the airport," he mumbled with a mouthful of food. "Oh, and the flight attendant gave me a few extra bags of peanuts on the plane."

I laughed. "Yes, I bet she did. You probably didn't even need to ask for them. Did she feed them to you too?"

He chuckled and shook his head. "Very funny, smartass."

I set my cake aside and poured him another glass of the champagne. The room had an iPod dock, so I plugged in my iPod, turning on some music for us to listen to while we ate.

After dinner, I pulled my pajamas out of his suitcase so I could change. He took them out of my hands and tossed them right back in.

"Remember our deal, Zoey? Two days, bed, no clothes," he shook his head and smirked at me, a big grin covering his face.

We both stripped completely naked and hopped into bed to watch a movie. I was just happy to be with him and it had been a long day for both of us.

Andy was exhausted, so he fell asleep within minutes. He'd been working overtime for more than a week and a half to finish his work, just to have one measly day off to fly to see *me*. He deserved to sleep, so I let him. I shut off the lights and the television, curled up with him, and fell asleep myself.

A few hours later, I woke up to Andy kissing my neck. His warm breath tickled just below my ear, but still caused a chill and goose bumps to break out across my skin.

"Andy, what are you doing?" I asked, knowing what his plan was.

"I was hoping to make love to my gorgeous, pretend wife," he said as he kissed down to my collarbone.

My heart thumped in my chest when he said *wife*. It was way too soon, but I did love the sound of it.

"By all means, please do," I whispered while pushing the covers off me, giving him better access.

He took his time, slowly kissing every inch of me. He returned to my lips finally as he positioned himself on his knees between my legs. With his hands on either side of my head, he hovered over me, not touching me anywhere except my lips.

He reached down and massaged my clit in a leisurely circular motion while he kissed me. I raised my leg up, wrapping it around his hip and pulling him down to me.

Once he was down, I pushed him over onto his back, straddling him. I wanted to be in control, so I gripped his wrists and pinned them up over his head.

"What are *you* doing, Zoey?" he growled, as he tried freeing himself from my grip.

"Oh no, you don't. Stay put. I promise to be gentle," I teased playfully, just before I nipped his ear with my teeth.

With a deep laugh emanating from his body, he grinned wickedly. "Don't be," he said as he rolled his hips upward, pressing himself against me.

"You like it rough, Andy?" I released my grip on his wrists, expecting him to reach out and touch me, but he entwined his fingers together and put them to rest under the back of his head instead.

"Do what you will," he said hoarsely, as that teasing, sexy grin of his slid over his face.

Gladly.

I slipped out of bed and turned on one lamp to the dimmest setting. There was just enough light in the room so he would still be able to see what I was going to do. I took one of the chairs from the table and set it in the middle of the room, then picked up his boxer briefs and tossed them over to him on the bed.

"Put these on, Sexy. When you're done, sit there," I directed, pointing to the chair.

"But what about the no clothing rule?" he asked curiously as he stood to put on his boxers.

"I guess it's meant to be broken. Besides, you won't be wearing them very long, and I *will* make it worth your while." I left him with an intrigued expression on his face and took his suitcase with me to the bathroom.

I fluffed my hair in a messy, tousled style, applied a touch of eye makeup and my favorite pink lip-gloss. I opened the suitcase to get the red lacy panties and matching bra he liked so much, but found that all of our clothing had been tossed around inside on the trip from the house. As I searched for the red lingerie, I found the sheer nightie and the panties I'd worn when I tried to surprise him before I left for Cabo.

Even though I'd thrown them away that horrid night, I smiled at his gesture. He retrieved them from the trash and brought them for me, but I wasn't going to wear them, not tonight anyway. What I had planned for him required something a bit racier, so I slipped on the red panties and bra set. I wouldn't mention I'd found my other lingerie in his suitcase, but I decided to surprise him by wearing it another time.

I turned off the bathroom light and opened the door. "Eyes closed, please,"

Peeking out at Andy to make sure he did as I instructed, I walked quietly past him to the iPod dock and found the song I wanted to dance to, "Sail," by Awolnation.

Originally, I planned to perform the dance I learned in class for him before I went to Cabo and then make love to him, but after the accident, I quit the class because of my injuries. Then my next plan with him was ruined because he wouldn't touch me. But that was a month ago and I was fully healed now. Not to mention, I was much more confident than I was before.

"Open your eyes and put your hands down at your sides."

Without question, he did what I told him to, so I pressed play on the iPod. As I dragged my short nails across his back from shoulder to shoulder, he shuddered and fidgeted in his chair at my touch. Standing directly behind him when the song started, I lightly ran my fingertips down each side of his neck and across his muscular shoulders.

The song had a great beginning. Several rhythmic notes of music played as I slowly made my way around to face him, dragging my fingertips across his back, then from his shoulder to his chest. As the first thump of the bass sounded, I straddled his lap and gripped the tops of his shoulders with my hands for balance. I arched my body over backward away from him, giving him a nice view of my tiny, red outfit. At the next thump of the bass, I whipped my head up quickly, making eye contact with him.

Sitting on him, I swiveled my hips, grinding myself on his lap, feeling the length of him against me. He groaned and reached up to grasp my hips. "Ah, ah, ah...no touching," I teasingly scolded him as I caught his hands and pushed them back down at his sides.

He took in a sharp breath as I ground against him again and found that he was hard beneath his boxers. The feel of his arousal on my already sensitive lady parts made me close my eyes and moan. There was no way in hell I was going to make it through the whole song without stripping off his boxers.

Leaning forward, I brushed my lips lightly across his. He tilted his head slightly in an attempt to press his lips to mine, but I was too quick for him. He groaned with frustration and called me a tease. I repeated the move before he figured out what I was doing and tried to kiss me again.

I stood up and spun around slowly, so I was no longer facing him. Standing with my legs apart, I swayed back and forth with a slight twist in my hips, giving him a nice view of the tiny, lace boy-shorts panties he liked so much. I straddled him again and gave him a little lap dance.

He was enjoying it, and so was I.

Facing away, I lowered myself to his lap and reclined back onto his chest, resting my head on his shoulder.

"*Please, Zoey.* Can I touch you now?" he panted in my ear, his stubble tickling my neck as I rubbed my ass against his erection.

Reaching down, I took his hands in mine and brought them up for him so he would touch me. Planting my feet on the floor, I rotated my hips on his lap as his erection strained the confines of his boxers. His hands roamed over my stomach. One hand went to my breast and the other slipped down between my legs.

I leaned forward for him as he unsnapped my bra with one hand. Just as he attempted to pull my panties to the side so he could touch me, I stood up to face him, sliding my bra straps down one at a time, doing a little striptease for him. He grinned, unable to take his eyes off me for one second.

After I slowly pulled off my bra, I draped it around the back of his neck then backed up so I was no longer touching him. I swayed from side to side, dancing for him. I was completely in to it and no longer thinking properly. I just let the music and my movements take over.

I danced around him as he hungrily watched every move I made. Standing behind him, I leaned over his right shoulder and raked my fingertips from his thighs, up over his abs and chest, then down his arms. Moving back around to the front of him, I pushed his knees apart, kneeling between them. Beginning at his abs, I kissed and licked my way up to his mouth as his hands roamed every inch of my body.

The song was almost over, so I took his hands in mine again, guided them up, and put his fingertips in the waistband of my panties, giving him permission to take them off if he wanted.

Without hesitation, he slowly pulled them down my legs, helping me step out of them. I was naked and wanted him to be naked too. I hooked my fingers in his boxers while he lifted his hips and I slid them down his legs to his feet. With a low growl, Andy grasped my hips and jerked me forward so I was straddling him once again.

His erection, standing at full attention, was too inviting, so I lowered myself down, guiding him inside me.

Andy had me so aroused, from the way he watched and touched me, an orgasm tore through me before I could take all of him inside of me. I wrapped my arms around his neck and he buried his face in my chest. He teased my nipples as my body clenched tightly around him.

As my orgasm slowly subsided, I began to move for him, placing my feet on the rungs of the chair for stability. His arms wrapped tightly around my waist, he pulled me down hard, entering me so completely I was sitting on his thighs.

"Ahh, fuck," he groaned, his breath ragged, and his cock pulsating as he came. I don't know why Andy saying that always turned me on.

"I love it when you say *fuck* when you come," I whispered. He groaned in response.

I didn't intend to get up, so I skimmed my tongue up his neck and kissed across his jaw line to his mouth. We sat there kissing, my hands running over his chest and shoulders, his hands massaging my body. Eventually, he broke contact.

"As much as I'd like to sit here doing this with you all night, this chair is hard, and it's hurting my ass," he laughed. "Can we go back to our soft bed?"

Giggling, I nodded. "Absolutely, I don't want anything making that fine ass of yours hurt."

He chuckled, then wrapped his arms around my waist and stood up with me still attached to him. We had kissed for so long, that he was getting hard inside of me again. *Yay. If today is anything like what the rest of our relationship was going to be like, this man is going to turn me in to a nympho. I can handle that.*

I wrapped my legs tighter around him, locking my ankles together as he stepped out of the boxers that were still at his feet. My arms and legs wrapped completely around him, I began kissing him again. I rocked my hips forward, taking his hardening cock further inside me as he slowly walked us toward the bed.

He groaned, "Again." I did as he asked, but instead of him going to the bed, he backed me up against the wall, where he drove into me with such mind-blowing force, we were coming together in no time.

I hoped our neighbors weren't in their room, because we were definitely not quiet.

We stood, with me pinned between him and the wall, catching our breath. His head was resting in the crook of my neck, with his warm face against my chest. When he finally pulled out of me, he let out a groan as the contact was broken. I slowly unlocked my legs from around him and he let me down to stand on the floor.

Standing on shaky legs, I kissed him, running my tongue across his bottom lip. "I'll be right back," I said and went into the bathroom to clean up.

While I was in the bathroom, I removed the makeup I'd applied before my dance and stood in front of the mirror for several minutes. The woman who looked back at me was not the scared girl from two months ago. There was natural color in my cheeks. I'd probably gained ten much needed pounds and I was completely in love with the man in the next room.

After a few more minutes of me absorbing all the changes and progress I'd made, there was a knock on the bathroom door. I opened it. "Are you alright?" Andy asked. From the look on his face, he must have thought I was stressed out and had locked myself in.

"Never better, actually." I smiled at him and gave him a quick kiss. "Bathroom's all yours." I brushed past him, smacking his well-built ass *hard* on my way by.

Andy caught hold of my wrist and pulled me to him. "You are by far the best thing that's ever happened to me, Zoey." His eyes held such sincerity in them my heart did a flip-flop in my chest. "I hope you know how much I love you." He kissed me on my cheekbone, then let go of my wrist.

Wow, I was not expecting him to say that. "And I love you," I whispered with my whole heart, meaning every word. That man was the reason I decided to get my life back and I owed everything to him. He was my second chance at life. I caressed his cheek before I turned away.

A few minutes later, he slipped into bed behind me, pulling me close. "So, is that what you were learning in your dance class?"

I rolled over to face him, and he began to run his fingers through my hair. "Yep, did you like it?"

He smirked mischievously, his blue eyes sparkling. "No, not at all. You should never, *ever* do that to me again."

We both laughed and I pinched his nipple gently for being a shit. He caught my hand and pulled it to drape my arm over his side.

"I couldn't figure out why the song was on the playlist you made for me, but now, I won't think of it the same way again. I never would've thought of it as a striptease song, but it was actually kinda perfect with the beat and everything," he admitted.

"I planned on doing that dance for you before I came to Cabo, but we saw how that worked out," I confessed with a sigh.

Saying nothing, he sat up on his elbow then leaned over and kissed my shoulder, ribs, and hip where my bruises had finally faded. "Now you're body has healed and so has your mind," he whispered before kissing me gently on my lips.

I moved closer to him, he wrapped his arm around me, and I lazily traced his tattoos with my fingertip. I'd missed doing it for a month, but we were back together in the flesh and making up for lost time. I was happy, sleepy, and relaxed, so I closed my eyes, falling instantly to sleep in complete bliss.

Chapter Eleven

The next morning, we decided to go to the beach. I showered while he ordered us breakfast from room service. By the time he was done with his shower, the food arrived, and I had it set up on the table for us.

"Andy, do you know how happy I am that you're here? When I talked to you on Valentine's Day, I almost packed up and came home."

He raised his eyebrows as he took a long swallow of his orange juice. "I'm glad you didn't," he laughed. "Last night was amazing, Zoey."

I felt my face flush. "Yes, yes it was," I chuckled as I pushed my plate away. I could not eat another bite with all the butterflies in my stomach. Until last night, I had never been so confident and sexually free with a man. It felt like we were truly one with each other. I knew there would be a lot of learning and experimenting with him, but I also knew we'd both enjoy every second of it.

While he finished breakfast, I changed into my favorite purple bikini, jean shorts, and a pretty, cream-colored cover up with tiny embroidered flowers. I fell in love with it when I saw it at one of the outdoor markets, and it was perfect for the beach. I left it unbuttoned because I would just be taking it off as soon as we hit the sand. I found a pair of Andy's shorts and set them on the bed for him, then packed a bag with everything we'd need for the day.

"We need to make a stop at one of the stores before we head to the beach," he said as he stood from the table.

"Did you forget something?"

"My sunnies. It was raining at home when I left, so I didn't think about bringing them."

I looked at him curiously, not knowing what he meant by "sunnies."

He noticed my confusion. "Sunglasses, Zoey," he laughed.

"Oh, I get it now." I giggled like an idiot. "A New Zealand word."

He nodded and kissed my cheek. "You're adorable."

Realizing I forgot mine at my aunt and uncle's, I decided to get some new "sunnies" too.

Once he was ready to go, we walked over to the shops at the resort and found a store that sold a variety of beachwear. We goofed around, trying on hats while we tried on sunglasses.

Andy knew what he was looking for and quickly found the sunglasses he wanted. He chose black, old school Ray-Bans, which he looked gorgeous in, of course. After trying on about ten styles of sunglasses, I was indecisive, so he picked up a pair of mirrored, aviator Ray-Bans and slipped them on me.

"You look sexy as hell in those," he stated sincerely.

"Really?" I never thought aviators were my style, so I never bothered picking up a pair.

He shot me a naughty grin as he squeezed my hip with his large hand and tugged me closer to him. "Abso-fucking-lutely," Andy said, just before he brushed his lips across mine.

We continued browsing around the store for souvenirs. I picked up a very stylish straw fedora hat with a black band on it and dropped it down on his head, then took his sunglasses and put them on him, too.

"Oh. My. God." I gasped and jokingly raised the back of my hand to my forehead, pretending to swoon. He really was breathtaking.

"I guess I'm getting the hat too?" he questioned with a chuckle.

"Uh huh, definitely. I'll buy it for you," I said. I think I might have even swooned for real.

He picked up a straw sun hat I would never pick out for myself and carefully set it on my head. "Now you're even more perfect. Let's get out of here and get to the beach, so I can see you in your togs again."

What in the ever loving hell is a tog?

Again, he noticed my confusion, so he looped one finger around the string of my bikini top in between my breasts. He stared me in the eyes as he moved his hand from side to side. His finger gently brushed the inside of each breast and my sternum. *Ah, togs equals swimsuit. Got it. Now that he's touched me like that, I want to go back to the room, strip off the togs and every other piece of clothing we wore and get down to business.*

"Adorable," he said again as I shook my head and grinned up at him. We made our way to the front of the store to pay for our hats and glasses.

I searched in my purse for my wallet. "I'm buying, wifey. Put your money away," he joked.

"No way. Between my sunglasses and the hats, my portion is about two hundred dollars. I can't let you pay for everything."

He whispered in my ear while the cashier rang up our purchases, "Love, will you let me spend a little bit of my money on you, please? You can pay me back later with another dance." He let out a deep, quiet laugh, and gave me a quick kiss on the cheek.

The cashier eyed us curiously. "You're newlyweds, aren't you?" she asked. I had forgotten we were still wearing the wedding bands.

"Yes, we are," Andy answered with a grin before I could even open my mouth. He glanced over and gave me a wink. God, I loved that man.

He paid for our hats and glasses and we strolled hand in hand to the beach wearing them. As soon as we stepped on the beach, he kicked off his shoes and carried them to walk barefoot in the sand.

We found a spot we liked and spread our towels out on the sand. I stripped down to my bikini and tied my hair back in a loose, twisted bun under the back of my new hat. Andy stripped off his shirt, then lay down on his stomach on his beach towel, propping himself up on his elbows.

After I situated myself on my towel, I noticed several women around us doing double takes of him as he absentmindedly picked up and sifted sand through his fingers. With his gorgeous face and body, sexy tattoos, his new sunglasses and hat...I couldn't blame them really.

He was completely oblivious to them.

I didn't want him to sunburn, so I found my sunscreen and dropped myself down to sit on his butt. I squeezed some on my hands and rubbed it onto his back, neck, and shoulders.

"Flip over. Let me do your front," I said when his back was done.

He started laughing. "I'm afraid you've already done something to my *front*, Zoey. If I turn over now, I'll be arrested for indecent exposure. Besides, I think there was a sign somewhere saying tents aren't allowed on the beach."

Did he really just tell me he pitched a tent in his shorts? Oh my God. I laughed heartily, slipped off him, and back to my own towel. As I moved away, I smacked him on the butt. "Well, when your front has *subsided*, let me know. I can put sunscreen on your sexy chest and abs. Then you can do me too," I whispered, with a double meaning he definitely understood by the look on his face.

After a few minutes, I could still feel eyes on us from people nearby. "You seem to be attracting quite a bit of attention from the ladies, Andy," I said quietly so they didn't hear me.

He turned over and sat up with his muscular legs stretched out in front of him, "Come here," he said to me.

I picked up the sunscreen and crawled over to him on my hands and knees. "Sit." He patted his thighs with his hands, motioning for me to sit on his lap. I did and immediately had the best seat on the beach. I squeezed sunscreen on my hands and began rubbing it over his tattooed chest.

He pulled my face close, kissing the tip of my nose. "You are the one attracting all the attention, not me. Besides, the only attention I want is yours."

Yeah, I could live with that. I grasped his face in both hands and planted the most sensual kiss I could muster up on his parted lips. I broke the kiss when I realized we were still on the busy beach with lots of people around.

I held the sunscreen out to him. "Do me?" I smiled deviously, pulling my sunglasses down a tad to look over the top of them at him.

"You are so bad," he said with a smirk. I sat right where I was while he rubbed sunscreen on my shoulders for me. When he was done, I hopped back over on my own towel.

We lounged on the beach for a while and just enjoyed the day. The people sitting closest to us started packing up and leaving for the day or went down to the water.

"Zoey, did you bring your iPod?"

I put down my book and checked my bag. "Nope, I left it in the room," I said. "Sorry, my love."

"I'm feeling a little left out, with you over there reading." He tipped his chin, indicating toward the book I held in my hand.

Right then, I felt like an ass. He had worked so hard to get a day off to come and spend the weekend with me, and there I was *reading*. That was not one of my brighter moments in life. *Duh, Zoey, spend time with your gorgeous boyfriend on the beach before you have to go home.* I dog-eared my page and shut the book, tossing it in the direction of my beach bag. I rolled over onto my stomach so my body was partially on his towel.

"What can I do to make it up to you?" I asked him, resting my head on his shoulder.

"Sing me a song?"

"Here? Are you serious?" I asked and sat up cross-legged. I was surprised he asked me to sing to him.

"Yeah, would you? You've never sang anything for me before, you know?"

Crap, I hadn't. Sure, I sang while he was with me, but I hadn't sung *for* him.

"Sing anything, whatever you feel like," he said. "Don't laugh, but hearing you sing along to any song that's playing when we're at home is one of the things I've missed most since you've been gone."

Right then, I wanted to do anything to please him. "I would never laugh at the words that come out of your mouth, Andy. That is the sweetest thing anyone has ever said to me."

"It's because I could listen to you sing all day long, Beautiful," he admitted. "What are you going to sing?"

Of course, I started out with something easy and chose to sing, "I'm Too Sexy," by Right Said Fred, just to see him smile. He laughed and grinned the entire time I sang to him, and it brought back so many memories from the weekend I met him. When I finished the song, he gripped my face in his hands and planted a noisy kiss to my lips.

"That was hilarious and I fucking love you for it," he said with a chuckle. "Let's go for a walk."

As he let go of me and we stood up, a little girl ran up to us. She looked up at me with her big brown doe-eyes. "Hi! You sing real pretty!" she squealed.

Holding back a laugh because of my song choice, I knelt down to meet her at eye level. "Aww, thank you," I said, smiling at her. "Do you sing too?"

She nodded and started singing, "Twinkle, Twinkle, Little Star." It was the cutest thing I had ever heard. When she finished, we clapped for her. "That was very pretty," I voiced, just as her mom came up to collect her.

"Sorry, she heard you singing to your husband and wanted to sing too," she laughed.

"It's okay. She's adorable," I said. "Keep practicing, sweetie, and someday you'll be famous."

"Bye, bye!" she yelled as her mom packed her off.

I looked over at Andy, who was grinning from ear to ear. "What?" I asked.

"Oh, nothing. I think I've just been replaced as your number one fan. It's cute."

"No way," I said. "You'll always be number one to me." The grin that took over his face when I said that would forever be embedded in my memory. Andy truly looked happier than I'd ever seen him and it made my heart flutter knowing I was the cause.

After dusting the sand off my legs and pulling on my cover-up, we headed to the edge of the water to cool off. We walked down the beach, splashing around in the water a little bit when it got too hot. We relaxed, took our time walking, and hung out together.

After arriving at a secluded area of the beach, Andy glanced over at me, took my hat and cover-up off me, and dropped them onto the sand. He took my hand in his and we waded out into the ocean until the water reached my chest.

"Sing me another song, but this time, I want you to sing a serious one...Please?" He gave me a little pout for teasing him with my previous song choice.

Being me, I needed to pick the perfect song for him, so I thought long and hard about it before I made my decision.

My song choice was "Break In" by Halestorm. The lyrics were perfect for the entire situation, singing the song to him would show him how much everything he'd done meant to me.

Andy came all the way from California to bring me home. He'd broken down every single wall I'd put up to keep him and everyone else out. He let me fall apart when I needed to and gave me the reason to put myself back together. If it weren't for him, I would still be a miserable, lonely person. Because of Andy, I wasn't. In the time I had been gone, I healed, both mentally and physically.

Of course, I would always face challenges because life always had its way of knocking us back a bit, but I knew if it did, I would have the strength and courage to knock it back without falling.

Andy knew me like nobody else and I was completely at ease with him. He would always be there for me, as I would be for him. He made me whole.

So I sang...I sang my fucking heart out to him as I stood chest deep in the Pacific Ocean with my gorgeous man in front of me. I would remember that moment for the rest of my life. Andy ran his fingers through my hair, caressing my arms and shoulders while I sang the song.

"Thank you, Zoey," he whispered when I finished. He took his hat and glasses off and kissed me with so much passion and love, my body ached. "Let's go for a walk along the beach so we can talk."

He put his hat and glasses back on, took my hand in his, and we walked back out of the water. When we reached the beach, he pulled me into his strong arms and just held me without saying a word.

I knew I made the right decision to go on my vacation. We needed the time apart to get ourselves right. And we did it...we fucking did it, and it was time to move forward.

We walked along the beach, away from the crowds of people. After walking a while, I could tell there was definitely something heavy on his mind, but I felt more love from him than ever before, so I wasn't worried that it was something bad.

"Zoey, can I ask you a question?" His voice sounded serious, yet thoughtful at the same time, as we made our way down the beach.

"Sure, what's up?"

"Um, don't read anything in to this, please."

I stopped walking and turned to face him. I took my sunglasses off and looked up at him, waiting to see where the conversation was going.

"You told me before that you had a miscarriage," he started a little nervously.

I eyed him inquisitively, wondering what he was asking.

"Shit, I'm sorry. I won't pry. Never mind." Andy seemed a little uncomfortable and started to walk again.

Reaching out, I caught his wrist. "Oh, no you don't. You cannot start a conversation like that and then tell me *never mind*. What do you want to know?" To prepare myself for his question, I sucked in a breath then let it out and said, "I'll tell you anything."

His brows furrowed just before he spoke. It was almost as if he was scared to ask me the question, which of course, made me worry more.

"Can you still have kids?"

Whoa, I did not see that one coming. The air left my lungs as I exhaled and closed my eyes for a few seconds to absorb his question. Not because he upset me, but because he caught me completely off guard.

"I know for some women they have issues—"

I reached out and squeezed his arm for reassurance. "It's okay, and it was most likely a one-time thing. It's very common actually. The doctors checked me out and everything is in proper working order. Is there something I need to know?" I grinned up at him, eagerly awaiting what was coming next.

He sighed uncomfortably. "I don't know, Zoey. It's probably just me thinking crazy thoughts because I've been wearing this wedding band since last night, we've both been married before, and I just love you so much. Ugh, fuck. I have no idea what I'm even saying." He laughed, clearly exasperated, and maybe a little embarrassed by his own rambling.

"So, are you saying someday you're *really* going to marry me and make babies with me?" I laughed to let him off the hook and ease his mind.

He smiled, and I swore his eyes lit up. *Yes, there is the grin I need to see.* I wrapped my arm around his waist and we went back to our towels.

"Let's go eat. I'm hungry," he stated, instead of answering the question I'd asked him.

I shook my head and smirked as I picked up my beach towel and began folding it. "You eat more than any person I know."

Andy packed up our belongings and we headed back to our room for lunch. We decided to take a shower to wash off the sunscreen, sand, and salt water. After our shower, we fell into bed to take a nap after being out in the hot sun all morning.

After a few hours of napping, I woke up before Andy. He was lying on his stomach facing me, both arms down at his sides, like he had just fallen face first onto the bed. He was completely naked and I couldn't help myself.

Propping myself up on my elbow, I laid next to him while running my fingertips lightly up and down his back. He didn't stir. He must really be tired if *that* didn't wake him up.

I decided to let him nap a while longer, but not for too *much* longer. I rolled over and closed my eyes to relax and enjoy my time with him, even if he was asleep. I wanted him, but I would wait until he woke up.

Chapter Twelve

Later on, I woke to Andy's hand gliding from my naked hip to my belly, his erection pressed against the back of my thigh. I reached behind me and grasped his hip pulling him harder to me. His hand slid down between my legs.

What a pleasurable way to wake up from an unplanned nap. I tried to turn over on my back, but he was too close, so I could only turn part of the way toward him. I raised my left leg and laid it over the top of his leg, which allowed me to turn a bit more. It worked out perfectly because he had better access to touch me.

He pushed two fingers in, then pulled them out, seeing if I was ready for him, which I definitely was. He massaged my clit in slow circles until I was panting and close to orgasm, then he stopped, not letting me go over the edge.

"Not yet," he whispered from behind me. He scooted down some and lifted my leg, so it was back up over his hip. I was able to roll onto my back. He rubbed the head of his cock over me, wetting the tip of it and then pushed himself inside me. *Oh my*. He slid his leg between mine, so we were in what I could only explain as a side-by-side scissor type position.

Once he began thrusting slowly into me, I felt sensations I'd never experienced before. It was a new position for me, but then again, everything was going to be new to me with him. I'd heard about the position before and always wanted to try it out, but never had the courage to with Rob since he was so selfish in bed.

Andy started rubbing me again with his fingertips, intensifying the sensual feelings coursing through me. I wasn't able to face him, so there was no kissing or touching him. It was all up to him to please me, and he did. Within minutes, I was moaning his name and clenching hard around him. I found if I spread my legs further apart, I could reach down and massage his balls lightly. He began thrusting harder as I touched him, and he groaned as he came inside me.

We lay there for a while afterward, our legs entwined, his chest to my back, and his arm now draped over me. The simple fact that we were so in tune with each other, no words needed to be spoken. Just lying there together, so wrapped up in one another, was perfection.

"I can't believe I have to go home tomorrow. I was ready to go, but now that you're here, I just want to stay here with you and forget about home."

He scooted up and laid his head on my pillow. "Zoey, we can be like this when we get back to Sacramento," he said as he smoothed my hair down and kissed my neck. "There is no reason why we can't."

Andy was correct, of course. We had worked out everything between us and were definitely great now. I rolled over to face him. "I love you. You're right. I think we are both in a good place now. There's no reason we can't do this."

He leaned over and kissed me. "I love you, too."

"Hey, can you go somewhere with me?" I asked. "I want you to meet Josie and Smoke."

He propped himself up on his elbow. "Of course. Do you want to go now?"

I nodded.

"You know, we were *supposed* to go at least two days with no clothes. I'm afraid you're not holding up your end of the bargain." He slowly dragged his hand down my body, gently massaging my arm, side, and leg. There was nothing sexual about it at all, just simply touching me in a loving way.

Playfully, I pushed him over onto his back and moved to lay full length on top of him. "Sorry, but I want you to meet them before we go. Who knows if we'll ever get back down here?" He ran his hands up and down my back as we talked.

"Then we better go before you try and take advantage of me again." He chuckled and kissed the top of my head. I rose up to straddle him, my hands on his chest. Looking him in the eyes, with a devious grin on my lips, I bent down and kissed his chest, then trailed the tip of my tongue over to his nipple and sucked it into my mouth.

Before he could do anything, I released his nipple and jumped off him. I giggled at the shocked expression on his face. I pulled my bikini, shorts, and cover-up back on in case we decided to go back down to the beach afterward.

"That's fucked up, Zoey," he growled and gave me an adorable pout with his delicious lips.

"Don't worry. I'll take good care of you later. I promise." I even traced a little X over my heart with my finger as my promise to him. While he pulled on his shorts and a T-shirt, I grabbed our hats and sunglasses and we drove to the stables.

When we arrived, a tour was just getting back so there was a lot of chaos between the tourists snapping final pictures and people trying to leave.

Fortunately, Josie had a full staff and spare time to talk with us.

"Josie, *this* is Andy. He flew down yesterday to surprise me."

Josie's eyes lit up as she held her hand out to greet him. "Andy, I've heard so much about you. It's good to meet you."

He smiled and shook her hand. "It's great to meet you, Josie. I can't thank you enough for what you've done for Zoey."

She looked up at him with a genuine smile on her face. "I was lucky to have her here to help *me* out."

We talked to Josie until it was time to start the next tour. I was happy these two very important people in my life had the chance to meet each other. Over the time I'd been away, I told Andy about all the conversations between Josie and me, so he knew how much she'd helped me on my path to healing myself.

After we said goodbye to Josie, I took my man's hand, interlacing our fingers together. "Let's go see Smoke now."

We found him in a corral, eating. He was more worried about having his snack than visiting with us seeing as he just came back from the last tour.

I showed Andy around the stables where the horses were kept, explaining to him the jobs I did while I worked there. We wandered around and I showed Andy the small arena where I led the smaller children around on ponies because they were too young to go out on the beach rides.

After we toured the entire property, we went down the trail to the beach.

"This is where I rode Smoke for the first time. We were right over there when Jess took all the pictures of us," I said and pointed down the beach.

"I loved the picture you sent me, Zoey. I had a copy made and framed it."

His admission made my heart swell in my chest. He had a picture of *me* in his apartment amongst the photos of his family. "I still can't believe we're here...together." I wrapped my arms around him.

Andy took his cell phone out of his pocket. "Let's get a picture of us *here*."

We posed as he used his phone to snap pictures of us together. Then he decided he wanted a few of me by myself, so I sat on the beach and posed for him. He made me feel beautiful, and when I looked through the photos, they reflected the undeniable love that I held for him in the deep, blue depths of my eyes.

After our impromptu photo shoot, we left the stables and went back to the resort. It was our last night in Cabo and we were trying to decide what to do after dinner.

"There's a nightclub close by if you want to go dancing," Andy suggested.

"You want to take me dancing?" I asked curiously.

"Actually, yes, I do."

"Well, then let's go dancing."

We dressed up in the nicest clothes we brought with us and headed to the nightclub. I wasn't sure what to expect at the resort, so I packed the dress and sandals I had worn when Jess, Sasha, and I went dancing. Of course, Andy brought his black Affliction shirt that I was so fond of him wearing.

The club was within walking distance, so both of us could drink and not worry about driving. Once there, we went straight to the bar, each of us ordering Johnnie Walker. We clinked our glasses together and enjoyed our drinks, then we had a few more.

"Let's dance!" I shouted over the noise and pulled him out into the crowd of people.

The bass was thumping as we found a spot on the dance floor. We danced to a few songs, bumping and grinding on each other, like everyone else. We were having fun and my man could *move*. Of course, it made me want to take him back to the room, strip him down, and have crazy, hot sex with him.

I thought back to all the activities I could never do when I was married to Rob. We never danced, and never sang to him. Hell, he didn't even care enough to hear me sing anything for that matter. Even in high school, he never went to any of my choir performances.

That night, I felt like a very lucky woman. *That's because I am a lucky woman.*

The nightclub was playing a variety of music, so I thought I would see if the DJ would play a song for me. I stood up on my toes to tell Andy where I was going and that I'd be right back. I left him on the dance floor, went to the DJ, and put in my request.

Back on the dance floor, I found Andy sandwiched between two women who were bumping and grinding on him. He caught my eye and a look of panic washed over his face. He was dancing with them just to be polite because it's just how he was, but I could tell he was not happy about it.

I wasn't a jealous person when it came to him. He'd proven many times he was only interested in me. The look on his face conveyed to me he was *not* enjoying himself at all and he was more worried he was going to be in trouble with me. Silly man, he should know me better than that.

I stood there for another minute, watching the women do their best to get his attention.

His eyes were begging me for help by the time I weaved my way through the people on the floor. I wedged myself between him and the girl who was dancing in front of him, giving her a little bump with my hip so she had to move.

He grinned and shook his head at my antic. He slipped his arms around me to squeeze my butt then planted one hell of a kiss on me.

The girl flipped her hair over her shoulder and stomped off. The other girl behind him mouthed "Sorry" and left. I shrugged my shoulders and smiled at her.

"Did you have a nice dance, Andy?" I teased.

"Thank you for saving me."

"Called Out in the Dark" by Snow Patrol came blaring out of the speakers a minute later. I pulled him close, he wrapped his arms back around me, and we danced.

After the song ended, I was hot, sweaty, and very thirsty. "I need another drink!" I hollered when the next song started. He took my hand, spun me around once, and led me back toward the bar.

The club was very busy, so there was a long line at the bar for drinks. Waiting at the end of the line, I stood up on my toes to talk because it was so loud in the room, but it didn't help.

Both of us had a nice buzz going and I wanted to keep drinking with my man, but we were not getting any closer to the bar for more drinks. "Let's get out of here," I said as the song ended and it became quiet for a moment.

We headed out the door. "Where to now, Zoey?"

"A liquor store for some Johnnie Walker. You game?"

He nodded and took my hand in his. We made it back to our room with our purchase and got shit-faced drunk together.

The next morning, I woke up to us both sprawled out, face down on the bed, stark naked. *Okay, so his favorite sleeping position is pretty comfy.* The sheets were a tangled mess and the rest of the blankets were lying in a heap on the floor. My inner thighs felt like they had been thoroughly pounded by the sex-god sleeping next to me.

Damn, I wish I could remember that. The last thing I did remember was us laughing and him pulling my dress over my head.

I sat up too quickly and immediately became nauseous. I stumbled naked to the bathroom and snatched a robe off the hook on the back of the door. I wrapped myself in it right as the saliva in my mouth began to sour. I flung myself onto my knees on the cold tile floor, and heaved into the toilet. *Ugh, it's been a long time since I've been drunk enough to puke.*

When it finally felt like there was nothing left in me to throw up, I rose from the floor, rinsed my mouth, and brushed my teeth. My face was clammy, so I splashed it with cool water. After drying off, I made my way back to bed and crawled in carefully to avoid making myself sick again.

Andy woke up as soon as I made myself comfortable. "Were you just getting sick in the bathroom?" he asked without opening his eyes.

"Yes, unfortunately I was. How are you feeling?"

He propped himself up on his elbows and appeared to be in deep thought. His hair was standing on end in all different directions, his eyes were barely open, yet he still looked gorgeous.

"I feel fine. How are you?"

"I think I'm done puking for the moment, so that's good. I should eat something though. Do you want me to order you something too?" Duh Zoey, of course he did. My brain was still fuzzy, so I wasn't thinking straight.

Andy stood up from the bed and his hair wasn't the only thing standing on end.

The sight of him made me laugh. "Dude, put that thing away. My thighs feel like punching bags."

He looked down at himself. "Sorry, Beautiful, it happens every morning," he joked, but made no attempt whatsoever to cover himself on his way to the bathroom.

As his fine ass walked away, I noticed several red scratch marks across his back and perfect ass cheeks. *Oops.* Guess I got a little carried away.

The room felt like it was spinning, so I threw my arm across my eyes to make it stop and banned all traces of light from seeping in to them. I don't know how much later it was, but I remembered I was supposed to be ordering breakfast. I eased myself to the edge of the bed to pick up the phone to call room service.

As soon as I sat up, I became nauseous again, but wasn't sure if I was going to be sick or not. Just in case, I went to the bathroom and knocked on the door. "Can you hurry, please? I might get sick again."

The door flew open and Andy was standing there with his toothbrush hanging out of his mouth. He had already taken a shower. My mouth started watering and I dropped to my knees, hanging my head over the toilet again. I didn't care if he was standing there.

Out of my peripheral vision, I could see he was still naked. Did the man just like being naked? I didn't mind, of course. I could stare at his body all day long. He finished brushing his teeth as my nausea got the better of me and I was sick again. He kneeled, naked, and pulled my hair back for me as he rubbed circles over my back with his strong hand.

"Seriously, you're holding my hair while I puke my guts out. Who *are* you?" I tried to joke.

"I'm the guy who loves you, even when you're on the floor puking your guts out," he replied as he continued rubbing my back.

Slowly and carefully, I stood up. "I think I'm okay now. Can you order breakfast while I take a quick shower, please? I think I can handle some toast and coffee."

He kissed me on top of the head and left the room. I brushed my teeth again and swished some mouthwash, just in case, then took a nice, cool shower. When I came out in my robe, breakfast was on the table, and our clothes were packed with the exception of an outfit he set out for me. I dressed and sat at the table next to him.

Andy ordered himself a full breakfast again, and it made me want to gag, just looking at it. He set a plate of toast in front of me, poured me a cup of coffee, adding sugar and creamer to it just the way I liked it.

"Thank you," I moaned as I laid my head on the cool table.

Then the smartass patted my back and cooed, "Poor baby," at me. He joked about me being a lightweight and about how badly I sucked at holding my liquor, but he was nice enough to rub my back as he ate one-handed.

After breakfast, we checked out and returned to my aunt and uncle's to find them eating lunch in the kitchen. "Zoey, Andy, you made it back. How was the resort?" Aunt Maria asked.

Huh? "How did you know about the resort?" I asked, confused.

I looked at my aunt and uncle, then at Andy. They were all smiling.

"What's going on? You're all looking very guilty for some reason."

"Sorry, Zoey, they were in on it too. I asked your mum for help, so she called to let them know I was coming down here." Andy grinned proudly at his sneakiness.

I looked back over to his partners in crime. "You two didn't go on a trip to a job site, did you?"

They both shook their heads. "No, we went out to dinner and a movie so he could come to get you. We've been home all weekend. Did you have a good time?"

"You guys are sneaky," I laughed. "Especially you." I reached out and pulled Andy into a hug.

"Do you want to sit down for some lunch before you head to the airport?" my aunt asked.

Of course, Andy said yes. I decided I could handle some warm tortillas with butter and a Coke. I needed some bubbles to settle my stomach.

"Are you feeling sick, Zoey?" Uncle Victor asked with a knowing smile on his face. I think he knew I had a hangover.

Andy and I started laughing. "Yes, we drank a little too much Johnnie Walker last night. I admit I'm a little hung over." *And my inner thighs are killing me.* Everyone laughed at my expense, but I didn't care.

After lunch, Andy helped me finish packing for the trip home. He let me stash all my souvenirs in his suitcase, since he had more space in his than I did in mine.

We gave my aunt and uncle one last hug goodbye then drove to the airport to go home.

Chapter Thirteen

June 2012

It was a nice, warm, Northern California night as I sat down on the bleachers at the drag strip with Jess. Andy was going to be racing his '69 Camaro that night. He'd made a few more changes to it over the last couple of months and it was going to be his first race since he finished. Noah was with Andy in the tech line, waiting for the safety inspection that had to be performed before they could race.

Several cars were through tech and already racing. Two diesel pickups were on the track doing burnouts in the burnout boxes to get their tires hot and sticky for better traction for their race. Thick plumes of black exhaust boiled out of their giant smoke stacks. We couldn't even see down in to the pits anymore because there was so much black smoke in the air.

It was Andy's first race of the year so I was excited and nervous for him. I sort of felt like I was the cause of him not racing because we were spending so much time together.

The week before, I had been horribly sick with a nasty flu bug that had been going around. All the employees at my store caught it as well. I pretty much banned everyone from my apartment so they didn't get sick too, which gave Andy plenty of time to get his car ready.

Jess and I watched the light tree count down through the yellow lights. The second the light turned green the diesel trucks shot down the track, billowing thick, black smoke behind them. The crowd went crazy. There were several newer diesel drag racing clubs around the area and everyone loved them.

"First race tonight, huh, Z?" Jess asked anxiously. "Is Andy excited to see what his car can do?"

I nodded. "Yes, very excited. They put it on the dyno and it's looking like it might be pretty fast. We'll see what happens."

We watched several more cars race until the track officials stopped the races and hopped in their truck to spray the track with VHT. The last couple of cars in the lane closest to us were having some traction issues and sliding sideways instead of moving forward. With the VHT liquid down, the tires would stick to the track better and not spin out.

Andy's Camaro was three rows back in the staging lanes; it looked like he passed tech and was going to race soon.

I pulled my cell phone out and sent him a quick text.

Good luck! Be careful too. Love you!

He sent me a text right back.

Thank you. Love you more. Meet me at the truck when it's over.

The cars started pulling forward once the VHT was down and the track was ready, so I didn't text him back.

I watched as a '62 or '63 Nova and a '71 Camaro pulled into the boxes and smoked us all out with their burnouts.

Jess and I both took in a deep breath and exhaled. "Ahh, nothing like a little tire smoke to make a girl happy," I joked as Jess rolled her eyes at me, laughing. It was a James family joke.

The two cars staged and sped down the track. Two more cars to go, then Andy was up.

I glanced at the car Andy would be racing. *Shit*. It was a black 1967 Chevelle, which if I was not mistaken, used to belong to me.

"Ah shit, Jess, look at the car next to Andy's. I think it's Rob."

She dug in her purse, pulled out a tiny pair of binoculars, and looked through them. "Yep, it's Rob. Do you think Andy knows it's him?"

I didn't dare ask why she carried binoculars in her purse, but I did wonder what else was in there. I had visions of Hermione Granger pulling all kinds of crazy shit out of that tiny bag she carried in one of the *Harry Potter* movies, and let out a little chuckle.

"Oh, he knows" I finally responded. The next two cars staged and raced down the track. "At least I know what the Chevelle will do and Andy's car is definitely going to be faster, so that's a plus."

We hadn't heard a word from Rob since the prank call when I was in Mexico back in February. I assumed the punches that Andy landed on him shut him up. I hoped it stayed that way. I heard the unmistakable sound of Andy's car start up, and then watched as he pulled into the burnout box. Rob pulled up next to him in his own lane.

"Oh God, I can't watch, Jess!" I covered my eyes with my hands and took in a deep breath. My heart pounded in my chest as I peeked between my fingers to watch the cars pull up to the start line. Unable to see inside either of the cars, I had no idea if Rob even knew it was Andy next to him.

The pre-stage light blinked on and I held my breath again. The Camaro's engine revved up. The stage light flipped on next and I cringed. Andy's car started to tilt slightly from the torque of the engine. As the next three yellow lights flipped on, one right after the other, I uncovered my eyes completely and stood up.

Green light!

Andy's car lurched forward and the front tires slightly came up off the ground, while the Chevelle's tires hooked up and the car started moving down the track. Rob was already at the hundred-foot mark, so Andy had a little distance to go to catch up to him.

Since it was his first race after he made several improvements to his car, he was taking it a little easy. By the time Rob hit the half-track mark, he had gained three car lengths on Andy. Andy shifted his car into third gear and caught up to the Chevelle quickly.

At three-quarters of the way down the track, Andy shifted his Camaro into fourth gear and flew past Rob, like he was standing still. Andy beat him by four car lengths. The reader boards showed Andy's time at 10.90 at 128 miles per hour, not too bad for his first time.

He would do even better the next time. We jumped up and down, cheering along with half the people in the bleachers. I heard shouts of "Damn, that guy got smoked." and "Did you see that?" There were even a few laughs heard.

My dad and brothers built the Chevelle for me, and I actually raced it a couple of times, but it was no match for the Camaro. We made our way down the steps of the bleachers and walked to the pits to wait for Andy to make it back to his car trailer.

About ten minutes later, he pulled his car up to where we were waiting and shut it off. He hopped out and walked over to where we were standing. Andy and Noah talked about how the car handled for a few minutes, while Jess and I waited.

When Noah and Andy finished their discussion, he held his hand out to me. "Come here."

He wrapped his arms around me, picked me up off the ground, and nuzzled his face into the crook of my neck. "Are you still feeling good?" he asked. "I'm glad to see you out of the apartment finally, even though you lost too much weight."

I nodded, wrapped my arms around his neck, and planted a kiss on his lips. "Nice job," I said, a little more smugly than I probably should have. "Four car lengths, that was pretty impressive." I was damn proud of my man.

Andy chuckled and shook his head. "I wasn't gonna let that idiot beat me in front of my girl," he joked as he put me down.

"Are you going to go again?"

"Yeah, I want to check under the hood first then I'll head back out to the staging lanes."

He popped the hood and lifted it up to check something in the engine compartment. Noah stuck his head under the hood too, and they started checking belts and hoses and who knew what else. I was more interested in the view.

"Would you look at that, Jess?" I joked, watching my gorgeous man's ass as he bent over the fender of his car. "Sheer perfection."

She started giggling. "Yes, they're both quite the vision with the way they're bent over the car, aren't they? Zoey, how does a man get a butt like that anyway?"

I shrugged my shoulders because I had no clue. All I knew was Andy's ass was amazing to look at both in *and* out of clothing. They looked over their shoulders when Jess and I busted up laughing.

"What's so funny, babe?" Noah asked over his shoulder.

Jess grinned. "Oh, nothing, baby. You're both the *butt* of a private joke, that's all."

It went right over Noah's head, but the expression on Andy's face told me he knew what Jess meant. A smug grin spread across his face before he turned back around and bent over his car again.

Thank you, Jesus, for an ass that nice.

A few minutes later, Andy put the hood down on his Camaro and went inside his car trailer. He came back out with a second helmet. He held it up and shook it in his hand. "Zoey, you want to ride with me this time?"

I hadn't been down the track in ages. I squealed because I was so excited. I think I may have even jumped up and down a couple times in anticipation. He smiled, shaking his head at me, then handed me the helmet.

"Should I take your excitement as a yes?"

"No, you should take it as a fuck yes!"

Andy chuckled as I ran around to the passenger side of the car and hopped in while he sat in the driver's seat. Instinctively, I reached over my shoulder to grab the seatbelt, when I realized he had racing seats in the car and a five-point racing seatbelt.

I immediately started laughing. I was wearing a skirt. A very short skirt at that.

"Um, Andy?" I said as I pulled the seatbelt up where it was supposed to go.

"Ah, fuck me," he said after he looked down and realized my predicament. He ran his fingers through his hair as he stared down at my lap.

One of the seatbelt straps was bolted to the floor under the edge of the seat, which meant it had to come up between my legs to buckle over my stomach. I giggled as I pulled my skirt up a few inches and started to buckle myself in.

"Wait, it's not quite high enough. You should raise it a little bit more. Make sure you can get your seatbelt nice and tight. Wouldn't want it too loose, now would we?" he questioned as he stared hungrily at my bare legs, then up my body to look me in the eyes.

I smirked and pulled it up as high as I could, then buckled myself in. "Better?" I asked.

"Yes." He reached down and adjusted himself in his pants.

"Can I help you with that?" I smiled as I playfully batted my eyelashes at him.

He started up the car, pushed in the clutch, and put it in first gear. "You definitely can later."

He drove over to the staging lanes and parked while we waited our turn. "So, Andy, wanna make out while we wait?" I teased. "I'm kind of pinned in over here. You can do whatever you want to me."

He looked over at me and shook his head. "I'm about ready to take you back to my car trailer right now, Zoey," he said seriously. "It feels like I haven't touched you in a month."

Now there's an idea. "Promise?" I asked.

The two cars in front of us started their engines and pulled forward. "We're up next!" I said excitedly.

He looked over at me curiously. "Are you really that happy to be doing this?"

"Hell yes, I'm excited. It's been forever since I've even been at the raceway, and even longer since I've actually been *down* the racetrack."

A surprised expression washed over his face. "You've been in an actual drag race?"

I nodded. "I raced the Chevelle before. It's how I knew your car would beat it. The boys and my dad built it for me to race. It's pretty basic, but it was enough for me to drive."

The two cars in front of us raced their way down the track.

"You never cease to amaze me, Zoey."

I laughed. "Hey, you're lucky I'm not begging to drive your car."

He raised his eyebrows. "Maybe I'll let you next time," he said as he put on his seatbelt and helmet.

"You'd really let me drive your car? In a *race*?" I pulled on my helmet and turned to him. I was shocked.

Andy started the car back up, shifted into first gear, and pulled forward into the burnout box. He just smiled and didn't answer me. After he did a nice, smoky burnout, he pulled the Camaro up to the line. While he messed with buttons and toggle switches, I looked over at the car next to us. Luckily, it wasn't Rob again.

My adrenaline started pumping when the pre-stage light came on and Andy revved the car up, getting ready to go. I felt the car shift slightly from the torque, and rev up higher as the lights on the light tree quickly counted down to green.

My body vibrated with excitement, fear, and honestly, there was a whole lot of lust mixed in as I looked over at my man in the driver's seat.

The second the light turned green, Andy slammed on the gas and released the clutch. The front of the car raised up as the tires came up off the ground again, and like a rocket, he launched us down the track. I squealed with excitement as the G-force pushed my body back against the seat. It was exhilarating and I could not stop smiling.

I watched Andy as he smashed the clutch and gas pedals as he shifted through the gears. And as quick as it started, it was over. I checked the reader board; he gained some time and speed with the second pass leaving the other racecar in the dust.

The car turned down the return road and we took our helmets off. "That was so fucking awesome!" I yelled over the noise of the motor and exhaust system.

He looked over at me with a sexy grin on his face. "I'm glad you enjoyed it. You ready to go home now?"

Watching him race, pounding pedals and shifting gears, turned me on. He was in his element at the track, and seeing him race like that had me wanting him right there. I nodded and squeezed his thigh. I was ready to take him to bed, and the way he was looking at me, I was pretty sure he was thinking the same thing I was.

We made our way back to the car trailer, where Jess and Noah were waiting for us. I quickly unbuckled myself and pulled my skirt back down to a decent length, then hopped out of the car.

Noah helped Andy load the car in the trailer, while Jess and I waited.

"I'm so excited for my bachelorette party this weekend, Zoey," Jess squealed. I think it finally hit her that she was getting married in less than two weeks.

"I can't believe it's already June," I said in disbelief. "Let me know if you need me to help with anything else, alright?"

The months that had passed since Andy and I came back from Cabo were amazing and perfect. Time was flying by since then, and every day was definitely getting better for us.

Jess smiled up at me sweetly. "I'd love it if you would sing at the wedding, Z. Anything you want."

Not taking the bait, I simply smiled back at her. Little did she know I had a big surprise for her and Noah. I *finally* convinced Andy to sing a song with me at their wedding.

After saying our goodbyes, we went home. Andy pulled through the gate at the shop and backed the trailer into the space next to the fence. I jumped out and unhooked the trailer for him so he could park his truck.

After seeing me change the tires on my car after Rob slashed them months ago, he thought it was hot when I helped with things like that. I opened the side door of the trailer, then flipped the light on inside to get the small ice chest and a few other items we had packed for our night at the drag races.

When I turned around, Andy was standing in the doorway of the trailer. He had *that* look on his face. *Oh my*. He stepped inside and pulled the door shut behind him.

"Do you know how fucking hot you looked with your skirt hiked up around your hips, strapped down in my car?" he asked as he stalked over to me.

Andy backed me up against the front of his car. I was so ready for whatever he planned on doing to me. I wrapped my arms around him as he ran his hands down the back of my thighs to lift me up onto the hood of the Camaro. He kissed me fiercely, his tongue darting into my mouth, licking and tasting.

He broke our kiss just long enough to pull my shirt off over my head. Swiftly, he unsnapped my bra and pulled it off, tossing it onto the hood of the car.

I pushed his shirt up and he pulled it the rest of the way off for me as I undid the button and zipper of his pants. I pushed his pants and boxers down over his hips to free his cock. He backed up long enough to reach up under my skirt to pull my panties off. I kicked off my sandals to put my feet on the front bumper for balance. He pushed my skirt up my hips then lifted me up and forward so my ass was at the edge of the hood.

He kissed me again before he pushed me backward so I was lying on the hood. He knelt down in front of the car, gently pushing my legs apart. *Holy fuck...I am gonna enjoy the hell outta this.*

As soon as my legs were far enough apart, his mouth was on me. His tongue probed inside me, then moved up to tease my clit. He groaned as he sucked my sensitive clit into his mouth and then licked his way back to my center. He slid one finger in at first, sliding in and out, before slipping a second finger inside me.

It felt like I was sliding off the car a little, so I reached up over my head and grabbed the cowl of the hood to hang on to.

He pulled away and stood back up. "Fuck, Zoey, I'd love a picture of you like this. You look so fucking beautiful up there."

"When we're done, I'll let you take one."

He groaned as he pushed his hard cock inside of me. I gasped as I lay on the hood. His hands gripped my hips as he plunged into me hard and fast. My body was burning hot, ready to ignite. I began to tighten around him as he slowed his movements. He was still thrusting hard, but slow, and I felt the car rocking on its tires from the motion of us on the hood.

His hips swiveled and he ground himself against me, sending me pummeling over the edge. My body clenched and unclenched around his cock as he ground his hips again. He thrust hard once more before he shuddered his own release.

Andy collapsed over me to rest his elbows on the hood, his forehead on my chest as he emptied himself inside me. I grazed my fingers down his back and his body twitched, oversensitive.

"Ahh...fuck, I love you," he groaned, grinding his hips against me one last time.

Giggling at his words, I wrapped my arms around his neck and we lay there, panting and sweaty. Finally, he stood back up, pulling me with him.

"If I'd known how much fucking me on your car would turn you on, I would've suggested it a long time ago," I whispered in his ear. "Where do you want me for the picture?"

"You're really going to let me take one?" he asked in disbelief.

I chuckled, because I think it shocked him so much that I was letting him take a naked picture of me on his car, he hadn't even realized what I said about fucking me on it.

"Only if I can take one of you too." I lay back and slipped my skirt off over my hips, letting it drop to the floor. "Where do you want me?"

"Right where you are. Just spin around and put your feet up on the glass," he instructed as he pulled his cell phone out.

He posed me on the hood the way he wanted, helping me position my arms and legs in such a way that my breasts and other private parts were covered.

After he snapped a few pictures he was happy with, he showed them to me.

"I can't believe that's me," I said, in awe of the photos.

He took the photos from an angle so the front end of the car was in the picture, with me lying on the hood, my hair spilling over the edge, looking like I was just thoroughly fucked. Which I had been.

It was his turn for me to take a picture of him. He was wearing my favorite jeans, so I asked him to lean against the front of his car facing me, with his hands on the hood next to his hips. His jeans were unbuttoned, his chest bare, and his tattoos on full display.

All he needed to do was stand there. Andy had a gorgeous, sexy, just fucked look on his face too. I snapped one picture. I didn't need another.

Chapter Fourteen

Even though we were still living in separate apartments, we slept together every night, at either my place or his. We tried to stay at our own places separately on occasion, but one of us would always give in and crawl in the other's bed during the night.

Simple fact was, we slept better when we were together. I actually slept, which was nice. Besides, we couldn't keep our hands off each other. I'd never had so much sex in my life and I loved every second of it. He never once made me feel neglected or unloved. Everything was perfect between us.

We had two more days of work, and if they were anything like the last few days, we were going to be busy. It was almost summertime and everyone seemed to be working on their cars. I was working mostly at the store because we were so busy, plus it was time to do inventory.

I would be working after hours doing inventory that night and the next night. Saturday was Jess's bachelorette party, where the bridal party would be going out dancing. It was going to be a long week.

By Friday night, I was dead tired, felt like shit, and praying I was not getting sick again, especially so close to Jess and Noah's wedding. When I came down with the flu in May, it completely zapped everything out of me. I had been so sick I lost all the weight I gained while I was in Cabo.

Inventory was not going well at all. I should have done it much sooner. The order I needed to place was huge and the store was a mess.

Andy volunteered to help me, but I turned him down because it was easier for me to concentrate and stay organized if I did it by myself. I finally finished at around two a.m. and made my way up the stairs to my apartment. I figured he would be there asleep, but he wasn't.

All I wanted to do was crash, so I did. By myself.

Horrible dreams interrupted my sleep the entire night. Dreams of my birth mom, watching her get high right in front of me, watching her take disgusting men into her room. I dreamt of the sickening noises they made while I sat crying inside my closet, all the times I had to scrounge around for food, and of being thankful that when I *did* make it to school, I at least ate a hot meal.

Saturday morning, I woke up late, crying. I was alone and needed Andy, but he wasn't there. It wasn't his fault, of course. I should've just gone to his place to sleep the night before when I realized he stayed home.

I wondered where he was, so I peeked out the window, and across the parking lot to Andy's apartment. His truck wasn't in his space, and I had no idea where he would have gone. I found my cell and hit the button on the screen to call Andy, but it remained lifeless. *Shit, dead battery.* I located my charging cord and plugged in my phone, but it was so dead it wouldn't even turn on.

Leaving it on my nightstand to charge, I went to my dresser to get some clean clothes, then hurried to the shower. As I walked through my bathroom door, I stubbed my toe on the doorjamb. I hopped around on one foot as tears rolled from my eyes.

"Fuck," I growled as I sat down on the lid of the toilet to inspect my poor pinky toe. I'd peeled a few layers of skin back and it was bleeding like crazy. *Damn, that fucking hurts.*

Once the bleeding stopped, I stepped into the shower, immediately turning the jets on to massage my back to try and relax. I sat on the shower seat for what felt like an hour. While I sat, I shaved my legs since I would be wearing a dress when we went out dancing.

Of course, I cut the hell out of myself right behind the knee where it hurt the worst. What else was going to happen? After my shower, I was getting a headache, so I took some ibuprofen. Deciding to take it easy the rest of the day, so I didn't accidentally kill myself, I pulled on some clean pajamas then decided to watch a movie.

I was craving chocolate chip cookies and considered baking some, but the thought of burning my building down was not appealing to me. I settled for some cold cereal, spilling the milk while pouring it. I was going to make some coffee, but apparently, I was out of creamer.

Fuck my life right now.

My cereal tasted like cardboard, but I ate it anyway. I crawled back in bed under the covers to watch the movie, but it was a big mistake watching a sappy love story. I was bawling my eyes out as the credits rolled at the end. I flipped the television off and closed my eyes to take a nap.

I woke up several hours later, tired, but I had slept without dreaming so that was good. I rechecked my phone and the battery was fully charged. I had a voice mail from Andy and a few texts. I listened to the voice mail; he was wondering if I was okay, since he hadn't seen or heard from me since work the previous day. The texts were much the same, except the last one asked if I was mad at him. I replied to his text.

My phone battery died. Not mad at you, I had a bad night. Today is not looking much better. TTYL.

I hit send, then decided I was hungry and needed some real food. I put a piece of chicken in the oven and made a salad. I didn't burn the chicken or slice a finger off while making my salad. After I ate, I was still grouchy, so I found a book to read, turned on my iPod, and curled up on the couch. My eyelids grew heavy, and I wanted to close them for only a minute. Evidently, the minute turned in to hours.

When I woke up, it was eight-thirty. Jess and the rest of the girls were picking me up at nine-thirty. They rented a limo to drive us around to a few clubs. Will and Justin were going with us, as they were best friends with Jess too.

Because I only had an hour to get ready, I jogged to my room and proceeded to ram my shoulder against the doorjamb. Beginning to feel like the entire day had some sort of a vendetta against me, I decided I'd better slow down so I didn't gouge my eyes out putting on my makeup, or light my hair on fire when I straightened it.

As I was slipping into my short, red, backless dress and high heels, the intercom buzzed. I gave myself a once over in the mirror. *Dang, I look good.* Especially considering all the crap that happened during the day and the mood I was in.

Tossing my cell, ID, and money into a tiny black purse, I rushed out the door. Fortunately, Will and Justin came out their door at the same time, and with their help, I made it down the stairs in one piece by linking my arms through theirs. We piled into the back of the limo and Sasha thrust a glass of champagne at me.

"Let's party, bitches!" she shouted. I downed the whole glass in one swallow and held it out for someone to pour me another. I was ready to party after my shit-tastic day.

We hit a few clubs, danced, and drank. Justin brought all of us those crazy beaded necklaces with tiny penises in between the beads. We were wearing those, while Jess wore a cheesy veil and a sash that said "Bridezilla" on it. The rest of us ended up with white feather boas, even Will and Justin. I had a nice buzz going on, so I had no idea where they came from.

Our last stop for the night was going to be our favorite bar, Hooligans. Jerome, a former high-end, club bouncer from Hollywood owned it. He wanted to get away from the celebrity lifestyle and own a place where nobody was turned away at the door. There was no waiting in long lines outside, and no picking only the 'it' crowd to let in.

It had been ages since I'd been there, and I hadn't realized how much I missed the place. We walked into the bar and it was packed wall to wall.

The enormous back room boasted a large dance floor, a booth for the DJ, and several booths with tables around the edges of the room. It also had a large bar, while out front there were tables, booths, and another bar. We called the week before and reserved the biggest booth for our get together.

Since it was Saturday night, the DJ played requests from everyone. The deal was, no matter what song you requested, the DJ would play it. Whether it was country, hip-hop, rock, or whatever, the DJ played it. Thank God, they didn't get many requests for country music.

All of us were out on the dance floor shaking our butts with Jerome to his favorite song, "I Like It" by the band Foxy Shazam. Ever since the song had come out, he played it every Saturday night without fail at one a.m., and if you knew what was good for you, you went out on the floor and danced with him.

Jerome was in the middle of the bridal party, all six-foot-eight of him, and he was dancing his ass off. He looked like an NBA basketball player, wearing loose jeans and a Sacramento Kings jersey.

The song ended and I was hot, so I went up to the bar for another drink and a bottle of water. I squeezed into the only spot left at the bar to get the bartender's attention. As I waited, the guy on the barstool to my right started talking to me.

"Are you having a good night?" he asked as his eyes traveled from my face down to my boobs. "You look hot."

Um, really? Did he mean I looked hot as in it was hot in the bar, or hot as in *hot*? I decided I wanted it to be because it was hot in the bar and not some pick up line.

"Yes, it is hot in here, isn't it?" I asked as I fanned myself with a napkin from the bar.

The bartender came and took my drink order, so I sat and waited for it.

"What's your name?"

"Zoey," I responded, not asking his name.

"So, Zoey, you interested in getting out of here with me?" he asked as he leaned in closer to my face and swept my hair back over my shoulder with his hand.

He actually ran his fingertips down my bare back. Seriously? Did this shit ever work for this guy?

"No, I'm not interested, actually. I have a boyfriend and I'd appreciate it if you didn't touch me again," I asserted with a slight glare in his direction.

"Fuck," he growled, "You don't have to be such a bitch."

I wasn't really in the mood to be called a bitch by a complete stranger, so I turned and faced him. "Oh, I'm sorry, did I offend you? What do you expect? You can't just ask a girl her name and in the next breath, ask her if she wants to go home with you."

Something caught the creepers attention over my shoulder. Then I heard a deep, angry voice say, "Leave." He stood up and left. I turned around to see Andy standing there, with a not so happy look on his face.

"What the fuck, Zoey?" he growled.

That pissed me off. I was waiting for my drink, minding my own business, and he's mad at *me*.

"What?" I replied. "I was waiting for my drink."

My drinks arrived, and I dropped my money down on the bar. Andy sat on the barstool the creeper had just vacated.

"Are you sure about that?"

"Am I sure about what?" I asked, the irritation very apparent in the tone of my voice.

"I saw that guy touching you. What the hell was that about?" He was really pissed, and because of it, so was I.

"For your information, *Andrew*, I let the guy know I had a boyfriend and I'd appreciate it if he kept his fucking hands to himself."

Grabbing my bottle of water in one hand and my margarita in the other, I took a long drink, and spun the barstool around with my feet to go find my friends. Andy reached out and grabbed my upper arm, causing my drink to slosh over the side of the glass. The liquid flowed over my hand, down my arm to my elbow.

"Great, thanks a lot," I growled at him as I set my drink back on the bar and picked up a bunch of napkins to dry my arm and hand off.

"Zoey, I'm sorry. I didn't like him touching you, that's all."

I didn't want to hear it. He had no reason to be jealous. I shook my head. "You should know better, Andy. What are you even doing here anyway?"

He took a napkin off the bar and cleaned my glass off, then handed it back to me.

"We're crashing Jess's party."

Oh yes, he was with my brothers and their friends at Noah's bachelor party. "I see." I was still pissed. I finished my drink and set the glass back on the bar.

"Sorry, but I haven't seen you since yesterday. You didn't want my help with inventory, and today I don't hear anything from you except for one text. Then I come here and it *looks* like some guy is all over you. What am I supposed to think?"

I raised my eyebrows in disbelief. "You're *supposed* to think your girlfriend loves you and can be trusted. Are you actually mad at me for what that asshole did?"

He shook his head. "No, I'm not mad at you. I couldn't see what you were doing. I just saw him touching you and I didn't like it."

I let out a breath. "I took care of it."

He slid off his barstool and pulled me close. "I'm sorry, Beautiful. I overreacted."

I looked up into his eyes. I could never stay mad at him because I knew he was sorry.

"Yes, you did overreact. Please don't turn in to a jealous boyfriend. Promise?"

He sat back down so we were face to face. "Promise. I know you're my girl and I'll never have a reason to be jealous. I know you love me."

Leaning over, I kissed him. "*Only* you," I whispered against his cheek.

My arm was sticky from my drink, so I excused myself to go to the bathroom and wash up.

On my way back to Andy, Nicole stepped from the crowd in front of me. She was so drunk, she swayed on her feet, and I was surprised she didn't fall over. Her lipstick was smeared and her mascara had started to run, so she'd obviously been drinking for a while.

"What's wrong, Zoey?" she asked with a smirk on her face. "Did you run off *another* man? Maybe if you weren't such a frigid bitch, you could keep one."

Really? What the fuck did she know?

I glared at her and tried to go around her, but she blocked my path.

"Fuck off, Nicole." I brushed past her and when I did, she rammed her shoulder against mine.

Okay, that's it. I'm done with this shit.

Since we returned from Cabo, I hadn't had a chance to say anything to her after the sex call she and Rob made to me from Andy's phone, so the bitch had had it coming for a while.

I made it two steps past her, turned around, and backhanded the skanky bitch right across her nasty-ass face, knocking her backward a few feet.

She put her palm against the cheek I'd smacked and her eyes grew as big as saucers.

"You bitch!" she cried.

Since one hit didn't feel like enough, I started toward her to hit her again when two of her slutty friends grabbed her arms and dragged her away.

I'd never hit anyone before and was shocked at what had come over me, but it felt damn good to smack her.

When I turned back to the bar, I made eye contact with Andy, who was jogging toward me with Justin and Will on his heels. They'd witnessed the whole altercation. Andy slowed to a walk and raised his eyebrows as a wide grin slowly spread across his face. The boys must have decided that Andy had everything under control, so they went back out to the dance floor.

Shrugging my shoulders, I smiled back at Andy as I walked toward him. We met up as "New York" by Snow Patrol came on.

Did he really ask them to play me a song? None of my friends would have asked the DJ to play Snow Patrol but me, and I hadn't asked, so it had to have been Andy. I took his hand and led him out onto the dance floor, where I pulled him in close.

"Did you ask them to play this for me?"

He nodded and kissed my forehead, holding me tight. "Yeah, I heard they took requests, so I asked them to play it as soon as I got here. Then I tried to find you...and here we are."

His lips brushed over mine as we swayed together on the dance floor. I laid my head on his chest and closed my eyes, breathing him in. I loved the feel of his heart thumping beneath my cheek and his hands caressing my bare back.

"I love this dress, Zoey," he said as he kissed me behind my ear, sending chills down my spine. We held each other and slow danced to the music, even when the song was over and a fast song started. It felt so good to be in his arms after the shitty day I'd had.

When the next song was almost over, he pulled back from me.

"That was a nice bitch-slap back there, by the way. What was that all about?"

I told him what Nicole said to me and then rested my cheek against him again.

"My girl...she's a beautiful, bitch-slapping badass," Andy whispered in my ear. I chuckled and kissed his chest through his shirt.

Two songs later, someone tapped on my shoulder. "The limo is here to take us home, Z, are you ready to go?" Sasha questioned.

I was definitely ready. "Please, let's get out of here." I looked up at Andy. "I need to go. Do you want to ride with us, or do you want to stay with the guys?"

Sasha interrupted. "Actually, some of the guys are coming with us. Noah is ready to go home with Jess. They're getting pretty hot and heavy out there on the dance floor. Will and Justin are having too much fun, so they're staying with a few of the girls."

Andy smiled. "I'm going wherever you go, Zoey." I gathered up my purse and my feather boa from our booth and we headed out to the limo.

Andy climbed in first and pulled me onto his lap when I tried to slide in next to him. He wrapped his arms around me, burying his face in my hair. I didn't realize he had been drinking too, and we were both about to fall asleep.

The limo drove around, dropping everyone off. As the car emptied of people, I stayed right where I was on Andy's lap. He ran his fingertips up and down my back as we drove around. Nobody was paying us any attention, so I nestled into the crook of his neck, kissing him gently.

His hand slipped inside the back of my dress, where no one could see. His other arm was around me, resting on my hip. It was loud in the limo with it being half-full still, but I heard him moan quietly as I snuck my hand up under his shirt to touch bare skin.

Eventually the limo slowed to a stop. "Z, this is your place," Jess said from across the car.

"Thanks for a great night, girls," I called back as Andy and I stepped out of the car.

Chapter Fifteen

We made it upstairs, and Andy let us into my apartment with his key. Once in the bedroom, he turned down the covers while I took off my shoes. I went straight to his side of the bed and stood in front of him.

"Sit," I directed, pushing him down gently to sit on the edge of the bed. I knelt down in front of him on my knees and pulled off his shoes and socks. I slipped my hands inside the legs of his jeans to knead my fingers over his bare calves. His leg hair felt coarse against my palms.

He reached out and gently massaged my shoulders with his strong hands as I unbuttoned his shirt, pushed it off his shoulders, and tossed it to the floor. Leaning forward, I kissed his muscular stomach, then took one of his hands in mine, turning it over to kiss his palm. I set his hand down on the bed next to him and undid the button on his pants, then his zipper.

"Are you alright, Zoey? Talk to me."

"I'm fine, but I want to show you how much I love you. I hate the fact that you thought for just a second—"

He put his fingertips over my lips to stop me. "No, don't say it. I was being a dick. I hadn't seen you all day, so I went looking for you because I wanted to dance with you like we did in Cabo. I misunderstood what was going on and you set me straight. Okay?"

I nodded.

He gripped my elbows and pulled me up to stand in front of him. He reached up and slid the zipper down on my dress. "Tonight you looked so beautiful. Let me make this up to you, please."

Andy stood up and pushed my dress off my shoulders, letting it drop to the floor. He hooked his thumbs in the top of his pants and boxers then pushed them down. He stepped out of them and sat back down on the bed.

As I stood in front of him wearing only my panties, Andy eased me closer to him and kissed my collarbone, then down to my breast, sucking my nipple into his mouth gently, causing my breath to quicken. His hands roamed from my ribs down to my panties, sliding them down my legs to drop on the floor with my dress. He lay back on the bed, pulling me on top of him, kissing me hungrily as he rolled over on top of me.

I wrapped my legs around his hips as he slid himself inside me. He didn't start thrusting or moving. He was still, inside me, as he kissed me.

"I love you, Zoey," he whispered in my ear as he slowly started rolling his hips.

The slowness felt wonderful, but I desired more from him. After the day I'd had, I needed a quick release.

"I need you hard and fast. *Please*," I begged hoarsely as I gripped his firm ass, pulling him hard against me.

He caught on to my desperation, pulled out of me and flipped me over onto my stomach, then grabbed my hips and pulled me up on my knees. I braced myself on my forearms as he centered himself and slammed inside me from behind.

"Ohhh fuck," I cried out from the rush of pleasure coursing through me.

With his hands gripping my hips, he pulled his body back so far he almost slipped out of me. He jerked me back hard against him as he thrust forward, his balls slapping up against my clit.

"Again, *please*," I pleaded with him. *Oh, sweet Jesus, that was amazing.*

He did as I asked, slamming into me over and over again, until I was practically screaming his name and tightening around him. Andy held himself back from his release until I was completely satisfied and then pulled out of me, easing me over onto my back.

He took a couple of pillows, arranging them under my hips. Then he put his arms under my legs, so he had my knees hooked over the bend of his elbows. Once he had me stable and still enough, he pushed inside me again. I cried out as the desire took over my body and my mind shut off completely. With my hips raised in that position, he was hitting my g-spot each time he thrust. My brain turned to mush with all the sensations I was feeling below the waist.

Within minutes, I was coming again. He thrust one last time as he finally let go himself. "Ahh fuck," he hissed out as he came. He wrapped my legs around his hips, and I wrapped my arms around him, pulling him down to me as his body shuddered over mine.

"Thank you. I needed that," I breathed out with a slight chuckle.

"You'd tell me if I was too rough, wouldn't you?"

"Mmm, you were perfect," I whispered as I pulled him into a kiss.

The Saturday morning of Jess and Noah's wedding, I woke up early. Andy was sleeping soundly beside me, and James was sleeping on my feet. I picked James up and took him to the laundry room to feed him, then stopped to use the bathroom and brush my teeth on my way back to bed. Andy was still asleep, so I slid into bed behind him.

"Wake up, my love," I sang quietly as I kissed his back and wrapped my arm around his waist.

He shifted slightly. "Mmm, what time is it?" he murmured sleepily, his voice deep and gravelly, his accent more pronounced.

A sleepy Andy was a very sexy Andy.

"It's time for you to get up." I shifted my hand down lower, wrapping it around him. "I see you're already up though."

I pressed my body against his. Never one to turn me away, he reached around behind him and found me with his fingers. While he slid his fingers in and out of me, I slowly glided my hand along his length while I kissed his muscular, tattooed back.

He shifted away, rolling to his back, so I climbed on top of him and guided him inside me. I rested my hands on his tattooed chest, moving slowly up and down on him, as his hands gripped my hips.

"You feel so good, Zoey," he groaned as he pulled me down to lie flat on his chest.

He wrapped his arms around me tight as he continued to thrust into me. I would never have enough of this man. Neither one of us bothered with pajamas anymore. We would wake up during the night to make love and our clothes just got in the way. I literally could not be in the same bed with him and *not* touch him.

I had no self-control, but neither did he. Gripping my hips, he pulled me harder and faster to meet his thrusts. The heat low in my belly began to travel lower until I was gasping, constricting around him in the throes of orgasm.

He slowed his thrusting, but not the intensity of them. Slow and hard, he groaned with the start of his own release as I came. He continued to push into me until his body trembled, emptying himself completely inside me.

Not five minutes later, my phone rang. I rolled off Andy and whispered a satisfied hello into the receiver.

"Zoey, it's Jess. We have a big problem!"

"What is it? What's wrong?" I asked, worried.

"Heather is totally fine, but she went in to labor and Jason obviously can't be in the wedding now."

My sister-in-law went into labor two weeks early. "Jess, what do you want to do?" I asked. "If you're worried about an odd number of people in the bridal party, I can step back and not be in it. I'll do anything you want. Just ask."

She sighed loudly. "Z, you're my best friend. You have to be in my wedding. We need another groomsman. Do you think Andy would do it? He's been a good friend to Noah."

I asked Jess to hold on a minute while I spoke to Andy. "Heather went in to labor. Can you fill Jason's shoes as a groomsman?"

"Of course," he said. "What about the tux?"

"Jess, he'll do it. What do we do about the tux? He and Jason are similar in size, so it might work, but with the difference in height, maybe not."

"I've talked to the tailor already, and she can alter it if he gets to her store within the hour," she replied, relieved.

"We're on our way," I said and hung up.

We hopped out of bed, quickly dressed and rushed to the tuxedo store. "Do I get to walk down the aisle with you, Zoey?" Andy asked as I drove my Audi down the freeway like a bat out of hell.

"Yes, actually you do. We walk down separately, but after the wedding we meet up and walk back down the aisle together."

I peeked over at Andy to gauge his expression.

He grinned back over at me. "Good, it will be the best part of the day for me."

God, my man was adorable when he wasn't being so sexy.

While the tailor was taking Andy's measurements, I walked outside and called my brother. "Hi, Jay. How's Heather doing? Is she feeling okay?" I heard her in the background talking to someone, which eased my mind.

"She's doing great, Zoey. The baby is being monitored, and everything is progressing the way it's supposed to. She's just going to be early."

She? "You're having a girl?" I squealed. "Finally, another girl in the family."

Jason chuckled at my exuberance. "Yeah, sis, we're having a girl this time. It's going to be awesome. I can't wait to meet her."

My eyes became a little teary at his sentiment toward his daughter. Eeesh, the day was going to be full of emotions. I was tearing up at my brother talking about his unborn daughter, and my best friend was getting married to my other brother. *Today is going to be a great day.* I was ecstatic for my brother and Heather. They both wanted a girl, and they were going to have one.

"Jay, don't worry about the wedding. We have everything covered. All you need to do is take care of your wife and baby girl. Let us know when she gets here. Love you, Bro."

"Love you too, Z. I'll call you as soon as I can. Have a great time at the wedding and make sure nobody worries about us. Heather's family is here if we need anything, so everything is alright."

We ended our call and I went back inside the tux shop. The tailor was a freaking miracle worker. I came back in just as she finished letting down the hem of Andy's pants.

"Wow," I said when I saw him all dressed up.

He smiled at me and straightened his bowtie.

The tailor stood up and gave Andy a once over. "Alright, Mr. Tate, off with your pants so I can hem them up for you, and you can be on your way."

I raised my eyebrow at Andy as he dropped his pants for her without even a hint of embarrassment. He stepped out of them and handed them to her then took off the rest of the tux and hung it in the garment bag.

He redressed in his shorts, T-shirt, and leather flip-flops. "I'll need thirty minutes to get these done," the tailor said.

"We'll be back in a bit, then," I said.

We went next door to the donut shop, where Andy and I sat down together and downed two dozen glazed donut holes and coffee, while we waited for his pants to be finished.

I sent Jess a text, letting her know we were going home to take showers, and then I would meet her at the salon to get my hair and makeup done with her and the rest of the girls.

"I think I might shave, Zoey," Andy said unexpectedly. "What do you think?" He ran his palms over his jaw. He had let his stubble grow out a bit more, so it was a little longer than usual.

"Why?" I shook my head quickly. I didn't want him to shave. I loved that gorgeous, unshaved face of his more than anything. I loved the way it felt as it grazed over my body when we made love.

"What's going through that head of yours right now, Beautiful?" Andy questioned with a devious grin on his face. "You're thinking pervy thoughts about me, aren't you? I can tell."

Damn that man. He always knew when I was thinking about the amazing things we did to each other in bed.

No way in hell was I going to admit what I was thinking, so I simply said, "I love your face exactly the way it is, Andy. However, I'm not going to tell you what you can and cannot do with your body, so...it's your decision." I laughed to hide my embarrassment.

"Uh huh, sure," he said, dragging out the last word. I wadded up my napkin and chucked it at him, but he caught it and threw it back at me, hitting me on the boob.

"Ha, boob shot! I win," he said triumphantly.

"You better watch it, Tate," I warned. "You might not get to see them later if you don't stop gloating."

He raised his hands in surrender. "Not gloating again, I swear. Even though I know you'll let me see them anyway."

Andy quickly stood up from the table before I could retaliate. He tossed all of our trash onto the tray then dumped it in the trashcan.

After we made it back to my apartment, we hopped in the shower together, making sure to hurry since I had a couple of hours of hair and makeup ahead of me. Andy didn't fail to tell me it took less than an hour before I was flashing him my boobs.

He was being a smartass, but he was in such a good mood I just went along with whatever he said and teased him right back. It was the story of our relationship; playful, goofy, lots of hot and romantic sex, and we loved each other unconditionally.

Since I was helping Jess and the other girls with whatever they needed, we had to get a move on. We were running just a bit late. I gathered up my bridesmaid dress, which was an elegant, above the knee, black dress. The wedding was going to be very stylish. There would be no tacky sea-foam green anywhere.

Jess picked out the color for the dresses, but she let us pick the cut and style that best suited our bodies. I took her with me when I shopped for my dress, and she watched as I tried on several. We both loved the dress I bought the second I put it on.

We hopped in my Audi, and Andy drove me to the salon to meet the rest of the bridal party. He kissed me goodbye then drove over to Noah's place to get ready with him and the other groomsmen. I was the last to arrive at the salon. Fortunately, everything was running smoothly, so I was able to get my hair and makeup done on time.

"Zoey, thank you so much for helping out this morning," Jess said. "I don't know what I'd do without you and Andy."

I smiled at her as the stylist fastened her veil to her hair. "You're welcome, Jess. We'd do anything for you," I said honestly. "Wow, you look exquisite. My brother is one lucky guy." My eyes started tearing up again because I was so happy for my brother and my best friend.

"Don't you *dare* cry, Zoey Lynn James," Jess growled at me.

"Sorry, I'm truly happy for you and Noah," I sighed. "I'm glad your day is finally here. The wedding is going to be perfect, and we'll have a new niece sometime today too."

Jess's eyes lit up. "They're having a girl?"

I nodded excitedly, a huge grin on my face. "Yep, Jay told me when I talked to him earlier. They're thrilled."

We packed up our belongings then headed to the church in the limo to get dressed and wait for the wedding to start.

Once we arrived, we gathered in a large room at the back of the church to finish getting ready. I helped Jess into her gorgeous wedding gown. We still had a while to wait before the ceremony started, when someone knocked on the dressing room door.

Sasha opened the door and spoke to whoever was on the other side. "We're all decent. Come on in," she joked, laughing.

My man came through the door, holding a tiny gift bag in his hand. He looked around at all the girls. "All of you look lovely," he said before turning back to Jess. "I brought a gift from Noah for you, Jess."

Andy stepped over to her and handed her the bag. He hadn't shaved, but it did look like he took some clippers and trimmed his facial hair.

"Thank you, Andy, for bringing this to me," Jess said to him. He gave her a kiss on the cheek then turned to duck out of the room. He winked at me as he left.

"Oh my gosh, who was that?" Jess's cousin, Kristen, asked. She was obnoxious, but Jess's mom gave her a major guilt trip to put Kristen in the wedding. "I'll be taking *him* to the backroom later, bitches. Just wait and see. You know what they say about the bridesmaids and groomsmen hooking up."

Wow, *really*? Jess and Sasha's jaws dropped as they stared over at me to see my reaction. They probably thought another bitch-slap was coming.

"Yeah, good luck with that guy, Kristen," I said sarcastically.

"What, Zoey, you think you've got a chance with someone like him?"

Actually, yes, I do. I have a good chance with him and a perfect life with him.

Tears pricked my eyes for the third time that day. *What the hell has gotten in to me?* Not wanting to be the cause of any drama on Jess's day, I dropped it.

Jess opened her gift from Noah. I clasped the sparkling, diamond bracelet around her wrist for her. There was another knock at the door about fifteen minutes later. It was Jess's dad.

"Jessie, it's time," he announced, beaming down at his daughter in her wedding dress with tears in his eyes. They had a father-daughter moment, while the rest of us gathered up our bouquets and lined up at the door.

Sasha and I were going out first, so we hugged Jess and made our way up the aisle to our pre-assigned places. I walked slowly holding my flower bouquet, and made sure I remembered to smile like I was expected to.

As soon as I saw Andy, I became a little teary again. He looked so handsome standing in line with my brothers and Noah's friend, Tyler, who was the best man. I was finally close enough to the front of the aisle so he could see me. He watched me with the biggest smile on his face.

I grinned back at him as I took my place on the bride's side of the church and waited for the rest of the girls and Jess. Once all the girls were lined up in their spots, the bridal march started, and Jess walked down the aisle with her dad.

All eyes in the room were on them, but mine. They were on Andy, and he would not take his eyes off me. He mouthed, "I love you" to me, making me blush.

Sasha poked me in the ribs to make me pay attention to the bride like I was supposed to. She bent her body sideways toward me and whispered, "Z, you're going to be next. Mark my words." She had her usual shit-eating grin on her face as Jess made her way up to where Noah stood waiting for her.

The wedding party turned to face the pastor after Jess's dad handed her over to my brother. Several minutes later, Jess and Noah said their vows to one another, and they were married. Once they were pronounced man and wife, they had the most romantic wedding kiss I'd ever seen.

It was so romantic, everyone in the entire church started clapping for them. They walked arm in arm down the aisle of the church, then the rest of the wedding party made their way behind them.

When Andy and I met to walk out together, he held my face in his hands and planted a sweet kiss right on my lips. "You look beautiful," he whispered. He linked my arm under his and we walked out behind the rest of the bridal party.

We even earned a few cheers when we walked by my family.

Chapter Sixteen

The wedding party met in a huge room at the back of the church, where we hugged Jess and Noah and congratulated them. While Sasha and I struggled to tie up the train of Jess's wedding dress, I noticed Kristen make her way over to where Andy and Jeremy were talking. She introduced herself to both men.

We watched as she ran her hand down Andy's arm. He backed away from her a step and folded his arms across his chest, blatantly snubbing her.

Jess looked over at me. "Zoey, feel free to go slap the shit out of her, then let's get to the reception. I'm ready to par-tay!"

"Thanks," I smiled and walked toward Andy.

He saw me coming and excused himself from the conversation with Kristen, who turned around to see where he was going. Andy walked right up to me and stopped.

"I know I already told you, but you look so beautiful, Zoey," he said as he wrapped his arms around me and picked me up off the floor.

It was probably childish of me, but I fought my own demons very hard for that man, and I was not taking any shit from anyone. I wrapped my arms around his neck and laid the most impressive kiss on him I could.

Our lips parted and I dipped my tongue inside his mouth to meet his. I pulled away with a little moan emanating from my throat as he set me back on the floor.

"We're ready. Let's get out of here and to the reception!" Jess hollered as I gently wiped my lipstick from Andy's lips.

Andy kissed me on the cheek. "I don't know what that kiss was all about, but you can do it again, anytime." I just smiled up at him and linked my arm through his to leave for the reception.

On our way past Kristen, I glanced over at her and she had her mouth hanging open, glaring at me.

"Guess you better try another groomsman, Kristen." I smiled sweetly, just to be a smartass. "This one is mine."

After I walked a few steps, another thought popped into my head. I stopped and let go of Andy then turned back to Kristen.

"I take that back," I stated. "Since two of the other groomsmen are my brothers, I suggest you stay the fuck away from them too."

Not waiting to see her expression, I turned on my heel and went back to my man.

We hopped into my car to make our way to the reception venue. "What was that all about, Zoey?" Andy asked curiously. I explained to him what Kristen said earlier about me not having a chance with "someone like that."

"Why would she even say that? I'm just a dirty, greasy mechanic," he said, a hint of disgust in his tone.

I was floored. "Andy, why would you even think that? You are attractive, hardworking, and never greasy *or* dirty for that matter. Did I mention you are the sweetest, kindest, and most loving person I know?"

He took my hand in his and kissed the back of it. "Thank you. I guess being told I was pretty much worthless for two years by my ex-wife's family kind of stuck with me."

Are you fucking kidding me?

"They sound like a bunch of arrogant assholes." Why would anyone even say that to him? We never really talked about his ex before, but I was very curious about her and why she left the way she did. *I guess this explains it.*

"Why would they think you're worthless?"

He sighed. "They're very wealthy, Zoey. They thought I was after their money or something. They hated the fact their daughter wanted to be with someone who worked under the hood of a car for a living. They never even tried to get to know me or find out anything about me." He smirked and shook his head.

Why were some wealthy people such jerks? It was as if having lots of money made them better than someone with no money.

Noticing the indignant expression on his face, I reached over and rubbed his arm. "All I can say is their loss is my gain, Andy. I don't know where I would be if you hadn't come in to my life." I was getting a little teary again. He was my rock and my *reason* for everything.

He noticed I was upset, so he pulled into the closest parking lot and stopped the car. He put the Audi in park and unbuckled his seatbelt, then reached across and unbuckled mine too.

Andy embraced me tightly over the top of the console. He had a rather intense expression on his face. "I love you more than anything. You are the great love of my life, and you always will be. I don't *ever* want to be away from you...I have a quest—"

Overcome by the sweet words spilling from his lips, I didn't let him finish his sentence. I pulled away just enough to kiss him hard. "It's a good thing we'll never need to worry about that. I'll always be yours," I said, slipping back onto my seat.

"Come on, Sexy. Let's get to the reception so we can eat, slow dance, and sing our song."

"Ugh, don't remind me," he grumbled quietly.

"Don't be nervous. If you need to, pretend you're singing it to me. You'll be great."

He drove us to the reception, and we walked in holding hands as the DJ announced for the wedding party to gather in our designated area for wedding photos. Andy and I had a few pictures of us taken together all dressed up, so we would have photos other than the snapshots we took on our phones. After the pictures, we had a delicious dinner with everyone laughing and having a great time. The best man and maid of honor did their toasts for the bride and groom, then mine and Jess's parents said a few words.

When the toasts were over, it was time for Andy and me to perform our song. The DJ made the announcement for Jess and Noah to come out on the dance floor for their first dance, as we made our way up onto the stage.

There were two barstools waiting for us next to our acoustic guitars and microphones. Andy was nervous, so I let him know I would do all the talking.

The DJ handed me his microphone. "Hi, everyone," I said to the crowd as Jess and Noah stood in the middle of the floor staring up at us, wondering what was going on.

"I'm Zoey. I'm Noah's only sister and one of Jess's best friends, and this is my wonderful boyfriend, Andy." I motioned to him as he settled on his seat next to me. "I was finally able to convince him to do a special song with me for Jess and Noah's first dance. They didn't know we were doing this for them."

Jess looked up at me with tears in her eyes as I spoke. "Thank you," she mouthed to me. "Jess, Noah, we are so happy for you. We love you both and hope you enjoy this song for your first dance. It's called "My Light.""

I handed the mic back to the DJ, and we settled in front of our own microphones on the barstools with our guitars. Andy was a great guitar player, much better than I was, so he started the song, and I backed him up.

He began to sing lead while I sang harmony with him. I had to admit, we sounded great together. The barstools were set up to where Andy and I were almost facing one another, so we could see each other as we sang.

Andy was extremely nervous that for his first time singing in public there would be over two hundred and fifty people watching him. It was very romantic. The crowd clapped along to the beat of the song as Jess and Noah swayed on the dance floor. Jess pretty much cried the whole time as Noah wiped her tears for her.

When we were close to the end of the song, I did most of the singing, while Andy sang harmony and played his guitar. By the time we finished, even I was teary. When we were done, we stood up to put our guitars back on their stands, and the crowd erupted in cheers. I took Andy's hand in mine and pulled him close.

"You did it. You were flawless."

He pulled me into his arms and laid a romantic kiss on me as he dipped me over backward in front of the entire crowd. They erupted in even more loud and crazy cheering.

"I love you, Zoey. I'm happy we did this together."

We walked off the stage, and Jess and Noah met us at the bottom of the steps.

"Oh my gosh, you guys!" Jess squealed with tears running down her face. "I don't even know what to say. Thank you so much. Andy, wow. Just...*wow*. I had no idea you sang." She pulled us both into a bear hug after she stopped dancing around with excitement.

The rest of the night, we danced and had a fantastic time at the reception. At midnight, Jess and Noah left for their honeymoon. They were spending a week in Hawaii.

"Have a great time and take lots of pictures," I called as they got inside their waiting car. We'd had a great night, but I was ready to go home. I was exhausted, and my feet were killing me.

Andy had shed his vest and jacket after our song. He was looking very scrumptious with his white shirt unbuttoned a bit and his untied bowtie hanging around his collar.

"Hey, handsome," I said as I snuck up behind him, wrapping my arms around his waist. "Why don't you take me home and help me out of this dress."

He spun around to face me, cupping my face in his hands. "That sounds like a great idea, Beautiful. Let's go." We found his jacket and vest, said our goodbyes, and began the drive home.

On the way, I checked my phone to find a text from Jason. It was a photo of his gorgeous, baby girl, Mya Rose, who was born just after ten p.m. After I showed the photo to Andy, I texted my brother back to tell him we'd visit them after Heather had some time to rest. I closed my eyes and began to drift off.

Once we arrived back at my apartment and stripped off our wedding clothes, we fell into bed, both of us worn out. We faced each other, and I noticed a serious expression on his face.

"Zoey, how do you feel about getting married again someday?"

Taken aback by his question, I tipped my head back to get a better look at his face. "Why do you ask?"

He reached up to brush my hair behind my ear and kissed me lightly.

"Well, I'm not getting any younger, you know? My birthday is coming up soon, and I'll be twenty-nine. I always wanted kids by the time I was thirty."

Shocked by his revelation, I felt my heart drop a little. I had no idea he wanted kids so soon. I didn't know what to say to him.

"I know we talked about this briefly in Cabo, Andy, but I just thought it was a general thing we talked about. I didn't know you actually wanted to do it soon. With *me*."

He propped his head up on his palm. "There's nobody else I'd rather do it with. I'm not asking you to go off the pill or anything, not right now, but we should talk about this. I'd marry you tomorrow. You know that, right?"

"No, I didn't. I'm not sure if I'm ready to share you yet. Babies are a lot of work," I replied softly, not wanting to disappoint him. I looked up into his big, blue eyes and imagined children with the same blue eyes, exactly like their daddy's.

My eyes welled up with tears at the thought. The perfect man lying next to me wanted to be married and make a family with me.

"Hey, what's with the tears?" he asked as he sat up. I sat up too, and reclined against the mountain of pillows behind me. He waited patiently for me to wipe my eyes.

"In one little moment, you've rendered me completely speechless, Andy. I guess now I am finally realizing this is all real, that we have a good chance to make a life together."

He scooted over next to me and wrapped his arms around me, so I rested my head on his chest. He took a deep breath. "Seeing you walk down the aisle today, Zoey…I just about lost it."

I smiled because I knew exactly what he meant. After seeing him in his tuxedo at the other end of the aisle, I wanted to marry him. But, a baby in the next year before he turns thirty? I wasn't sure how I felt about it. I finally had myself back together and couldn't imagine having to take care of a baby too.

"So what do we do now?" I asked, still stunned at how the evening had turned from Jess and Noah's wedding, to Andy telling me he wanted to marry me and have a family together.

"This conversation came out of nowhere, Andy. I wasn't expecting to talk about this, at all. I don't know if I'm ready for kids. I'm not even twenty-five yet."

He looked at me intensely, yet confused. "Zoey, you were pregnant before. I thought maybe you wanted kids while you were younger."

Why was this so confusing to me? I wanted to be with this man more than anything I'd ever wanted in my life. But kids? Soon?

"Andy, I do want kids. My pregnancy before was not planned. I thought you knew. I'm not sure I want them as soon as you do."

He reached over to stroke my cheek. "So you're not saying no, then, just not so soon. I get it."

I nodded. "Exactly. I want to spend as much time as we can together before that. Plus, we aren't even married, so there's that too," I laughed.

He blew out a relieved breath. "It's just a formality, Zoey."

I rubbed my eyes. I was worn-out and couldn't think straight. "Can we talk about this tomorrow? Give me some time, please. You've completely blindsided me and I need to think about this for a while. This is an intense conversation, I'm really tired, and I don't want to say the wrong thing right now."

He kissed me on top of my head, and we slid down under the covers. He fell asleep quickly, while I lay in bed thinking about our conversation for an eternity before falling in to a restless sleep. I woke up several times from dreams about my birth mom.

I dreamt I was going to be a horrible mother like she was. I dreamt I was going to fail my own children, as she failed me. I never knew my dad, but Andy would be a wonderful father if we did have kids.

It made no sense to keep tossing and turning, so I quietly slipped out of bed, pulled on some pajamas, and tiptoed to the living room. I picked up a book and my iPod then settled myself on the couch to read to get my mind off the baby conversation. I put in my earbuds and, of course, found Snow Patrol. I read a few chapters and finally grew tired again, so I set my book down and closed my eyes.

I woke up to sunlight streaming through my windows, and Andy was kneeling beside me, trying to untangle my earbud cords from my hair. I reached up and pulled them out of my ears. "Good morning," I whispered as he finally freed my hair and set my iPod on the coffee table.

"Hey," he said quietly as he maneuvered his arms underneath my shoulders and knees to pick me up. He carried me back to bed and gently laid me down. Without saying anything else, he stripped my clothes from me and tossed them onto the floor, then pulled the sheet up over us both, and we fell back to sleep.

Chapter Seventeen

August 2012

"Are you all packed, Zoey?" Andy asked when he walked into my bedroom.

It was Friday after work, and we were going to Sonoma for the weekend to visit his family. I would be meeting them for the first time and I was so nervous it was making me sick to my stomach. They were good people based on what Andy had told me, but I was psyching myself out bad.

"Yes, I'm finished. Are you ready to go?" I zipped up the suitcase lying on the bed and prayed I'd packed the nicest clothing I had. I wanted to make a good impression.

"Did you pack a fancy dress? My aunt wants to take us out to dinner tomorrow night at one of the vineyards for my birthday."

I laughed because that was the first I'd heard about us going out to dinner for his birthday. "Guess I'm not ready then. Let me find a dress and shoes real quick, and we can leave when you're ready."

He came up behind me and wrapped his arms around my waist as I was looking for a dress in the closet. He swept my hair to the side, started kissing my neck, then gently nipped my ear with his teeth.

"You know, if you keep doing that, we're going to get to Sonoma even later than we already are," I mumbled as I reached behind me and ran my palm across the front of his pants, giving his hardening cock a gentle squeeze.

"Join me in the shower?" he asked as he took the bottom hem of my sundress and pulled it over my head. Not waiting for me to answer, he unhooked my bra and slid it down my arms. Andy lightly ran the tips of his fingers down my back then rid me of my panties.

There I was standing naked in the closet, while he was still fully clothed in his work uniform.

I turned around and slowly unbuttoned his shirt, slipping it off over his broad, muscular shoulders. He pulled his white tank top over his head while I undid his pants. I kissed his chest, trailing a path of kisses and my tongue down to his nipple, lightly taking it between my teeth. He shivered after I released it and stripped off the rest of his clothes.

Andy picked me up high, so I wrapped my arms around his neck and shoulders. He held my legs around his waist and slid inside me as he backed me up against the wall.

We made it to Sonoma an hour later than we planned, but it was well worth the delay. I would be late to anything for a quickie with my man. I actually fell asleep in the car halfway there, so he had to wake me up when we neared his aunt and uncle's house.

He pulled my car up in front of a mini mansion in the hills of Sonoma; the house lit up inside as if there were a party going on.

"Wow," I uttered nervously as I stepped out of the car and looked up at the enormous house that towered over us. "You left this place for a crummy apartment over a garage in Sacramento? Are you sick?" I giggled as I rested my palm on his forehead, pretending to check for a fever.

He picked me up in his arms and spun me around twice, making me so dizzy I begged him to put me down. "It was the best decision I've ever made in my life, Zoey. I'd live under a bridge if I had to, to be with you."

Shaking my head, I laughed at his declaration. "You could always move in with me, instead of living under a bridge."

He raised his eyebrows and a hopeful grin spread across his face. "Is that an invite to move in with you?" he joked as he put me down. I didn't have time to answer him before we heard someone clear their throat behind us.

If I'd had the chance to answer him, my response would've been *yes*.

Andy turned around and pulled me along with him to meet his uncle. "A.J., it's good to see you back here again."

I adored that they called him A.J., but wondered why he never asked anyone in Sacramento to call him that. Maybe it was just a family thing. Andy let go of my hand and walked into a rough, but loving man hug with his uncle. It was obvious to me that the man loved his nephew very much by the way he hugged Andy.

"We've missed you around here," his uncle chuckled, confirming my suspicions about him missing Andy. "It's too quiet without you."

Andy had only been back to Sonoma two times since he moved to Sacramento, once while I was in Cabo, and the other time was when I was sick with the flu again. I had made him go the second time so he wouldn't catch it too, which worked out for the best since I stayed in bed the entire weekend and slept anyway.

"You must be Zoey," Andy's uncle said as he shook my hand.

"Yes, it's nice to meet you finally, Mr. Tate."

He was a giant of a man, bigger than Andy was, even. He was at least six foot five, long and slim though, unlike Andy's long muscular body. They had the same golden skin and blue eyes.

"Please, call me Hamish," he said politely. "This is my lovely wife, Sarah."

Andy's aunt stepped forward and hugged me. "Zoey, I'm happy to meet you. A.J. has told us so much about you."

I looked at Andy curiously, wondering what exactly he'd said about me. "I didn't tell them about any of your bad habits," he joked.

I laughed and smacked him lightly on the arm. "I'm sure yours are much worse than mine."

His aunt Sarah smiled at us. "Don't worry, Zoey. A.J. would never say a bad thing about someone he loves. It's just not in him."

She put her arm around me. "Let's get you inside. You've been driving for a while so I'm sure you're tired and hungry. Boys, get the luggage will you?" she called over her shoulder to Andy and Hamish.

Both Tate men started laughing. "We're here five minutes and she's already bossing me around," Andy joked as he pulled our bags out of the trunk.

I walked with Sarah up the natural stone walkway to the front door. The house was breathtaking. The stone from the walkway carried up several wide steps and on to the front of the house surrounding the entrance.

"Your house is beautiful, Sarah. You must love living here," I stated in amazement as we walked into the foyer. I followed Sarah's lead when she kicked her shoes off just inside the door.

The house looked like it belonged in a magazine. Andy's aunt and uncle obviously had loads of money. I would need to work on changing my views on rich people *all* being assholes. The Tate's were definitely not that way.

"I do love living here, Zoey, although it is a lot to take care of, and much too big for the two of us. We miss A.J. being here, but we know he's happy with you in Sacramento now, so that's all that matters."

Andy and Hamish came barreling loudly through the door with our bags.

"Hey, animal prints look good on you, Andy," I teased as he walked into the foyer with my zebra print purse slung over his shoulder. "Maybe I'll buy you one for your birthday.

Hamish clapped him hard on the back. "You know, she's right. I think you need some shoes to match."

Andy looked back and forth between Hamish and me, shaking his head at us. "Very funny, smartasses," he smirked as he handed my purse to me.

"A.J., do you two want to sleep in your old room, or would you rather sleep in the guest room? It's up to you," Sarah said.

Andy looked at me and I gave him a slight shrug, as if to say either room was fine with me. "My old room is perfect for us, Aunt Sarah. I kind of miss my bed actually," he replied with a laugh.

"Let's get your stuff upstairs then, so we can relax and get ourselves acquainted with Zoey after all this time," Sarah suggested.

We took our bags and ascended the stairs to his room at the end of a long, wide hallway. There were several family photos framed on the walls along the way. Photos of Andy, his parents, his sister, and his aunt and uncle as well. They all seemed so happy in the photos. Everyone was always smiling.

It made me sad for Andy because he lost so much. It also made me realize *why* he was ready for a family of his own.

How could I have been so stupid not to realize it before? All he had left of his family were the two people who lived in this house. They didn't have children, so he had no cousins or anything. Andy's mother was an only child. Her parents, along with his dad's parents were already deceased.

Yes, I would definitely need to rethink the kids by thirty idea.

We entered a large bedroom at the end of the hall. It didn't look like it had been touched since Andy left. The walls were a nice shade of blue that was eerily similar to the blue we painted his bedroom at the apartment. There were real surfboards hanging vertically as decorations on one wall.

There was a California King-size bed against the center of another wall, and matching nightstands adorned with lamps sat on either side of it. I realized why he missed his bed. It was huge, and it looked really comfy and expensive.

The room fit his personality. It was very masculine, but also laid back with the surfboards on the wall.

"This is a great room, Andy. Are they yours from New Zealand?" I ran my palm over one of the surfboards. He told me before he surfed a lot when he was growing up in "En Zed," as he referred to his home country.

"Yeah, those two are mine," he replied, motioning to the two surfboards closest to me. "This one here was my dad's." He pointed to the larger, older looking board that was directly in front of him.

Hamish set the bag he was carrying down on the bed. "We'll let you two get settled in. Why don't you come downstairs in a bit, and we'll raid the fridge and the wine cellar."

"Oh, that sounds great," I said. "We'll be right down."

They shut the door as they left the room. I turned to face Andy, who had silently crossed the room to stand behind me.

"Hey," he said in his low, sexy voice as he slid his arms around me.

"Hi, there," I whispered as I faced him and wrapped my arms around his neck. "Are you glad to be back here?"

"I'm glad to finally be here with *you*," he replied as he lifted me up. "I thought I'd never get you here to meet my family."

My legs instinctively wrapped around his waist, and he walked us over to his bed, where he collapsed on top of me. He stood back up, leaving me lying on his bed, while he looked me up and down.

"What are you doing?" I asked suspiciously.

"Oh, I'm not doing anything out of the ordinary..." Andy knelt down and ran his hands up the sides of my bare legs. "I'm admiring you on my bed, imagining what I'll be doing to you later, right on this very spot."

Oh my. I propped myself up on my elbows.

"Why don't you give me a little example then, so I know what to expect?" I teased as I ran my fingers along the top edge of my sundress strap. He didn't hesitate. Once the words were out of my mouth, he was on top of me, kissing me hungrily. He kissed a trail from my jaw, down my neck, to the top of my breast.

Andy hooked his fingers in my dress strap and slipped it and my bra down just enough to uncover me. My breast now bared to him, he sucked my nipple into his mouth, teasing it with his tongue until it hardened under his touch.

I moaned softly. "You make me feel so good." Our quickie before we drove from Sacramento only left me wanting him more.

He lifted my dress up and pushed my knees apart, settling himself between my legs, and pressing his hardness against me.

"You're torturing me, Andy." He didn't stop. I wrapped my arms around him and slid my hands down the back of his shorts, beneath them and his boxer briefs, to squeeze his bare ass.

Gripping him hard, I pulled him closer to me. He groaned as I slipped my right hand around, took his cock in my hand, and started stroking him. He left my breast alone after that and began kissing me.

I released him then pushed his shorts and boxers down over his hips to free his cock from the confines of his clothing.

"Zoey, what are you doing?" he mumbled as he began kissing my neck.

"You," I teased as I rolled him off me. I slid to the floor, where I knelt in front of him. He lifted his hips for me, so I pulled his shorts and boxers all the way off.

He scooted to the edge of the bed, to position himself so that I was between his legs. I took his cock in my hand again, and then guided him inside my mouth.

"I fucking love you, Zoey," he whispered huskily as he tangled his fingers through my hair.

I hummed in response to him, and he groaned from the vibration of my mouth on him. I stroked and sucked him vigorously, teasing him with my tongue, and within moments, he was coming hard in my mouth.

"Mmm," I moaned while I swallowed everything he gave me and carefully released him. "We better get downstairs for some food and wine." Not waiting for a reply, I stood up, took my bag into the bathroom, and brushed my teeth.

A few minutes later, I exited the bathroom. Andy had put his clothes back on and was sitting right where I left him. "You ready?"

He shook his head. "Not yet. Come here, Beautiful," he said, grinning from ear to ear. I walked over to stand in front of him. "I promise to take real good care of you later." He pulled me down to sit on his thigh and slipped his arms around my waist.

I giggled. "Oh, I *know* you will."

"I don't know how I got so lucky finding you, Zoey, but the fact that you like giving me blowjobs so much..." his voice trailed off as he smirked at me.

"Oh my God, you're such a perv!" I laughed and smacked his arm. "Here I was thinking you were gonna tell me how lucky you were for finding *me*, and then you go all pervy—"

He didn't let me finish before he busted up laughing. "You know I love you, Zoey, blowjobs or not."

I couldn't help but laugh, it *was* hilarious. "Don't worry. I like the way you taste, so have no fear, you will get them from me as long as you want them," I joked. "Now let's get downstairs before they realize what we're up to."

Chapter Eighteen

When we arrived in the massive, chef's kitchen, we found that Sarah had set up a small, but elaborate buffet of food for us on the large granite island. Andy stopped abruptly when he saw what she'd prepared. "You didn't need to go to so much trouble for us, Aunt Sarah."

She shook her head and shooed him toward the table. "It's no trouble, A.J. and you know that. I know you probably didn't eat dinner after you finished your day at work."

Andy's aunt had set out an array of wines, cheeses, fruit, and a variety of hors d'oeuvres. I didn't know where to start, so I carefully began arranging an assortment of food on my plate. Sarah was right. We didn't have time to eat dinner before we left, especially after becoming sidetracked while I was picking out a dress.

"Everything looks delicious," I said to Sarah as I picked up a fork. I was famished. Andy was sitting at a small table with Hamish, enjoying a beer, and talking about his car.

"Andy?" I said, waiting for him to respond.

He looked over at me. "Yeah, love?"

"Do you want me to make you a plate while you two catch up?"

He shook his head and stood up. "I can get it, but thank you."

After picking up a plate from the stack, he kissed my cheek. I noticed Hamish and Sarah watching us intently. They seemed pleased with what they saw.

Andy filled two plates with food and took a seat at the table with us. I swore I didn't know how he could eat so much and not gain any weight, but then again, he was very...*active*. Between work and me, the man probably burned every calorie he consumed.

"Zoey, A.J. tells us you own a business? Is that right?" Sarah asked after we sat down at the table and began to eat.

I swallowed my food and wiped my mouth with a real cloth napkin. "Yes, I own it along with my dad. It's an auto parts store for high performance race cars."

She nodded, understanding. "Oh yes, A.J. mentioned you were in the family business with your dad and brothers. I think it's excellent you two have that in common."

Andy smiled over at me and squeezed my leg under the table.

As we sat around the table talking, I realized I was the only one speaking without a New Zealand accent. It made me chuckle.

"What's so amusing, Zoey?" Andy asked.

I smiled. "I just realized I'm the only one here without an accent."

Andy shook his head. "Actually, Beautiful...you're the only one here who *has* an accent. You're a foreigner in a house full of Kiwis."

His revelation had everyone at the table laughing. I *was* the outsider at the Tate's since I was the only American. Too funny. I pouted jokingly, and he kissed me on the cheek then continued eating.

After I helped clean up dinner, we had dessert and coffee before we decided to head upstairs to bed. Andy stopped abruptly when we reached the staircase.

"I'll be up in a minute, Zoey. I need to talk to my aunt," Andy said as he twirled a lock of my hair around his finger.

"Sure, I'll go upstairs and get ready for bed then."

He shook his head. "Oh no, you won't. I want you naked when I get up there," he whispered in my ear. He gave me a tender kiss on the cheek, then turned and left me standing at the bottom of the stairs with my mouth gaping open.

After my brain began functioning again, I went to his room and freshened up in the bathroom while I waited for him. I found my iPod and shuffled my playlist, so I didn't have to worry about finding something to listen to on my own. I turned off all the lights except the bathroom light, stripped off my clothes as he'd requested, and slid under the covers.

Once I was comfortable, I thought back to all the photos in the hallway and Andy's wish to have kids by the time he was thirty. He was in my life now and I wanted to marry him, but I wanted to wait a bit longer than what he did for kids. I understood his reasons for wanting them by age thirty, but I needed to prepare myself mentally for sharing him. I felt like I was being selfish for wanting him all to myself.

We knew we wanted to get married someday, but we'd only been together for a little over eight months. He had brought it up a few times since Jess and Noah's wedding, and we agreed that it just felt *right* with us. Did we really need to wait to get married? Neither of us wanted a big wedding; only close friends and family.

I had so many thoughts running through my head. Could we get married soon and talk about kids after a year or so? Yep, we definitely needed to have a serious talk. It had been a long week and I was exhausted. My eyelids were heavy, so I closed my eyes for a minute.

I woke up to Andy, once again, untangling my earbud cords from my hair. He carefully pulled them from my ears, shut off my iPod, and set it on the nightstand.

"Andy?" I whispered. He turned back to me and looked me in the eyes, waiting for me to speak. "Let's get married."

His mouth dropped open in surprise. "Where did that come from, Zoey?" He crawled into bed next to me, already stripped of his clothes.

I nestled up to him. "I'm serious, Andy. Marry me? We can do it as soon as we can get our family and friends together, maybe even do it here. Do you think Hamish and Sarah would let us?" I asked, stifling a yawn.

He rose up on his elbow and brushed my hair behind my ear. "Hey, slow down. Where is all this coming from?" he asked, and I could see a little bit of panic on his face. "I think we should talk about this when you're not half asleep, alright?"

My heart thumped in my chest, and I was starting to worry at his lack of the word *yes*. "Did you change your mind?" I asked hesitantly.

He shook his head. "That's not what I'm saying, at all. Let's just talk about this another time, definitely not when we're lying here naked, okay? I can't concentrate."

My heart sank at his avoidance of the subject. Why didn't he want to talk about this? I sat up, pulling the sheet around me to cover my body. "No way, I'm wide awake now. Why are you avoiding the subject? Do you not want to marry me?"

He sat up quickly and pulled me in between his legs, so my back was against his chest. He wrapped his arms around me, resting his cheek against mine. "Hey, that's not what's going on here. Zoey, I want to marry you more than anything I've ever wanted. Can you *please* trust me on this for now? I promise we will talk about it tomorrow. It's been a long day and all I can think about is picking up where we left off a while ago."

I could feel his erection on my lower back. "Yes, I can *feel* it," I laughed. "Why are you so horny all of a sudden?"

He slid around me, and I fell back onto the bed as he settled himself between my thighs, his cock resting against me, so all he had to do was push his hips forward to slide inside me. His fingers lazily stroked between my legs, making me wet and anxious for him.

"It's not all of a sudden. I want you every second of every day. I'm not sure what you're doing, but I swear you're getting more beautiful by the day," he said. "Your body is amazing."

I rolled my hips upward, letting him know I wanted him. He pushed himself inside me and pulled out slowly, then kissed my neck and across my collarbone.

"So perfect," he groaned, then flicked my nipple with his tongue.

"Oh, God," I whispered when my body tightened around him. I clawed my nails down his back. He groaned as he thrust his hips forward and buried himself inside me.

He rotated his hips in a slow circular motion, grinding against me, making me orgasm. "Mmm, Andy," I moaned as my body trembled and constricted around him.

Not stopping his motion, he continued pulling out and slamming back into me, harder each time, until we both came together. Andy collapsed on me, resting his head in the crook of my neck.

"Fuck Zoey, I can't control myself when you do that with your nails. It makes me want to fuck you hard. I can't help it," he admitted, almost sounding ashamed. He propped himself up on his elbows, looking down at me like he was waiting for me to say something.

I pulled his face down to kiss him. "It's why I do it, Sexy. Sometimes a girl just needs to be fucked. *Hard.*"

A low, deep laugh emanated from his chest. "I can't believe you said that."

I wrapped my legs around him and pulled him back down for a kiss. I teased his lips with my tongue, gently biting his bottom lip.

"I can't help the way you make me feel...the way you make my body feel," I whispered. "The way you make my heart feel...I love you so much. Whether we're making love or getting kinda crazy and hot for each other like we just did, I know it's because we love each other, and no matter what, it's just the way we are together."

He kissed me passionately while he rocked his hips forward. His cock twitched, and he was getting hard again inside of me. "I love you, Zoey," he groaned as he grew harder and slowly began thrusting his hips.

"Do you love me enough to marry me?" I teased.

"Yes," he whispered. "Now shut up and let me make love to you. No more fucking tonight for my girl, she's gonna get it slow and easy now."

That night, I slept well. I was exhausted and completely satisfied, thanks to Andy. I don't know how many times we made love, or even what time we finally went to sleep. He was gentle, sweet, and passionate the entire night, worshipping my body like it was a piece of fine art that should be treated with care and appreciated for its beauty.

When I woke, I turned to face him in bed, but when I opened my eyes, he wasn't there. I sat up and looked around the room, wondering if maybe he was in the shower already. Checking the clock on his nightstand, I found that it was already nine-thirty.

Holy shit, I overslept. I was embarrassed, so I flew out of bed on weak, wobbly legs, took a quick shower, yanked a white, lacy dress over my head, and within thirty minutes, I was downstairs. It had been so hot outside in Nor Cal, I pretty much lived in dresses of some type. Granted, it was usually simple sundresses, but I was in Sonoma at the Tate's house, so I only brought my nicest dresses. Besides, it was too uncomfortable to wear anything that was even remotely snug.

The house was empty, from what I could tell. My stomach was growling, so I proceeded to the kitchen to find something to eat. I found an envelope with my name scribbled on it propped up against a wine bottle on the counter.

> Zoey, There's food in the fridge for you. Please eat whatever you would like. Hamish and Sarah are up at the winery working in the office. I have an errand to run. See you soon. I love you. Andy

Hmm, wonder where he went to so early. I didn't need to wonder long. When I finished eating a bagel, he came strolling into the kitchen.

"Good morning. Did you sleep well?" he asked as he folded his arms around me and kissed my neck.

"Yes, I did. You were right about the bed, too. It's so comfortable, I just woke up about an hour ago," I admitted.

He kissed my shoulder. "Are you sure the bed is what made you sleep so long?" he asked, grinning. "We did stay up late, remember?"

I sighed. "I'm sorry. I don't remember much from last night. You know...all the wine we drank. Maybe you can remind me?" The funny thing was I had only sipped on one tiny glass of wine.

He spun me around on the barstool, pushed my dress up my thighs, wrapped my legs around his hips, and picked me up. *Holy hell.* He jogged out of the kitchen with me wrapped around him, hanging on for dear life.

"Andy, put me down!" I shrieked as I scratched my nails up his back. I couldn't stop laughing, though, which of course, egged him on more.

"I am *so* gonna make you regret doing that with your nails, Zoey," he growled.

I was secretly thrilled with what he might do to me.

He carried me the entire way across the house, where he stopped at the bottom of the stairs. I had slipped down a bit from him jogging across the house with me, so he hoisted me up onto his hips again. He got me settled; I hung on tighter, and then he took the stairs two at a time.

"Andy, you're going to drop me," I laughed and was breathless from the ride. I didn't know how he hauled me up the stairs so fast.

"I'd never drop you," he said before he kissed away what breath I had left in me, all the way down the hallway to his bedroom.

Using my back, he pushed the bedroom door open, walked through it, kicking it closed with his bare foot. He finally tossed me onto the bed, stripped off his clothes, then pulled my dress and panties off. He had a very naughty gleam in his blue eyes.

"Do you need to be *fucked* again, Zoey?" he asked deviously as he crawled onto the bed on his hands and knees. *Oh yes, please.*

I scooted backward out of his reach, unsnapped my bra, and threw it to the floor. "As a matter of fact, I think

I do," I said, stifling a giggle. He reached across the bed and gripped my ankles then pulled me to him.

He pushed my knees apart and kissed from my ankle all the way up my thigh. I propped myself up on my elbows and watched him kiss my inner thigh. "You are so fucking hot," I whispered.

When he looked up at me, I noticed his gorgeous blue eyes had dimmed and filled with desire. He ran his tongue up to lick my clit while I watched him. I closed my eyes and let my head fall back. God that felt good. He edged in closer and delved deeper with his tongue.

After a few minutes, he slipped his fingers inside me and began sliding them in and out slowly. "Andy...*fuck.*" I was literally panting when he brought me to my first orgasm.

He tortured me with his tongue throughout my orgasm, so that when it was over, I still trembled. He sat back on his heels.

"Turn over and get on your knees," he said, his voice deep and gravelly. Without question, I did as he told me.

He gripped my hips and pushed himself inside me from behind. He groaned loudly and then sucked in a deep breath as he began pounding into me. "Ahh, fuck...Zoey," he mumbled as he continued to drive into me, his balls smacking against my clit each time.

He let go of my hips to run his hands up and down my back. My legs were still weak from our activities the previous night, and they were beginning to shake. Maybe I should take up running or something to strengthen them if I was going to keep up with this machine of a man.

"Andy, I need to lie down, my legs..."

He pulled out suddenly, making me gasp. "Sorry, Zoey," he said as he watched me flip over onto my back.

"Oh, it's quite alright," I said. "My legs feel like rubber from last night. Now get back down here and finish what you started." So he did.

We laid there for well over an hour, tangled up in the sheets, him on his back with my cheek against his chest, and me tracing his tattoos with my fingertip. "You still haven't taken me to get my tattoo yet."

"Are you still going to get your snowflakes?"

I nodded. "Mmm hmm...Yeah, that's still what I want."

"We'll make an appointment and try to go next weekend. But right now, we need to get dressed. There's somewhere we need to go."

"Where are we going?"

"Lunch."

Chapter Nineteen

We redressed and went outside to leave. I started walking to my car, but he took my hand and guided me over to the detached garage instead.

"Our ride is in here," he said as he pulled me through the door behind him.

He flipped a switch on the wall, bathing the garage with light. There were a few cars in the garage, but we walked past them to a bright red, side-by-side ATV.

"Andy, where are we going that we need to drive an ATV? Are you sure we can't take this Aston Martin instead?" I inquired when I noticed the gorgeous car sitting next to it. I'd never seen one in person.

He smiled at me, shaking his head. "Please get in, Zoey. I promise you, it will be worth it."

I pouted. "Can I drive?"

Andy handed me the keys then walked to the roll up garage door and hit the button to open it. He came back and sat on the passenger seat.

"Well, let's go, woman," he urged, with the happiest smile I'd ever seen on his face.

I hopped in the driver's seat and started the engine. Jokingly, I revved the throttle a little bit. He put on his seatbelt as he shook his head. I pulled my seatbelt on while I let the ATV warm up, then after a few minutes, I drove it out the garage door.

"Which way, Sexy?"

He told me to drive around behind the garage toward the vineyard. We passed through several rows of grapevines toward the foothills that surrounded the massive property.

"Go up this hill here," he instructed me, pointing to the left. We reached the top of the hill and drove into a grove of trees. "Keep going till you hit the clearing, then park."

He kicked his feet up on the dashboard of the ATV and crossed his ankles. I drove until I found the clearing in the trees. I parked toward the right side of the clearing and shut off the engine.

"Now where?"

He took my hand in his. "Right this way," Andy replied as he led me into the grove of trees.

I looked over at him inquisitively and joked, "You're not bringing me out here to whack me are you? Bury me somewhere nobody would ever find my body?"

"Nah, not today," he replied sarcastically. He put his arm around my shoulders and kissed the side of my head.

I looked at the area where he was leading me and saw there was a large picnic blanket and a few throw pillows spread out under the shade of a large weeping willow tree. It was the biggest willow tree I had ever seen in my life.

"Is this where you were this morning when I woke up?"

He nodded, grinning. "Yep."

We came closer to the tree and I saw an ice chest sitting next to it.

"Sit down, Zoey. Get comfortable. I'll get the food ready."

I giggled. "Hurry, I'm hungry."

"Jeez, hold your horses, boss lady," he teased as his blue eyes lit up with amusement.

He pulled out a small tray from a picnic basket next to the ice chest, then set out two wine glasses and poured us each a glass of chilled wine. Opening the ice chest, he took out everything to make my favorite Chinese chicken salad. He prepared our salads then handed me my plate and fork. I set my plate down and leaned toward him.

"Thank you, my love. Nobody has ever done anything like this for me before."

He pressed his lips to mine. "I do it because I love you, Zoey."

"I love you, too." I sat back down and enjoyed our lunch under the willow tree.

When we were finished eating, he put the salad away, stood up, and walked around the other side of the willow tree. When he came back around, he was carrying his acoustic guitar.

"What else are you hiding behind the tree?" I joked.

"Nothing else behind the tree, don't worry," he said as he sat down on the blanket with his legs crossed. "I'm going to sing you two Snow Patrol songs today so sit back and relax."

I nodded and waited for him to play.

"I know it's been months, but this song made me jump on a plane to get to you when I couldn't stand being away from you for another second. It's one of the best decisions I've ever made, and I won't ever forget that weekend, Zoey."

Andy started strumming his guitar and sang "New York" to me. When he finished the song, I was in tears because he sang it so perfectly. He set his guitar aside on the picnic blanket.

"Ready for some dessert?" he asked before I could say anything.

All I could do was nod. I was feeling emotional from his speech before the song because I hadn't realized how much it meant to him. I watched as he opened the ice chest again and pulled out a small, covered tray. Arranged on the tray were several different pieces of fancy dark chocolate. He took another bottle of wine out and poured us half a glassful each.

"Thank you," I whispered, as I looked him in the eyes. I walked across the blanket on my knees to sit on his lap.

"You're welcome," he replied, kissing me on the tip of my nose. "Now, let's eat some of this chocolate before it melts. My aunt says it's good with this wine." I didn't budge. I needed to be close to him.

I picked up a piece of chocolate off the tray and held it up to his mouth. He took it gently from my fingers with his teeth, then took a piece from the tray and fed it to me.

We shared the tray of chocolate and a glass of wine while we fed each other in between kisses.

When we finished dessert, he patted my leg. "It's time for my last song."

I gave him one final kiss then moved off his lap, back to the blanket. He stood up with his guitar in his hand and took a seat on top of the ice chest, resting his guitar on his thigh. There was no speech this time before Andy started the beginning chords of "Just Say Yes."

Throughout the whole song, he never broke eye contact with me. His eyes were almost pleading with me, and I didn't understand why. When he finished the song, he stood and propped his guitar against the tree. He held his hands down to me and pulled me up to stand with him.

"I have one more surprise for you. Close your eyes."

I closed my eyes and his lips brushed against mine before he released my hands. I heard him moving around while I waited, wondering what he was up to.

"Open your eyes, Zoey," he said so quietly I almost didn't hear him.

When I opened my eyes, I found him sitting back on his heels on the blanket in front of me. My heart immediately started thumping in my chest and I became lightheaded. Was he really doing *this*? I took a step toward him and he reached out, taking my left hand in his.

Oh my God, he is really doing this!

My eyes pooled up with tears as he began to speak, and goose bumps broke out all over my body even as hot as it was outside in the middle of August. I wanted to say yes to him right then, but he had planned such a special day for me that I needed to let him continue.

"Zoey," he said so nervously his voice shook with emotion. "I've never told you before, but I knew I loved you the first week I knew you. We've been through a few tough times, but we made it through because we didn't give up on each other. I can't imagine spending the rest of my life without you by my side."

He held a ring in his hand as he looked into my eyes with a gorgeous smile on his face. "Will you marry me, Beautiful?"

Tears were sliding down my cheeks before he even had the entire question out, and I couldn't breathe. Overcome with emotion, I was literally speechless, so I frantically nodded my head.

"Is that a yes, Zoey?" He chuckled, but I noticed his eyes were getting a bit watery.

I nodded again and covered my mouth to stifle the loud, happy sob that was on its way out.

"Come on. You know which word I need to hear come from your sweet lips." He was grinning at me, waiting for me to say *yes*. I removed my hand from my mouth and finally breathed out.

"Y-yes...yes, I'll marry you."

I dropped to my knees in front of him, threw my arms around him, and cried the most intense, happy tears of my life. He kissed the top of my head then wiped the tears from my face.

"Don't you want to see your ring?" he asked as he brushed my hair over my shoulders.

He could have given me a plastic ring from a gumball machine, for all I cared, but I noticed the blue Tiffany & Co. box sitting on the blanket next to him. I gathered myself together enough to stop crying, sat back on my heels in front of him, and nodded.

Andy took my left hand again, lifted it, and slid the ring onto my finger. It was a perfect fit.

I finally had the nerve to look down at my engagement ring and gasped the second I saw it.

It had a huge, princess cut diamond in the center with a diamond-encrusted band. I'd never seen a more beautiful ring in my life. It was stunning the way it sparkled in the sunlight that filtered through the willow tree.

"Andy...it's too much," I whispered, because I knew the ring cost him a fortune.

"No, it's not too much for you, Zoey. It can never be too much," he said candidly. He stood up and pulled me with him to wrap me in his arms. "Thank you. You don't know how happy you've made me today."

We finally tore ourselves away from each other after a while. He pulled my left hand up to his mouth and kissed my ring finger. "It looks perfect on you."

I held my hand out to look at it again. "It's a beautiful ring, Andy. I never expected this, and I know I was bugging you last night about getting married—"

With a gorgeous smile on his face, he put two fingers over my lips to shut me up. "Stop, I've had the ring since June. I've just been waiting for the right time to ask you...when I was sure you were ready."

Finally, I was starting to think clearly. *Did he just say June?*

"June?" I asked in disbelief. That was two months ago.

"Yes. I bought it the day of Jess and Noah's parties. That's where I was the day we didn't get to talk until we met at the bar."

I laughed at the memory because it was a shitty day for me, and there he was, out buying me the most exquisite engagement ring I'd ever laid eyes on.

"Is this why you said we'd talk about it later?" He grinned, and I knew I was right. "So, you've been planning this for a while then?"

He nodded. "I asked my aunt for help when I made our plans to come here. She helped me get everything ready last night so I could bring it out here while you were sleeping." He smirked. "I almost proposed to you that day in the car on the way to the wedding reception, when we pulled into the parking lot and had our talk, but you and your big mouth interrupted me before I could get the question out."

I loved the playful grin that spread over his face when he said that. I remembered the conversation clearly, and I *did* cut him off when he was talking to me.

"Sorry about my big mouth. Next time you have an important question to ask me, tell me to shut up, please."

"Next time, I definitely will," he teased.

"Hey, let's take a picture and send it to everyone to see if they notice the ring!" I was so excited to share the news with our friends and families. I smiled, still not believing everything he did for me.

Andy pulled his phone out of his pocket and readied the camera. He took several photos of us posing with my left hand and ring in the photo, but not focusing on it directly.

We decided on a photo of us facing each other, him kissing my forehead. Both of us had our eyes closed, with my left hand resting along his jaw line and neck. We sent the picture to my family, my friends, and Andy's aunt and uncle. Within minutes, we received several texts back from everyone congratulating us.

Andy shut off his phone and there, underneath the giant willow tree, Andy and I made love on the picnic blanket and celebrated our engagement, slowly and sweetly. We took our time loving each other. And afterward, we held each other close and reveled in our perfect day.

Chapter Twenty

Later that evening, I sat on the edge of the bed slipping on my high heels as Andy stood in front of the mirror, adding a little dab of gel to his palm to run through his damp hair. After our picnic, we came back to the house and lounged around until it was time to get ready for our dinner out.

I stood from the bed and walked to the mirror to check my makeup one last time before we left. Standing next to Andy in my strapless, purple satin dress, I watched him in the mirror. "You look very handsome."

He was wearing black dress pants and a black button up shirt with a black tie. As usual, his long sleeves were rolled to just below his elbows. His all black clothing set off his blue eyes, making them brighter. He smiled as his eyes met mine in our reflections. He turned to face me, took my left hand in his, and brushed his lips across my knuckles, where he stopped at my giant engagement ring.

"I can't believe this is happening," I whispered, my voice trembling slightly with emotion.

He looked at me apprehensively. "What do you mean?"

I let out a long, shaky breath. "I just mean...look at everything we went through at the beginning, and now we're *engaged*. I never thought this would be happening."

His large hands gently cupped my face. "Zoey, are you okay with this?" He thought I was getting overwhelmed.

"Yes," I said truthfully, because I was more than okay with it. I would marry him that minute if I could. "This whole year has gone by so quickly. I never thought I would be getting married again. Please, trust me. I am thrilled to be marrying you. Today has been the best day of my life."

I pulled him down to me and placed a light kiss to his lips.

"I love you, Andy. You are my life. I've never been happier, and I can't wait to be your wife. After we get married, I promise we will talk seriously about babies. Just give me until then, please."

He nodded happily, kissing me back. "Let's go out and celebrate then, shall we?" he asked as he took my hand and guided me out the bedroom door.

Andy started down the stairs, and I stopped at the top, forcing him to stop too since he had a hold of my hand. He turned back to me.

"What is it, Zoey?"

"Move in with me when we get home."

He walked back up the stairs and embraced me. "Yes. I will move in with you. I thought you would never ask." He kissed me gently and told me he loved me.

We went downstairs to meet Hamish and Sarah for Andy's birthday dinner. His birthday was still a couple of weeks away, but it was the only weekend his aunt and uncle had time to get together to celebrate with him. I was planning a surprise party for him at my place on the day of his birthday, but they couldn't get away from the vineyard to come.

"Look at you two all dressed up. Very nice," Hamish said to us when we met him and Sarah in the living room.

"A.J., you better keep an eye on this girl tonight. The rock on her finger can probably be seen from space," Sarah chimed in as she lifted my hand to inspect my ring. "I'm so happy for you both. A second chance at love doesn't always come around."

Of course, my eyes welled up with tears. I was deliriously happy. "Thank you, Sarah," I said as I hugged her.

"I hate to break up the hug fest here, ladies, but we need to get on the road for dinner," Hamish joked. We gathered our purses and headed out the door.

The four of us talked on the way to another vineyard about ten miles from the house. When we arrived, the parking lot was filling up quickly, but Sarah had made reservations for us the week before.

After we were seated, Sarah ordered a bottle of champagne for us to celebrate our engagement and Andy's birthday. We ordered our dinners and a couple of appetizers to eat while we were waiting.

"Zoey, do you have any ideas on what kind of wedding you would like?" Sarah asked.

I smiled and looked over at Andy. "Well, we haven't really had the chance to talk about it too much yet, but I think I'd like something small, probably with just our families and close friends. What do you think, Andy?"

He chuckled and shrugged his shoulders. "I'm so happy you said yes I haven't even thought about what to do next."

Andy took my hand in his and gently rubbed his thumb over mine. "I'll say yes to whatever you want to do though," he said as he gazed lovingly into my eyes.

"How about we find a justice of the peace Monday morning?" I laughed. "I'm ready now."

Our appetizers arrived, and as we ate, we talked about wedding ideas. We discussed everything from a huge wedding to a small wedding with only our family and friends at the Tate's house or the vineyard's main house.

I found myself watching Andy a lot through dinner. He never stopped smiling, never took his eyes off me or his aunt and uncle. He seemed to be genuinely happy and content. He even shared a few stories about his mom, dad, and sister. It had me thinking again about the 'kids by age thirty' thought of his.

By the time our dinner arrived, I was a little sick to my stomach from worrying about it. I told him we would get serious about it after the wedding, and I meant it. He had a ring on my finger and a promise to marry him, so I hoped it would be enough until then.

"Hey, you okay?" he leaned in and whispered in my ear.

I nodded my head, trying to get my brain to snap out of thinking too seriously about something that wouldn't happen for a while. "Yeah, I'm good. Just lost in thought, as usual," I replied as I gave his thigh a squeeze under the table.

We finished our dinner and decided to skip dessert. The food was delicious, and nobody left any room for it. Hamish opened the restaurant door leading to the parking lot, and as I passed through the doorway, something caught my attention.

More like *someone*.

A man was standing near our car, and he seemed to be waiting for someone. As we approached him, I heard Andy suck in a breath and mutter something I didn't comprehend.

The man took a few steps toward us. "Andrew fucking Tate!" he bellowed as he flicked a cigarette onto the ground. "What the fuck are you doing back in this area?"

I wasn't sure if he was a friend, a drunk, or just being a jerk. It was hard to tell but I could definitely smell the alcohol coming off him in waves.

I didn't need to wait long to find out the answer because he stepped closer to Andy and took a swing at him, nearly hitting me in the process. *What the fuck?* Andy was quicker, dodged the swing, and pushed the man away from us.

The man righted himself and whirled around to face Andy. "How dare you show your face around here after what you put my sister through?" he growled.

"What are you talking about, Corey?" Andy replied. "I didn't do anything to your sister except sign the divorce papers like she wanted me to."

Oh shit, the ex's brother.

We'd talked about her a bit. Her name was Michelle and she divorced Andy via papers left on their dining room table. She wouldn't even talk to him to tell him why she was divorcing him. She just cited "irreconcilable differences" on the papers. According to her lawyers, she wanted nothing from him except a quick divorce. No explanations, no hassle.

Corey stepped closer to Andy, so close that their chests were almost touching, and Corey's face was inches from Andy's. "I'm not talking about the divorce, you piece of *shit*," he spat. "I'm talking about Emma."

An extremely confused expression washed over Andy's face, and his brows furrowed. "Who is Emma?"

Corey took a step back away from Andy. "Are you kidding me?" he asked. His tone was cold enough to freeze water.

"I don't know who she is, Corey. Cut the bullshit," Andy replied, clearly irritated.

"Emma was your daughter," Corey growled.

Andy stepped back, as if he'd been slapped.

"What are you talking about, Corey?"

I felt like I was going to throw up. Why did Corey say "was" your daughter? *Does that mean...* My knees weakened, and I felt Hamish grab my elbow to hold me steady while I watched in confusion as the situation unfolded.

"You let my sister go through her entire pregnancy *alone,* knowing Emma wasn't going to live to take more than a few breaths."

My heart sank. *Oh no, no, no, this cannot be true.* As soon as the thought entered my head, it was as if a light bulb blinked on in Andy's mind...like he finally understood something.

"She was pregnant..." Andy whispered to himself as he brought his hand up to rub his jaw.

He took in a breath and shook his head slightly before speaking again.

"I don't know if I believe you. I need to talk to Michelle. She needs to explain this to me. Where is she?"

Unable to gauge his thoughts, I stepped forward and touched his arm. He looked over at me finally. The look in his eyes was complete disbelief. He reached up and ran his hands over his jaw line.

He hadn't done that in months, and now he'd done it twice in the last sixty seconds.

Andy turned his body toward me. "Zoey, I..." his voice faltered before he could get any more words out.

He spun back around to face Corey. "I need to talk to Michelle about this. Tell me how I can contact her."

Corey smirked. "You can't expect me to believe you know nothing about your own fucking kid."

Andy was getting ready to lose it. "I don't give a fuck what you believe. Just tell me how to get in touch with her," he seethed through clenched teeth.

"I'm not telling you shit, Tate. You stay the hell away from my sister!" Corey yelled.

Andy took a deep breath and calmed himself down. "Look, Corey, you come here and tell me I've done these things, and I don't know what you're talking about," he said, trying to stay calm. "You're telling me I have a daughter I know nothing about with my ex-wife?"

Rage flared across Corey's face. "No, you asshole. I am telling you that you *had* a daughter. She's *dead*, and you weren't even man enough to be there."

Oh, please no. This cannot be happening to him. My heart was absolutely breaking for Andy. Reaching out, I took his hand in mine, interlacing our fingers. I knew there was no way in hell he knew anything about it.

He was physically shaking. Andy opened his mouth to say something, but stopped. He was lost in his own thoughts and seemed to be in shock. His face was devoid of expression, and the ever-present sparkle he'd had in his gorgeous blue eyes all day was fading right before my eyes.

Then Corey stepped over to me. "This guy is a piece of shit. You better run while you can you dumb bitch," he muttered, the stench of liquor and cigarette smoke on his breath when he spoke almost made me gag.

Suddenly, Andy came back from his trance, let go of my hand, and landed a punch right on Corey's jaw, knocking his drunken ass to the ground. He dropped to his knees and seized Corey by the throat, pushing his head down onto the asphalt of the parking lot.

"Don't you fucking talk to her," he hissed at Corey. Andy punched him again, this time in the ribs.

Nobody saw the second punch coming. It happened so fast we were all stunned.

Hamish pushed past me, reached down, and grabbed Andy's arms. "A.J., come on. Get up. Let him go."

Corey's face was turning a gross shade of red by that time, but Andy listened to Hamish. He released his hold on Corey's throat and stood up. "Get the hell out of here," Andy growled at him.

Corey actually listened to Andy and walked away. He staggered toward the parking lot, coughing and holding his throat.

Andy turned to me. His face was pale. "Zoey, I'm so sorry," he whispered as he pulled me to him and wrapped his arms around my shoulders.

His entire body was trembling. I couldn't tell if it was because of his adrenaline from getting in to a fight, or if it was from the shock of Corey's revelations.

"Are you alright?" I asked, worried. He shook his head and held me tighter. He was definitely not okay.

I heard sirens in the distance. Great, someone called the cops. "We need to go now," Sarah said as she looked in the direction of the sirens. We hurried to the car and left, passing by the cop car as we pulled out onto the road.

Andy sat quietly in the back seat with the side of his head resting up against the window. He had his elbow propped on the armrest with his hand over his eyes, rubbing them with his fingers. I refused to sit and let him worry, but his aunt and uncle weren't saying anything.

Everyone was in shock, but he needed us.

"Andy?" I said quietly.

He shook his head as if he wasn't ready to talk yet. Thankfully, he held out his hand to me, and I took it in mine to comfort him. I unhooked my seatbelt and slid across to the middle seat. I wrapped my arms around him and tried to pull him closer. He wrapped his arm around me, but it wasn't to embrace me, it was to pull the seatbelt across me and strap me in.

I felt nothing but grief for him. The tears flooded my eyes and rolled down my cheeks. "Don't push me away," I whispered. He finally looked me in the eyes. *"Please..."*

He reached up and gently wiped the tears from my face. "Sorry, Beautiful. I didn't mean to make you cry."

I shook my head. "You didn't make me cry. My heart is breaking for you. What do you want me to do?" I asked. "I'll do anything to help you. Just name it."

I would toss my birth control the second we got home, if I thought it would make him happy again.

He let out a shaky breath and laced his fingers with mine before he spoke. "Can everyone listen to me for a minute, please?" he asked, his voice still wavering.

"Of course, A.J.," Sarah said as she turned around to face us with tears in her eyes.

We sat and waited while he gathered his thoughts, his thumb gently moved back and forth over my hand. "I want you all to know that I didn't know about Emma. I hope none of this is true."

Andy took another deep breath. "I swear on my parents and sister that I didn't know."

He exhaled loudly then turned back toward the window. He was still shaking. "I didn't fucking know..." he whispered, his breath fogging up the window.

The pain in his eyes, right before he turned away, reinforced to me he was telling the truth. He hadn't known about her.

Andy had once again been completely blindsided.

"A.J., you don't need to do that. Nobody in this car doubts you," Hamish said firmly. "I promise we'll help you get to the bottom of this."

Nobody spoke the rest of the ride home.

Chapter Twenty-One

We walked inside the house and sat in the living room, waiting for someone to be the first to speak. I found the bar and poured four glasses of Johnnie Walker. I handed Hamish and Sarah their glasses, then went back to the bar to pick up Andy's and mine. I joined him on the couch. He looked like his entire world had just fallen apart.

He sat staring straight ahead, his face pale and his eyes distant. I eased closer to him on the couch and handed him his glass.

"Here, drink this. Try to relax, please."

He looked at me and gave me a quick nod. "Thank you."

Andy downed his drink in one gulp, so I gave him mine. The four of us sat silently for what seemed like hours.

Hamish was the first to speak. "Maybe we should call it a night and take some time to let this sink in. We can figure out what to do in the morning."

Andy nodded and stood up as if he were on autopilot. He was there physically, but mentally, he was gone. I knew that feeling all too well, and it made me sick to see him going through this. Sarah and Hamish said their goodnights, leaving us alone in the living room.

"Hey," I said quietly, stepping toward him. "Let's go lie down. We don't have to talk about this tonight if you don't want to." He nodded and took my hand, leading me to his room.

I changed into my pajamas and brushed my teeth while he stripped down to his boxer briefs and slipped into bed. When I finished in the bathroom, I found him lying in the dark on his back, his hands underneath the back of his head, just staring at the ceiling.

I turned on my lamp and crawled into bed with him. "Do you want to be alone?" I asked hesitantly. "I can go sleep in the other room if you do." I was hoping he wanted me to stay with him, but sometimes people need to be alone to mull things over before talking to someone.

He reached out and pulled me down to rest my head in the crook of his neck. "Stay, please."

Thank God. I didn't want to leave him, but I didn't want to crowd him either if he needed space. I draped my arm over him and began tracing his tattoos with my fingertip.

I kept quiet because I was at a loss for words. 'I'm sorry' definitely wasn't sufficient for what was going on. His ex-wife had been pregnant with their child when she divorced him. It explained why she left the papers on the table while he was at work, and refused all contact with him.

She had to have been hiding it from him, but why? What was it Corey said? Something like Michelle went through the entire pregnancy alone, knowing Emma would only take a few breaths.

What happened to that poor, sweet baby to cause her death?

"Zoey, please don't think I abandoned my own daughter," Andy said, unexpectedly.

I sat up quickly and placed the palm of my hand on his chest over his rapidly thumping heart. "Never, *ever* think that. I know you. I know you would never do something like that. Why would you even think it?"

He sat up and studied me, searching my eyes with his. "I'm sorry. I just thought about your birth mom and your situation—"

I rested my palm on his cheek. "Don't even think it. You can't compare the two situations."

His blue eyes held unshed tears. One spilled over and slid down his cheek when he blinked.

My heart stopped beating in my chest.

I had never seen a grown man cry, and I definitely never thought I would see *him* cry. With my hand shaking, I brushed it away with my thumb.

"I love you so much, Andy. We'll figure out what's going on, and we'll get through this." I leaned in and lightly pressed my lips against his.

He kissed my forehead then brought his lips back to my mouth. He kissed me hungrily, and my lips parted to let him in.

"I love you, Zoey...I'm so sorry," he whispered between kisses.

Why did he keep apologizing to me? He didn't do anything wrong.

He needed me, and I wanted to take his mind off what was going on, for just a little while. We would need to talk about it, just not right then. I kissed him back as desperately as he kissed me. I put my hands on his chest and pushed him back on the bed, so he was lying on his back again.

Quickly, I stripped off my pajamas as he pulled off his boxers and tossed them aside. I straddled him and began stroking him gently while he watched me. I released him then crawled over his body to kiss him.

He gave my breast a firm squeeze before he ran his hand down my body between my legs. He began caressing and teasing me with his long, thick fingers. I ran my hand down his chest, over his abs, and began stroking him again.

"You ready for me, baby?" I whispered in his ear before I sat back and sank down onto him. The connection wasn't close enough. I needed to hold him to show him everything would work out, that we would get through this together. I pulled him up so he was sitting and wound my legs around his waist.

He wrapped his arms around me and clung to me. He was still shaking.

"Andy, look at me. Please?" I asked as I rocked my hips back and forth in a slow rhythmic motion. His eyes shot open, meeting mine.

My heart hurt for him. I slipped my arms around his shoulders as my body picked up speed with his hands guiding my hips. "We will get through this," I whispered in his ear. "I love you so much."

Gripping my hips, he abruptly stopped me from moving and let out a tortured sob. His body shuddered as he let go and wrapped his arms tightly around me.

I felt like I was going to die when I heard him cry. My own tears silently spilled over because I couldn't stand to see him in so much pain, but I needed to stay strong for him. He had been my lifeboat when I felt like I was sinking in a sea of depression. It was my turn to be his lifeboat, and I would do anything to keep him afloat.

My man was absolutely broken. I felt his tears on my collarbone where his face was buried in the crook of my neck.

Without warning, he flipped us over, so I was lying on the bed, with him between my legs. He centered himself over me and pushed himself back inside me, thrusting hard, as if he needed to be in control of *something* in his life right then.

Balancing with his elbows by my shoulders, our fingers intertwined above my head, he kissed me urgently. His falling tears mixed with mine on my face.

"Zoey...I'm so sorry...so sorry," he mumbled.

I squeezed my eyes shut to dull the ache from his continuous apologies. They were breaking me in two.

He continued to thrust in and out of me, seeking his release. Overcome with emotions and the heaviness of his weight on me, my body was on fire for him. I was so close—his breathing was coming rapidly, hot on my neck, his thrusts harder and faster, needing a final release, but not getting it.

My body began shaking and constricting around him. Moaning with my orgasm, I let go of his hands and scraped my nails hard down his back the way he liked.

"Harder please, Zoey," he mumbled. "*Please...*"

I did it again as hard as possible, not wanting to hurt him, but he would just beg me to do it repeatedly if I didn't. He ground his hips against me and exhaled loudly as he reached orgasm. His body collapsed on mine while he emptied himself inside me.

He pulled out and slid down to rest his head on my chest. His full weight was on me and I had a hard time breathing, but I didn't care. He could stay there all night. I was not going to let him carry the weight of the whole situation by himself. For him, I would carry it all. If he needed to be close to me, then so be it. I took in a deep breath and let it out, calming my nerves.

He rose up on his elbows. "Sorry, I'll get off of you," he whispered.

"No, please stay," I wrapped my arms and legs around him so he wouldn't move.

"I'm too heavy, Zoey." He slid off me part of the way, so half of his body was on the bed, the other half was still on me.

I ran my fingers over the back of his head and neck while he stayed there with his head on my chest.

"You called me baby..." he said quietly, his voice deep and hoarse.

"Hmm...I did?"

"You asked 'are you ready for me, *baby*' earlier," he explained.

"Oh yeah, I guess I did. Sorry," I said as I kissed the top of his head.

"It's okay, I liked it. You've only ever called me Sexy. Wait, I'm still sexy, right?"

I smiled. "Yeah, baby, you're still Sexy. Don't forget you're *my love* too."

He reached down, pulled the sheet up over us, and propped himself up on his elbow. He rested the palm of his free hand on my chest between my breasts. "I love you, Zoey...so much," he said as he looked down into my eyes.

"I love you, too," I replied. "I know this day didn't end the way either of us predicted, but you need to know that today under the willow tree was the best, most perfect day of my life. We *will* get through this."

He rolled over on the bed and laid his head on his pillow, so I rolled to my side to face him.

"Zoey, I feel like everything has been fucked up now," he said honestly. "The day we get engaged was supposed to be a good, happy memory...and it's been... ruined. We can't get that back."

"It's not *ruined*," I whispered, on the verge of tears. I was sickened at what he was telling me. "Please don't say that."

Tears fell from my eyes then, and I needed a minute alone to gather my thoughts. I jumped off the bed, snatched my pajamas from the floor, and went into the bathroom, slamming the door behind me. I backed up against it for support, trying to catch my breath and control my emotions.

After I cleaned myself up, I pulled my pajamas back on, went to the sink, and splashed water on my face. When I stood back up, patting my cheeks dry, he was standing in the doorway.

His eyes, brilliant blue rimmed with red, were bloodshot from crying. "I'm so sorry, Zoey," he said miserably, rubbing his jaw with the backs of his fingers.

"Will you stop apologizing?" I sobbed. "You have nothing to be sorry about. None of this is your fault. Don't you get it?"

He crossed the room in two strides and pulled me close. "I'm sorry. I'll try. I feel like everything is all fucked up. I wanted everything to be perfect for you."

I sighed. "Everything was perfect, Andy. I'm trying to keep what Corey said and our amazing day separate. We don't even know if what he said is true."

He shook his head. "Why would he lie? He has nothing to gain from it." I hoped he was wrong, but who would say something so horrible and lie about it?

"I don't know...I don't know," I sighed. "Let's go to sleep, and we'll try to find Michelle tomorrow, okay?"

I slept horribly and Andy did too. He tossed and turned constantly. I finally dozed off well after two a.m. The next time I opened my eyes, the sun was up, and I was alone in bed. I yanked on some shorts and a T-shirt then went to check on Andy.

I arrived in the kitchen to find Hamish and Sarah sitting on the barstools at the kitchen island still in their pajamas.

"Where is he?" In my gut, I already knew he was gone.

They looked at each other, as if they weren't sure what they should say to me. I saw the concern in their eyes when they turned back to me.

"He's gone, isn't he?" I asked, my voice shaking.

Sarah nodded. "I'm sorry, Zoey. He wanted to go talk to Michelle on his own. He wants you to go home."

I felt nauseous, like I was going to throw up, the acid building up in my mouth. "I need to talk to him," I mumbled as I turned around and ran back up the stairs to the bedroom to find my phone to call him.

I took my purse and turned it upside down, spilling the contents on top of the bed. "Where is it?" I cried, rummaging through my belongings. "Where the hell is my phone?" I threw the covers back on the bed then searched my suitcase for it.

"Zoey, it's right here," Sarah said from the doorway. "You left it on the couch last night."

I jogged to the door, and she handed it to me with shaking hands.

"When did he leave, Sarah?"

She seemed ashamed. "It's been a couple of hours. He woke up early and found out where Michelle is employed on the internet. She's living in San Francisco and working at a real estate company. He's planning on staying there tonight and going to see her at her job tomorrow."

"How did he get there, Sarah?" Andy wouldn't have taken my car if he wanted me to drive home.

The corners of Sarah's mouth turned down in a frown. "He took my car, since I don't drive it very much."

I sat down on the bed, not saying anything back to Sarah. I was so angry with her and Hamish for letting him go alone. Did they not realize he needed someone with him for support?

They had known him his entire life. Me, less than a year, and I *knew* he needed someone with him.

I dialed Andy's cell number.

"Zoey, please don't be mad at me," he said as soon as he answered the phone.

"I'm not mad, Andy. I am *worried* about you. I don't think you should do this alone. Where are you?"

He cleared his throat. "San Francisco." *Fuck!* "Please try to understand. I need to see her on my own, *if* she'll even talk to me."

What was I supposed to do? I couldn't force him to let me help. He didn't want me there. I didn't have to like his decisions, but I had to respect them. It wasn't my marriage, or my child.

However, it was my future and his at stake if this went bad.

"Fine, Andy. I can see you already made up your mind, but you didn't have to run out on me without talking to me. That hurts more than anything," I admitted, trying to keep the tears at bay.

"I'm sorry. I wasn't thinking straight and didn't mean to hurt you. I need to go, but I'll call you as soon as I find anything out. Go home and try not to worry about this. I'll get it figured out."

What choice did I have? "Alright," I acquiesced, feeling crushed. "Please be careful, and keep me posted. I love you. Don't forget that."

He let out a shaky breath. "Okay, Beautiful. Please be careful driving home. I'll miss you every day. I love you. Bye."

The line went dead, and our call was over. A wave of dread washed over me, and my mind automatically went on autopilot. I had to get the fuck out of there and back to my home, where I could try to deal with what happened.

I packed my belongings and found everything Andy had left behind and put it in my suitcase. He did not want me with him. I was emotional and just wanted to go home. I picked up my makeup bag, headed to the bathroom, brushed my hair, and then tied it back in a loose knot.

I stood in front of the mirror brushing my teeth when Sarah came in and knocked on the doorjamb. "Zoey, do you want to talk about it?" she asked.

At the same moment, I pushed my toothbrush back a bit too far and triggered my gag reflex. I launched myself toward the sink to spit out all the toothpaste then gagged again. My face was suddenly clammy and sweaty, and I became dizzy.

I propped my elbows on the cold bathroom counter for balance.

Sarah walked into the bathroom and put her hand on my back. "Zoey, are you alright? Are you sick?" she asked.

I shook my head. "No. I think I'm better now. That was really weird."

After rinsing my mouth and toothbrush, I splashed cold water on my face. Sarah handed me a towel to dry off.

"Thanks," I said as I took the towel. I was still feeling a little weird from my gagging incident. "I think I need to eat something before I leave, if it's okay." The whole situation was making me physically sick.

She nodded. "Of course, Zoey. Let's get you some food. If you want to talk about what's going on, please let me know." I nodded and followed Sarah downstairs to the kitchen.

I sat at the table, watching Sarah and Hamish eating their bagels. We talked about Michelle a bit, as I picked at my bagel. It had no taste and I was having a really hard time eating it.

Other than discussing their divorce, Andy never really talked about Michelle, so I didn't know much about her. Apparently, they eloped because her family disapproved of him.

Previously, he told me they didn't approve of him, but I had no idea they eloped.

It seemed as if Michelle was rebelling against them after she graduated from college, and Andy was her token 'bad boy'. I found that information slightly amusing, because there was nothing 'bad' about him.

Sure, tattoos covered most of his upper body, but they never even saw his tattoos because he'd gotten them all after his divorce. Her family mislabeled him as a *greasy mechanic*, but he was a great person. He came from a good family, from the right side of the tracks, so to speak. Michelle's family sounded like a bunch of rich, snobby assholes to me.

"Zoey, I know Michelle sounds like a horrible person, and I am not defending her actions, but she really did love A.J. She was getting a lot of pressure from her family. It took a horrible toll on their marriage," Sarah explained.

Why should it matter if she loved him? I shook my head in disgust. "That might be true, Sarah, but she kept a *child* from him. How could she do that if she loved him as much as you say she did? I love him more than anything, and I couldn't fathom doing something like that to him."

Hamish and Sarah nodded in understanding. "She had her reasons," Hamish sighed. "I can't imagine what they would be, but from what Corey was saying, it sounded like something was medically wrong with the baby."

I let out a long breath. "I really hope she'll talk to him, and he comes home soon."

Andy and I hadn't been apart for more than a weekend since we came home from Cabo at the end of February. It worried me that he was going through something so devastating by himself.

"I should really get on the road." I stood up to wash my plate. "My parents are expecting us for dinner, and I need to let them know what's going on."

Hamish stood and picked up my bag for me. I picked up my purse, phone, and keys. "Thank you for having us. I'm sorry our visit turned out the way it did."

Sarah reached out and gently squeezed my elbow for reassurance. "Zoey, it will all work out. A.J. loves you. I know you feel bad because he left, but he has always needed to work problems out on his own. It took him months to let us in after the accident. He believes it was his fault because they were coming back from one of his rugby matches. After his divorce, he went back to New Zealand for six months. He deals with matters the best way he knows how."

Great, I had to worry about him taking off on top of everything else. "Well, I hope everything turns out for him," I sighed. I didn't know what else to say, so I left.

Chapter Twenty-Two

It took everything in me not to tell Sarah how wrong she was about what he needed. She said he dealt with everything the best way he knew how, but the best way to deal with problems was to address them when they happened, not to leave and ignore them.

I needed to stay strong and focused so I could be there when he realized he needed me.

By the time I hit the Sacramento city limits, I felt horrible. I was sick with worry and exhausted from not sleeping the night before. I had too much time to think on the way home from Sonoma by myself. I convinced myself I would do anything to make Andy happy. Once I arrived at my apartment, I unpacked my suitcase and started a load of laundry. I decided to take a nice hot bath after putting my makeup and bathroom items away.

When I pulled my birth control pills from my bag, I stared down at them, took a deep breath, and tossed them into the trash. I would give him what he wanted most, if it's what would make him happy.

Besides, I only had a few days left before I needed to start a new pack anyway. I'd been on birth control for years and I was going to marry the love of my life. I would do anything for him, and he would for me. I just needed him to come home so I could tell him. Then we would get married and move on with our lives. Without a doubt, he would be happy with my decision.

I felt like shit from the stress I was putting on myself about what Andy was going through. Unfortunately, I still had to explain everything to my family since he was going to be off work. I took a nice long bath, trying to waste as much time as possible before it was time to go to my mom and dad's.

After a long while, the water turned cool in the bathtub, so I got out. Drying myself off, I noticed my breasts were a little tender. I was not looking forward to that every month. I used to get horrible tenderness and cramps until I started taking the pill.

I dressed and called Andy. He didn't answer, so I left him a message telling him I was going to explain what was going on to my family, and how I would split his jobs between my brothers at work until he came back.

I sent Jess a text.

> *Are you coming to family dinner? I need you. Something bad has happened.*

Not even a minute later, my cell rang. It was Jess. "Zoey, what's wrong?" I explained to her what happened in as much detail as possible. "Oh no, Z...I don't even know what to say."

I began crying, again. "Why does this shit happen, Jess? Couldn't she have been honest with him from the beginning? He would've dealt with everything by now and this wouldn't be happening to him. To *us*."

Jess sighed heavily. "I don't know. The whole thing is crazy. Are you worried he's gonna leave?"

Terrified. "I don't know what I'll do if he does, Jess," I whispered. "The only reason he was freaked out when I went to Cabo was because I was hurt. If I hadn't been, he would've been fine with it because he knew I needed time away. I think if he wants to go, I have to let him."

Later in the day, I drove myself to my mom and dad's house for dinner. I still hadn't heard back from Andy, so I sent him a text while I sat in the car before going inside to face everyone.

> *Hope you're doing well. I wanted to let you know I'm always thinking of you and I love you.*

My phone rang as I stepped out of my car. It was Andy. I slid my index finger across the screen to accept his call. "Hi," I said when I answered.

"Hey, how are you doing?"

Needing privacy for my call, I leaned up against my car door instead of going inside the house. "I'm sad. How are you doing?"

"Same."

"Andy?"

"Yeah, Beautiful?"

"I talked with Sarah and Hamish earlier this morning. I just wanted to let you know if you feel like you need some time away...you know, after you talk to Michelle..."

My voice wavered as tears spilled over and down my cheeks. I took another deep breath as he waited silently for me to finish. He needed to know I was okay with it if he needed time away. "I will understand if you do, but *please* don't take six months, okay?"

I heard him sigh. "Alright, Zoey."

There was no way in hell I could be away from him for that long, and there was no way I would let him deal with it on his own. I tried to deal with my problems on my own and look where it had gotten me.

Miserable, alone, and in therapy.

He told me he loved me, and we ended our call. I walked to the house, knowing in my gut that I wasn't going to see him again, at least not for a while.

I would not let him wallow in the same self-pity that I did for months before I met him, though. He had played a big part in dragging my ass out of it. In turn, I would do the same for him if I needed to. I would give him some time to absorb the news about Emma, but I was not going to let him grieve on his own.

When I walked in the door, my entire family was sitting in the living room waiting for me. Jess leapt from her seat and ran over to me. She threw her arms around me and squeezed me tightly.

"Z, I knew it would be hard on you so I let everyone know something happened. I didn't tell them what, but I didn't want everyone to start gushing over your engagement as soon as you walked in the door. I hope you don't mind."

She knew me well, and I appreciated what she had done more than she could have known. I sobbed on her shoulder, trying to gain some control before I spoke to everyone.

The next thing I knew, my entire family gathered around me, each one of them resting a hand on my shoulder, back, or arm to support me. *This* is what Andy needed; support from his family. My family was now his too.

"I wish Andy could have this...from all of you. He needs all of us to support him."

We sat in the living room, and I filled them in on what I'd learned so far, which wasn't much. I hoped I would know more tomorrow after Andy talked to Michelle.

When we sat down for dinner, I convinced everyone it was acceptable to look at my stunning engagement ring. I wanted everyone to enjoy their night and help me not to dwell on things.

We would get through this. I had to believe it.

During dinner, my dad's cell phone buzzed. He pulled it from his pocket to see who was calling. He made eye contact with me when he saw who it was, and I knew it was Andy. My dad stood and excused himself from the table to take the call in another room.

"Dad? Tell him I love him, will you?" He nodded and left the room.

When he returned a few minutes later, he gave me a weak smile before he sat back down.

"What did he say?" I asked quietly.

He squeezed my hand. "He wanted to apologize to me about missing work and to make sure I took good care of you."

I nodded and dabbed the tears in my eyes with my napkin.

I made it through one plate of food. Still hungry because I hadn't eaten since I'd left Sonoma, I decided to have a second helping of dinner. Adam came into the kitchen while I was filling my plate.

"Save some for me, Z. Since when do you eat seconds?" he joked as he started scooping more food onto his own plate.

I smacked him upside the head, hard. "Shut up, fucknugget! After living with Angie all these months, you should know better than to fuck with chicks who have PMS."

He took a step back. "Ah yes, please...take as much food as you want," he smirked. He held his plate out to me. "Here, do you want some of mine too?"

That earned him another smack upside the head from Angie, who had come into the kitchen too.

I gave her a high-five for it. "I got your back, Z," she joked.

For the first time that day, I laughed. "You know, Angie, we should probably rethink smacking your boyfriend upside the head so much. It seems to be giving him brain damage."

After dinner, I didn't feel like staying to visit with everyone. I wanted to be alone to think. I said my goodbyes to my family and went home. When I arrived back at my apartment, I was tired, both physically and mentally, so I decided to get in bed. It wasn't even dark outside yet, but I didn't care.

I pulled a T-shirt of Andy's out of his drawer in my dresser and slipped it over my head, then crawled in bed. James hopped up on the bed and cuddled up to me. I stuck my earbuds in, turned on my iPod, and stared at the ceiling for a while.

I picked up my cell phone so I could text Andy, but I didn't know what to say to him. As I lowered my hand to set my phone down, it vibrated with an incoming call. I looked at the display to find Andy calling me.

I jerked my earbuds out and flipped my finger across the slider to answer the call.

"Hey, I was just thinking about you," I spoke softly into the phone.

"Were you, now?" he responded with a chuckle. "Dirty thoughts, I hope."

He seemed to be doing better, so I decided to go along with his line of conversation.

"You know it, Sexy. You were definitely doing something dirty to me," I said in a low, deep tone.

He let out a long, slow breath, suddenly serious. "I miss you, Zoey. I'm sorry I left the way I did."

My eyes welled up with tears, but the tears were not for me. My tears were for him and for what he was going through.

"You know you can count on me for anything, right?"

"Yeah, I know. I just feel like everything I touch turns to shit." He sighed and then cleared his throat.

"Don't say that, please," I whispered.

"I'm sorry. I can't help it. It's stupid, but I feel cursed with bad luck or something. I lost my family, I almost lost you, and now I've lost a baby I didn't even know about. Everything was going so good for us, and the day we get engaged..." He paused for a moment. "I wanted everything to be perfect for you. I'm so sorry."

"You have nothing to be sorry for. This is not your fault. She had no right keeping this from you. Once you talk to her and find out what happened, we will try to move past it."

There was only silence from Andy for several seconds.

"I don't know how I can get past this," he admitted. "What if there is something wrong with me, you know? What if something in my genes or DNA is what caused her death? What about any kids we might have? I can't let it happen again."

He was jumping to conclusions.

"Andy, stop. You don't know what happened. Please try not to think that way."

With the way he was speaking, I was starting to freak out. I just wanted to go to him and help him.

"Where are you staying?" I asked. "I don't want you to be alone, or to try and talk to her on your own. I can drive down there tomorrow."

Silence.

"Andy?"

Silence.

"No," he said quietly.

My heart sank. He didn't want me there.

"I want to be there for you." I was ready to beg him to let me come to him at that point. "I don't have to go when you talk to her, but you *need* someone with you."

He cleared his throat. "Zoey, stop. *Please.* I need to figure this out on my own. I've already fucked everything up enough."

Why was he blaming himself? "This is not your fault," I cried. "You are not to blame. This is all on *her,* not you. You didn't do anything wrong."

There was nothing but silence on the line.

"Hey," I whispered. "Please say something."

After several more moments of quietness, he finally spoke. "I need to go so I can think. I'll let you know when I hear something."

So that's it, huh? He's completely shut me out. Now I knew how he felt all those months ago when I did the same thing to him. *It fucking hurts.*

"Andy...don't..."

"Goodbye, Zoey," he whispered right before he hung up on me.

Fuck! I was sick of him hanging up on me. I opened up a new text and sent him a song.

"There For You," by Flyleaf. Please listen to it. I love you.

Chapter Twenty-Three

The following week passed by in a haze of emotion. I tried to work, but my mind constantly strayed to Andy. How was he doing? Was he able to find out anything? I didn't want to push him too hard, so I only tried to contact him once a day, either by call or text.

Andy never responded, but I kept trying...he needed to know I was still there if he needed me. I was losing hope for him finding anything out. He should have called by now with something...*anything*. Still, nothing happened.

Saturday eventually rolled around, and on top of worrying about Andy, I still hadn't started my period. I was extremely concerned about it, so I pulled out the paperwork included with the box of pills, to see if I had missed something. Nope, same as the last type of pill I took. A few months back, I'd switched to birth control pills that stopped my period, so I was supposed to get only four per year.

My period should have started around the time I threw away the rest of the packet of pills. I was officially a week late. I was *never* late. What was I going to do if the new birth control pills messed up my system? I'd never taken pills where they actually stopped my period before, so I wasn't sure what to expect.

After I read the list of side effects, I was starting to stress out, so I called Sasha. I needed some girl talk from someone who would *not* baby me when I was freaking the fuck out. I had every side effect listed on the paperwork, from nausea, to sore and swollen breasts and mood changes, to being tired. The only fucking side effect I didn't have was a lighter period or spotting. I had *nothing*.

"Zoey!" she squealed when she answered her phone. "Girl, where have you been? It's been days since we've talked."

I laughed at her enthusiasm. "Sash, I am kind of freaking out here. Can you come over?"

She grew serious. "Of course. Are you alright?" I heard her moving around and her door slammed a minute later. "I'm on my way now. What's going on?"

I sighed. "I'll explain when you get here."

We ended the call, and twenty minutes later, I let her in my apartment.

"Sash, what the fuck are you wearing?" I asked when she dropped her gargantuan purse on my couch and I caught a glimpse of her outfit, or lack thereof. She was wearing what appeared to be a black silk nightie and nothing else.

It came down to about mid-thigh on her, and she was wearing knee high stiletto boots. Her black and purple hair was crazy messy.

"Did I interrupt something when I called?" I joked.

She let out a sigh. "I wish. Now what the fuck is going on?"

I was still looking over her outfit when she snapped her fingers right in front of my face, getting my attention. She grabbed the hem of her shirt/nightie and yanked it up.

"Look, *shorts*. I am wearing shorts. Shit, Z, you called and said you needed me, so I threw on the closest thing I could find and dragged my ass over here. Now spill it. What the fuck is going on?"

And that, my friends, is why I called Sasha over *any* of my other friends.

She seized my hand and dragged me over to the couch, where she shoved me backward until the backs of my knees hit it, and I fell onto my ass on the cushions.

"Speak!" she bellowed.

"Holy fucking hell, Sash. Relax. I am not a dog. There is no need to get physical," I teased.

"I'm about to slap a bitch, Zoey James," she warned as she grinned from ear to ear.

"Okay, sorry. Here goes." I took a deep breath and closed my eyes. "My period is a week late." I opened one eye at a time waiting for her to have some sort of an epic sized, Sasha freak out.

Instead, she narrowed her eyes at me and a smile slowly began to form on her face.

"So?" she smirked. "Are you trying to tell me you're pregnant?"

No. Yes? I don't know. What the fuck?

"Sasha, I've been on the pill for years. I can't be." I was officially in disbelief.

She shook her head. "Zoey, yes you can. The pill doesn't always work, you know. My sister-in-law baby cousin Tracy—"

"Sasha!" I yelled. "This is no time to be quoting that crazy bitch from the *Friday* movie. This is serious."

Okay, it was funny.

But still.

Holy-mother-fucking-shit!

"I was on the pill when I was married to Rob. I'd stopped taking it because I quit having sex with him and didn't see the point. I was on it for years and nothing happened."

"So how the fuck did you get pregnant if you weren't having sex with him, Zoey?" Sasha questioned.

Oh God, this is embarrassing. "He was out partying with his friends and came home drunk. Well, while he had been gone, I drank a bottle of wine, and we ended up...you know...and we didn't use protection."

She nodded as I hung my head in shame. "Right, so we are fairly certain that isn't the case then. Did you miss any pills?"

I shook my head. I hadn't missed any.

"I switched three months ago to the pills that stop your period for three months, so I haven't had my period since May."

"Where is that handsome boy toy of yours anyway?" she asked, looking around for Andy. "Why are you talking to me about this and not him?"

"I haven't seen, or talked to him in a week."

Confusion and concern washed over her face. I explained Corey's story to her before I stood up to get a drink. I went to the kitchen, leaving her on the couch so she could absorb everything that happened.

I brought two glasses of sun tea back into the living room and set them on the table. When I turned back to Sasha, she was looking at me curiously.

"Z, I don't mean to be a bitch, but are you *sure* you're not knocked up?"

"Yes, I am sure," I hissed as I scrubbed my hands over my face in frustration.

She was still looking at me strangely.

"Why are you looking at me like that?"

She stood up, took my hand, and dragged me down the hallway to my bedroom, where she yanked the hem of my tank top up over my boobs, baring my torso.

Sasha grabbed my hips then spun me around to face my mirror.

"This is why I am looking at you like that, Zoey," she exclaimed as she yanked my shorts down my thighs. Thank God my panties stayed in place.

"Look at your stomach."

I slowly looked my body over. She was right. Fuck. My normally flat stomach was rounded slightly now. *Barely noticeable. Shit!* Weight gain was on the list of side effects, too, but with Andy and I having dinner together every day, I was obviously going to gain weight, so I ignored that side effect.

It was a very inappropriate time, but I needed to laugh.

"Maybe it's a toomah," I joked, rubbing my belly and doing my best impression of Arnold Schwarzenegger from the movie *Kindergarten Cop*.

Sasha burst out in hysterics. "It's not a toomah!" she yelled.

"Zoey," she finally said seriously. "You need to make an appointment with your OB to get checked out."

I pulled my clothes back on, grabbed my laptop off my dresser, and sat on my bed.

While we waited for it to boot up, she asked me what I was doing.

"I'm gonna Google this shit," I said, referring to my barely noticeable stomach and the birth control pills.

An hour later, Sasha and I were both in a panic. I was going to die. It was official. I for sure had cancer. Or a cyst. Or endometriosis. Or I was secretly growing the twin I never knew I had.

Okay, that was a bit far-fetched. I'd read one too many Stephen King books and seen one too many movies about a dude who carried his detached Siamese twin around in a basket and let it kill people.

Fuck me. "Sasha, remind me next time that Google is *not* my friend."

I closed my laptop and tossed it on my bed.

"My twin is hungry. Let's take your nightie and go to lunch." I jammed my feet into some flip-flops as Sasha scowled at me, and we went to lunch.

I drove to the deli Andy and I went to the first weekend we met.

It was only fitting that as soon as we sat down with our sandwiches, my cell phone started blaring "Sex on Fire."

"Finally," I grumbled. I hadn't heard his voice in almost a week.

"Hey," I said as I put my cell up to my ear.

"Zoey, it's good to hear your voice," he replied hoarsely.

"How's everything going?" I stood up to walk outside for some privacy.

He sighed with frustration. "Not so great. I don't know any more today than I did last week."

I pushed the door open and stepped outside. "Nothing? Were you able to talk to her at all?"

"No." He sighed loudly.

The tone of his voice told me he was irritated.

"I went to her work every day, but she wouldn't see me. After a couple days, security escorted me out and threatened to arrest me for trespassing and harassment."

That fucking bitch!

"So I waited down the street from her work, to see if I could talk to her when she left, but a security guard walked her out every night. I felt like a fucking stalker."

"I'm so sorry. I can't believe she won't even talk to you," I replied. "So, now what?" I wasn't sure if I wanted to know the answer.

"Are you going to your mum and dad's tomorrow for dinner?"

With everything that was going on, I hadn't really thought about it. "I don't know. Are you coming home?"

"I'll come back tomorrow."

Thank God. "Okay then. Do you want to come to dinner too? I'm sure everyone will be happy to see you."

"I'll let you know tomorrow. When you find out what time you need to be there, text me and let me know, okay?"

I promised to call my mom as soon as we hung up.

Once I was off the phone with my mom, I sent him a text, telling him I needed to be there at two to help with dinner and I hoped he would come too. I went back inside the deli to eat.

"Well, what happened, Zoey?" Sasha asked impatiently.

I told her everything Andy said as I ate my sandwich and chips. We finished our lunch and left.

As we walked out the door, Sasha turned left, grabbed my hand, and began to drag me behind her. For such a tiny thing, she sure was strong.

"Um, my car is the other way. Where are we going?" I questioned, confused.

"To the fucking pharmacy to buy a pregnancy test."

Oh, hell no.

I stopped abruptly, jerking my hand from hers. "No way in hell, Sash. I cannot be pregnant. It's not possible," I groaned. Literally, fucking groaned.

"Zoey, I just watched you down an entire foot long sandwich and a bag of chips. By. Your. Self. You are so fucking pregnant," she blurted cheerfully.

Skank! Why did she have to say that shit to me? As if I wasn't freaking out enough, she tried to convince me I was pregnant too. Why did this happen?

After five minutes, I was finally able to convince her I was most definitely *not* going to get a pregnancy test, and I would be making an appointment with my doctor first thing Monday morning.

We went back to my apartment, and Sasha left to go home. I was alone again for the rest of the day, so I took a long, hot bath to relax. Andy would be home sometime the next day, and I could talk to him face to face. I hoped someday he would get past the heartache he was feeling from losing a child he never knew about. I would never understand how his ex could be so cruel to him.

After I stepped out of the bathtub and dried off, I stood completely naked in front of my full-length mirror and placed my palms on my belly. *Is it possible that I am pregnant?* What was Andy going to do when I talked to him about it once he came home?

He is going to freak out, Zoey. That's what he's going to do.

He was going to go absolutely nuts, and from what he had said, I didn't think it was going to be in a good way. I worried about what he mentioned to me before, about genes and DNA, and I began going nuts myself. What in the hell was I going to do? I already knew what I *wasn't* going to do.

I would *not* be like his ex.

As soon as he was home, I would talk to him. The possibility of being pregnant was definitely not something I wanted to tell him over the phone.

Chapter Twenty-Four

The next morning, I woke up late and hopped in the shower after I fed James and started another load of laundry. While I was showering, James had curled up in a giant orange fluff ball on the middle of the bed. I dressed myself and played with him while I waited for the laundry to finish.

Once I took care of the laundry I made some French toast and scrambled eggs for breakfast. I still had a couple hours before I needed to leave for my mom and dad's house, and I wondered if Andy was on the road yet to come home. I sent him a text, asking where he was, and then decided I needed to keep busy, so I cleaned my entire apartment from top to bottom.

Since I was kind of a neat freak, it didn't take very long, so I went over to the shop and cleaned the office.

When I arrived home from the shop, I had a text from Andy that I missed by about five minutes. It said he was just getting on the road and to head over to dinner by myself. He would see me when I came home.

It would be a couple hours until he was home, so I had no reason to hang out and wait. I went to my parents' and found my mom in the kitchen cutting up the meat for dinner.

"Hi, Mom," I said as I hugged her from behind.

"Hola, Mija," she replied cheerfully. "Where's our Andy at? Did he not come with you?" My dad came into the kitchen and gave me a big bear hug.

"No, he's not home yet. Things didn't go so well in San Francisco. He still doesn't know anything."

My mom shook her head and muttered something under her breath in Spanish as she turned back to finish cutting up the meat. With my knowledge of the Spanish language, I understood that she called someone a fucking bitch.

Yes, she was where I acquired my foul mouth.

My dad and I chuckled when we heard what she said. I explained to them what happened with Andy trying to go to Michelle's office and security getting involved. As I spoke, my dad sat shaking his head, unable to believe what was happening with Andy.

When my mom was finished with what she was doing, she washed her hands and turned to me. "I'm so sorry this is happening to both of you, baby girl. Andy is part of this family and it hurts to know we can't do anything to help him. Just know we're here for you and here for him when he comes home. Please let him know that."

Tears flooded my eyes because my family had accepted him as one of their own, like they had me when I was adopted. "I will, Mom. He's coming home today, so I'll make sure he knows."

As I helped my mom cook dinner, the rest of my family began arriving at the house. When it was ready, and everyone was updated on Andy, we gathered around the table to eat.

Jess sat next to me, leaned over, and whispered in my ear. "Is there something you need to tell me?"

I narrowed my eyes at her. What was she talking about? So much had happened since I saw her last.

She rolled her eyes at me. "Seriously, Z? I talked to Sasha."

As visions of murdering Sasha went through my head, I let out a breath. "Fucking blabbermouth," I muttered so only Jess could hear. "Later," I whispered.

Jess let me get through dinner but cornered me in the kitchen when I went in for seconds. Yes, seconds. Again.

Of course, right as I heaped more food on my plate, Adam walked in the kitchen.

"Dang, Z, seconds again, huh? Looks like you've put on a couple pounds too."

Yep, he was fucking brain damaged. I took the serving spoon full of refried beans I was holding and flung them at him.

A moment later, Angie walked in the kitchen and found her boyfriend covered in beans.

She shook her head at him. "What did you say this time, Adam?"

He unbuttoned his bean-covered shirt, pulled it off, and began wiping beans off his face and from his wavy, chin length hair with it.

"I said something I promise never to say again, that's for sure. I don't particularly enjoy wearing food," he grumbled.

While he cleaned himself off, my mom came into the kitchen, took one look at him, muttered *"idiota"* then went about cleaning the kitchen.

After he was done, Adam walked over to me and squeezed me tightly. "You know I'm just messing with you, right, Z?"

I nodded. "Yes, and you know you deserved what you got in return, right?"

He kissed my cheek loudly. "Yep, I think we're even," he joked and left the room.

My mom sang while she cleaned, so Jess and I were able to talk quietly without her hearing. "Why didn't you buy a pregnancy test yesterday? Are you crazy?" she asked in disbelief.

"Jess, I don't see how I could be...*you know*..." I raised my eyebrows at her, willing her to understand what the fuck I meant. I was afraid to say the word *pregnant* now because it made me nauseous.

"I am calling the doctor first thing in the morning," I said as I shoveled in a mouthful of food.

She looked at me and smirked, like she just knew I was pregnant. Frustrated, I tossed my fork down on the counter and jogged to the bathroom.

I heard Jess call my name before I slammed the bathroom door and locked it. With my two best friends convinced I was pregnant, I was beginning to second-guess myself too. I was positive I hadn't missed any pills, and I was so careful taking them at the same time every day.

Oh God, what if Andy was right? There could be something wrong with our baby if I were pregnant. Would we be able to handle it?

There was a knock on the door.

"Z, I'm sorry," Jess said quietly. "Please open the door."

I unlocked it and let my best friend in. I sat on the lid of the toilet while she settled on the edge of the bathtub. I explained my newfound fears of a possibly sick baby.

"Oh, Zoey," she cried. "I am so sorry. I didn't think about that."

After I unrolled a few squares of toilet paper for both of us, I dried the tears from my cheeks as she dried hers. "It's okay. It's all hard to deal with right now, especially without him here and not knowing anything about it."

We talked for a few more minutes before my nephew Jake started pounding on the door because he needed to use the bathroom. We went back to the kitchen for dessert, but I took mine to go, instead of staying to eat it.

I was so over the day, and just wanted to go home. I hoped Andy was home waiting for me.

It took a while to say my goodbyes to everyone, but I eventually left to drive home. I pulled my Audi through the Dutch Bros. drive-thru and bought a small, decaf Cocomo.

Jesus H, now I was convinced I was pregnant and ordering decaf fucking coffee. I checked my phone while I waited for my order. Nothing from Andy.

As soon as I was home, I parked on the street next to my building and ran up the stairs. All I needed was to see him and tell him of my suspicions. I didn't want to waste time messing around with the gates to get into the parking lot.

I unlocked my door and went inside the apartment. I was expecting him to be sitting on the couch waiting for me, but he wasn't. James was wandering around meowing for no apparent reason, so I picked him up and walked through the apartment to see if Andy was in another room.

When I walked into my bedroom, I found an envelope laying on my bed with my name scrawled across it in his handwriting. Next to the envelope was a key ring with a few keys on it and his cell phone. I dropped James down on the bed and picked up the envelope.

In my heart, I knew it was bad. Very, very, bad.

Inside the envelope, I found a long, handwritten note and the Tiffany & Co. receipt for my engagement ring.

Oh, please, no. No. No, no, no!

Anxious to find out what the note said, I sank down onto the bed and unfolded the paper.

Zoey,
I can't even begin to tell you how sorry I am for everything that has happened. I've been wracking my brain all week trying to come up with a solution, for a way to fix this, but I've realized I can't. There is nothing I can do. My hands are tied.

Not knowing what happened to Emma has made my decision about having a family of my own final. I know you didn't want children right away, but I can't take the option away from you in the future, when you decide that you are ready.

I'm sorry I didn't have the courage to talk to you face to face, and that I had to write you a letter. I know if we talked in person, I would never be able to leave you. I love you so much, Zoey.

I know in time, you will find someone new, someone who is worthy of you and won't have all the baggage that I do. I need a clean break, so I've left my cell here, and the phone company will shut it off in the next few days.

I also left the receipt for your engagement ring, so you can return it if you want to. I don't care what you do with the money if you decide to return it.

I know my decision to leave is going to hurt you, and for that, I am so, so sorry. I hope that one day you will forgive me. Just know I will always love you more than anything.

Andy.

Oh my God. I dropped the letter on my bed, picked up his keys, and ran out my front door as Will and Justin came out of their apartment. I skidded to a stop before barreling into Will. He reached out and gripped my shoulders to steady me so I wouldn't fall down the steps.

"Zoey, what's going on?" he asked, his voice panicked.

I shook him loose. "He's fucking gone!" I cried as I righted myself then ran down the stairs and out the lobby door. I continued running until I hit the parking lot between the apartment building and the shop. There, I stopped.

His truck and trailer were gone.

Will and Justin were running behind me, calling my name, but I ignored them and began running again. I took the stairs up to his apartment two at a time until I missed a step and fell to my knees on the landing at the top of the stairs.

I picked myself up, my knees and hands stinging from my fall, and found the keys I'd dropped.

"Zoey, stop!" Justin called out to me as they made it to the bottom of the stairs.

I ignored them again, walked on shaky legs over to the door, and unlocked it. I paused because I wasn't sure if I wanted to see what was, or was not, on the other side of it. I pushed the door open, but couldn't force myself to go in. Will and Justin came up behind me and stopped.

"He's gone. I can't believe he left me," I whispered as tears began to fall, and my heart shattered in my chest.

Will brushed past me, shooting me a sympathetic glance as he went inside the apartment. Several minutes later, he came back out. I looked him in the eyes anxiously, waiting for him to tell me what I already knew.

He shook his head from side to side. "I'm so sorry, Zoey. All of his personal belongings are gone."

Will locked up the apartment, and my friends walked me home.

They sat me down on the couch, one of them sitting on either side of me. I buried my face in my hands and began bawling.

"I knew he would leave, but I thought he would come back."

The letter he left said he wasn't coming back. *Ever.* Justin stood up and went into the kitchen, while Will sat with me as I cried. A few minutes later, Justin came back to the living room with three glasses of Johnnie Walker. He held a glass out to me.

"I can't drink that, but thank you," I whispered. He looked at me curiously and raised his eyebrows in question.

"Everyone thinks I'm pregnant, Justin," I said and started crying again.

Will pulled me over to him hugging me tightly. They were having a silent conversation behind my back, trying to figure out what the hell was going on.

"Call Sasha, the blabbermouth," I muttered. "She'll tell you everything."

Justin stood up from the couch and went down the hallway to my bedroom. Ten minutes later, he came back out, made a cup of hot tea, and brought it to me. I finally calmed down enough to talk to them.

After a while, Sasha and Jess showed up. Four of my best friends surrounded me because my world was turned upside down, because my other best friend left me.

Andy was gone, and he destroyed my heart in the process.

The five of us talked through the night, in to the early morning. They were able to talk some sense in to me. I started the evening completely heartbroken, and by the time we all fell asleep at my place, I was downright mad.

I was mad at Andy for leaving the way he did. He fucking lied to me when he told me to go to family dinner without him. He said he'd see me when I came home, when what he was really doing was getting me away from my apartment while he packed up and left me.

I was mad at his ex for being the chicken-shit bitch, who was so fucking heartless she hadn't told him about Emma. I was mad at him for leaving his cell phone, with no way for me to contact him.

All my life, I had lain down and let whatever happen to me, happen. I was no longer that person.

This time, I chose to fight. I was going to fight for Andy with everything that I had. I wasn't going to let him go as easily as he had let me go.

I placed the palm of my hand on my stomach, and in my heart, I knew there was someone else I had to fight for.

To be continued...

The third and final part to Zoey and Andy's story will continue in the upcoming book

"Beautiful With You"

Author Bio

Jen Andrews was raised in a small town in Northern California, and still lives in the same county where she was born. She is a self-proclaimed music and lyric addict. She grew up in a 'car family' so her life has been spent around old hot rods. She and her husband, Jake, even have a few of their own. In her spare time, Jen loves to travel wherever she can. She finally lived her dream of traveling to New Zealand to see her favorite rugby team, the All Blacks, play. Jen loves to do photography as a hobby and continues to write.

Find Jen here:

https://www.goodreads.com/author/show/7762025.Jen_Andrews

https://www.facebook.com/AuthorJenAndrews

https://www.facebook.com/jenandrewsauthor

https://www.goodreads.com/book/show/20755729-the-reason

https://www.goodreads.com/book/show/22585630-just-say-yes

https://twitter.com/jennysnowflakes